CRASY

GIBSON BOYS BOOK #4

ADRIANA LOCKE

Cover Image: Adobe Stock
Cover Design: Kari March
Editing: Marion Making Manuscripts
Jenny Sims, Editing 4 Indies

ALSO BY ADRIANA LOCKE

The Exception Series

The Exception

The Connection

The Perception

The Landry Family Series

Sway

Swing

Switch

Swear

Swink

Sweet

The Gibson Boys Series

Crank

Craft

Crave

Crazy

Dogwood Lane

Tumble

Tangle

Trouble

Restraint- Coming Soon

Standalone Novels

Sacrifice

Wherever It Leads

Written in the Scars

Lucky Number Eleven

ONE

Peck

"IT'S *YOU.*"

A pair of red flip-flops come to a stop next to the truck. Dust billows from the harder-than-necessary halt to movement and flows under the truck and right into my face. I wave my hand in front of me and cough.

"Yeah?" I ask. "What's your point?"

Toenails painted the color of grass on a spring day tap against the gravel. A thin gold ring adorns the second toe.

"Are you proud of yourself?" she asks.

The tone she's using nixes any ideas I may have had to scoot out from underneath this vehicle. It has that flair to it, that you've-done-and-gone-screwed-up-but-I'm-going-to-make-you-wallow-a-while thing that turns men's blood to ice.

The only problem is that I can't figure out what I've done. Or who she is.

I drop the wrench in my hand and study the tanned legs visible

1

from my disadvantageous position. They're short and tanned, the muscles in her calves flexing as she pops one foot up on her toe.

The voice—one that's clearly annoyed with me for some reason—isn't familiar, nor are the legs. A quick scan of recent activity doesn't unearth a woman who should be pissed. Not that a woman needs a reason to be pissed, but still.

"Well," I say, "it depends on why you're asking."

"What's that supposed to mean?"

"It means that if you're asking if I'm proud of the fact that I diagnosed and will have Dave's truck fixed in under an hour—minus the time I spend in this conversation with you—then yes. I am. Or if you're asking about the black lines down the middle of Main Street, I'm proud of that too. I—"

"That's not what I mean, and you know it."

"Do I?" I scratch the top of my head.

Staring at the undercarriage, I attempt to figure out what the heck is happening here. The day has been a doozy already. Between Nana calling me at four in the morning because she couldn't get out of bed and my cousin Walker's pissy mood when I got to work at his mechanic's shop Crank, I should've just called in sick. I should've stayed in bed instead of trying to make the best out of the day.

Sometimes, you just know better. I knew better this morning. I'm just not smart enough to listen to myself.

"You're a jerk, you know that?" she says with a huff. She shifts her weight from one foot to the other. "No, I take that back. You're more than that. You're a jackass."

"What in the world are you talking about?"

"You know what I'm talking about."

"Um, nope. I really don't."

"Yes, you do. Now come out here and face me like a man."

"If you insist," I mutter.

Pressing my heels into the gravel, I roll myself out from under the truck. The sun is bright, almost blinding me with its early afternoon rays. I shield my eyes and look up into the face of a woman who looks like she wants to kill me.

Her bright green eyes widen just a bit before resuming their narrowed position. A set of full lips are pressed together in a hard line. Her face is framed by a couple of unruly strands of sandy brown hair that's fallen from a lopsided ponytail.

I bite back a smile. I'm one hundred percent certain I'm supposed to be intimidated and not entertained right now, but I can't help it. She's fucking adorable.

"Well, here I am," I say.

She takes a step back. Her eyes release from mine and drag down the length of my body. When they return to my face, she narrows them again. "You're a jackass."

"You've said that." I get to my feet and brush off my hands. "Look, do I know you? Not that I don't love being yelled at by a stranger …"

"You are incredible," she says, dropping those pretty little lips of hers open.

"Thanks." I smile. The gesture does not get returned. "If you're Tad's daughter or something, tell him I put the gas cans back. It was an emergency. I swear. Just tell him they're behind the shovels in the barn, and I'll pay him back. Okay?"

She cocks a brow. "And you steal gas too. Wow. What a winner."

"You're awfully judgy for someone who doesn't even know me."

"I know all I want to know about you."

"That's a shame," I say, sliding my hands down my jeans.

A gasp sneaks through the air as her hands fall to her sides in exasperation. I take a step back for self-preservation. Just in case.

"Are you hitting on me?" She blinks once, then twice.

"No," I say. "I mean, if you want me to, I'd—"

She throws her hands up in the air. "She said you worked fast and would move on without thinking twice about it, but I had hoped that she'd be wrong."

"Who? Who said that? I have no clue what you're talking about."

She lets out a little laugh that's anything but funny. I wait for steam to come out of her ears, but the only thing rolling off her is the scent of oranges.

I glance around for cameras because this has to be a joke. Surely, one of my cousins is setting me up. But the longer I look, the more it becomes apparent: she's as serious as a heart attack.

"You're exactly like she said you'd be," she says.

I rub my forehead, wishing once again I'd have stayed home. I have a good twenty minutes left on this truck and then a fifteen-minute drive back to Crank to clock out. Then I need to check on Nana and make sure she got lunch before I can go home and get a shower and close my damn eyes. But before any of that can happen, I have to figure what the hell this girl is talking about.

Blowing out a breath, I focus.

"Let's just restart this whole thing," I say. "What's your name?"

"We're really doing this?"

"Doing what?" I hold my hands in front of me. "What are we really doing? I don't get it."

She flashes me a disapproving look. "You're really asking my name?"

"That's what ya do when you don't know somebody. At least it is around here."

"Fine. I'll play along. I'm Dylan," she says as if she's talking to a baby. "And we talked last week about how much you love my best friend."

The last part of that gets loud. Really, really loud. She takes my cringing as a sign of weakness.

She moves toward me, her eyes flashing her fury at me like bolts of lightning. Her finger jabs me in the chest.

"You better be scared of me," she says. "Thinking you're gonna ghost her like some careless asshole after she opens up to you about—"

"Whoa, wait—"

"No, I'm not gonna wait." She jabs me again, harder this time. Her face twists when I don't budge. "I shouldn't have even shown up out here because that probably will make your ego explode."

My brain scrambles with her accusation but gets even more fogged up with the look in her eyes. Worry is etched on her face.

"Listen, I'm sorry about your friend. Honest. But—"

"I highly doubt that." She takes a deep breath, the passion starting

4

to wane as she thinks her point has been delivered. "You better stay away from her. Do you hear me?"

I have no idea what we're doing here, but I feel bad for Dylan. And her friend. And for the guy who ghosted her friend if Dylan ever catches up with him.

A part of me wants to maintain my innocence, but I'm not sure it matters.

"I get it," I tell her. "Your friend is hurting, and you're ready to go to battle. I respect that. Lord knows the battles my family has gotten me in. But I ..."

This placates her a little. She opens her mouth, but no words come out. Another deep breath is taken, causing the tiny chip of diamond in her nose to shine.

She's pretty. This girl with her golden-brown skin and long eyelashes and personality for days would have me chasing after her if I didn't want to run out of fear for my life.

The venom in her eyes subsides. She reaches up and brushes back a strand of hair that came out as she railed me, and I see a tattoo on her wrist. It's the word *family* written in a delicate script. I think about my brother, Vincent, and how many times I've gone to war for him or my cousins.

I consider telling her I'm not who she thinks I am. But if I do that, she's going to start shouting again, which means I'll just be here longer fixing this damn truck. Besides, I did nothing wrong, so maybe I'll let it go. Let Dylan get it off her chest and move on. I have broad shoulders. Besides, the guy, whomever he is, probably wouldn't give a shit anyway from how it sounds. It'll probably make her feel better to think the guy feels bad—at least a little.

"I'm sorry," I say. "Is there anything I can do to make this better?"

"Stay away from her."

"I will. Promise. Cross my heart," I say, acting out the gesture in front of her. "Anything else?"

She nods, looking around Dave's front yard. "Well, you could bring her pots and pans back. They were the first nice thing she ever bought for herself, and it makes it easier to save money if you can cook at home. I'm sure she'd like to have them returned."

"Okay," I say, wondering why some dude would take a woman's kitchen equipment. "I'll see what I can do."

I bite my bottom lip, trying to figure out how to get a set of pans back from a guy I don't even know. Dylan scrutinizes every move I make. Finally, she shakes her head.

"You pawned them, didn't you?"

"No," I insist, slightly offended. "I wouldn't pawn someone's pots and pans. Who do you think I am?"

"A jackass."

I roll my eyes. "Right. I forgot."

"And you could bring me a bottle of Jack. After all, I'm helping her pick up all the pieces of her heart that you so thoughtlessly threw against the wall. So thanks for that."

"You're welcome."

She scowls. "Really?"

"Look, I'm doing my best here," I say with a chuckle. "Give me some credit."

Her arms cross over her chest as she considers this. "Fine. I'll give you *some* credit for at least *sort of* taking responsibility. That's it. That's all you get."

"Good enough, I guess."

With a satisfied nod of her head, she starts to turn away, but then she stops before she gets too far. "One more thing," she says, looking at me over her shoulder. "Don't tell Navie I was here."

I blink once. Twice. Three times.

Navie? Bartender Navie? Navie-Who-Works-At-My-Cousin's-Bar Navie?

My friend Navie?

Navie knows Dylan? And Dylan doesn't know me?

Am I being set up here?

I grab at my temple with my right hand.

"You won't, right?" Dylan asks when I fail to answer.

"Yeah. Sure. I, um, I won't say a word," I say, trying to piece all this together.

Her shoulders relax, the V-neck dropping low enough to see the cleavage that I would enjoy any other time except right now when I'm mentally marinating Navie knowing Dylan and Dylan thinking I'm some other guy.

I run a hand down my face and, once again, regret not going back to bed.

"It's a shame you're such a jackass," she says.

I drop my hands. "Well, thanks. But I'm not one really."

"I beg to differ."

"Suit yourself," I say. "But tell Navie that if she needs to talk—"

"Nope. If you want to talk to her, you do it. Be a man. Prove me wrong." She walks toward her car again. "And bring back her pots and pans. Do you hear me?"

"If I can find them."

She stops at her car and flings open the door. Her eyes narrow again. She's so damn cute, and this entire thing so bizarre that I can't take it. I laugh.

"If you don't find them, I'll come find you," she says.

"Could you warn me first? And let me schedule that into my day because I'm running about a half hour behind right now."

She fights a smile as she climbs into her car. She pulls away just as quickly as she arrived, and I'm left standing next to old man Dave's truck, wondering what the hell just happened.

TWO

Peck

I tug my hat down to block out the early evening sun. Stepping over a broken piece of sidewalk that the town of Linton hasn't bothered to fix in at least fifteen years, I make my way toward Crave.

My cousin's bar is my usual haunt after work, and today is no exception. What is different about today, though, is that I have a reason to be here besides not just wanting to be alone.

My face breaks into a grin as I remember the little spitfire. Her finger pressed against my chest as she leveled warnings makes me laugh. But as entertained as I am with Dylan's moxie, an uneasiness settles over me when I think of Navie.

I would like to think Navie and I were close enough that I'd know if she was seeing someone seriously enough for them to steal her cookware. And I'd really hope she knows she could ask me for help if she needed it because if this guy is the jerk that Dylan seems to think he is, then what else has he done?

The door chimes as I tug it open. Eighties rock music is playing on the speakers, letting me know my cousin Machlan, the owner of the bar, is still here. Pieces of streamers and popped balloons are stuck on random nails and pictures from Machlan's birthday party that got a little out of control last weekend.

"Hey," Machlan says from the other side of the bar. "You're in here early."

"Long day."

I plop down on a barstool. Machlan slides a beer down the bar, and I catch it with one hand.

"Tell me about it," he says. "Hadley woke up mad at me for something I did to her in her dream last night. And then Navie was an hour late and about as happy with me as my girlfriend for some unknown reason. I can't win."

I take a long sip of beer. The glass has the perfect level of dew on the outside. Setting it back on the bar, I look at my cousin. He doesn't seem to know things he's not telling me, but Machlan is good at hiding shit.

"What's going on with Navie?" I ask with as much nonchalance as I can muster.

"Fuck if I know. I've learned it's best not to ask." He leans forward, his elbows resting on the counter. His lips turn up into a smirk. "Tad was in here earlier looking for you. Said something about gas cans and a note left scrawled on a two-by-four in spray paint last night?"

"I left a damn note, and I returned the gas cans. I don't see what the big deal is."

"Maybe that you broke into his barn," Machlan offers.

"I did not." I look at Machlan. He's still wearing that stupid smirk. "What? The door was open. That officially makes it not a break-in."

"Pretty sure Tad and all relevant legal definitions don't agree with that assessment."

"Well, common sense does. Think about it. I didn't have to break anything to enter, and I returned everything—except the gas, but there wasn't much in there, really."

Machlan doesn't look convinced.

"Besides," I say, "he would've given to it me if I'd have asked."

"Which is what you should've done."

I shrug, taking another drink. It was a couple of gallons of gas. If Tad is really that pissed about it, I'll just remind him of this the next time he calls me with a broken down tractor at dark.

Machlan chuckles. "Well, you owe me twenty bucks for the gas. I paid him to keep him from coming to find you."

Eyeing him curiously, I tip my bottle from side to side. "Why are you being nice to me?"

He rolls his eyes as he starts to respond, but he's interrupted by a loud crash from the storeroom. It's followed by a loud string of profanities before Navie comes marching into the room.

Her hair, streaked with bright pink strands, is a haphazard mess on top of her head. She comes to a halt in front of Machlan.

"If you want me to serve tequila tonight, you're gonna have to get it off the top shelf yourself because I'm not screwing with it. I almost just died." She gives Machlan a don't-mess-with-me look before flipping her gaze to me. Her irritation eases a bit. "Hey, Peck."

"Navie," I say with a tentative nod.

She flips me a forced smile before refocusing on my cousin.

"Why does he get a smile," Machlan says, pointing at me, "and I get yelled at?"

"Because Peck didn't set a death trap for me in the storeroom," she replies. "And he's cuter than you. And nicer. And—"

"And I sign your check," Machlan counters.

"And I'm cuter." I grin as they both look at me. "What? She said it. Not me."

Machlan sighs, handing Navie a white bar rag. "I beg to differ on that, Peck."

"It's true," Navie says. "I'd be all over him if he didn't feel like my brother on some level. That and he has that thing for Molly McCarter. That makes me a little concerned about his well-being."

She rolls her eyes so hard that it has to hurt.

"Never understood the Molly thing either," Machlan says.

"Let's keep my girl out of this," I say. "She's never done anything to either of you."

"Because I keep my pants zipped up when she's around. Otherwise, there's no doubt she'd have done things to me that she's done to every other guy who lives in this half of Illinois," Machlan says. "When are you going to let that whole thing go?"

I take a drink of my beer and set it down with a thud. "Never."

The two of them go into an already-heard, overly tired tirade about Molly. They share a venom with the rest of the town against the woman I've always defended.

Molly was my first crush. Since the first night she crawled in my bedroom window when we were six, I've had a soft spot for her. It's crazy, I know, and the sentiment hasn't exactly been reciprocated, but I can't help it. I like her. Period.

Machlan looks at his watch. "I'll go get your tequila, but then I gotta head home. Add twenty to Peck's tab for gas." He shoots me a look before heading toward the storeroom. "Behave."

I take another drink as Navie pulls out a white takeout box from Carlson's Bakery from behind the counter. She sets it on the bar.

"I know it's bad manners to bring food from one establishment into another, but this sandwich is my breakfast, lunch, and probably dinner," she says, "so I don't care."

I lean against the counter and study her. Besides her annoyance, there's no sign she's been through something like Dylan described.

Dylan.

I grin.

"What are you smiling about?" she asks, picking the onion off her sandwich.

"Oh, nothing. Why didn't you just cook?"

"Busy."

Unhelpful.

"Do you usually cook?" I ask, prodding a little harder.

She quirks a brow as she shoves a bite of turkey and cheese into her mouth. "Sometimes."

"What's your favorite thing to make?"

"What is this? The Spanish Inquisition?" She rips a napkin out of a container in front of me. "Why do you care what I like to cook?"

"Gee, take it easy," I say, leaning back. "Just making conversation."

And probing you for information, but I'll keep that to myself.

Her face falls. She tosses the wadded-up napkin on the counter. "I'm sorry. Bad day."

"Wanna talk about it?"

"Nope." She takes another bite, a bigger bite, to keep from talking. "I'm fine. I'm always fine."

Frustration is written across her face. I look at the television hanging above the coolers and try to hide mine. Why won't she just tell me what I want to know? It's not like I can just blurt out that her friend Dylan accosted me today and told me all her secrets.

Thinking of Dylan with her hands on her hips makes me grin again.

"Machlan said your brother was coming to town," Navie says, dabbing a napkin against her mouth.

"Yup. Vincent and Sawyer are coming in for a couple of days."

She raises a brow. "Sawyer? Do you have another brother I didn't know about?"

"Sawyer is Vincent's son," I clarify. "He's a cute little shit."

"So is this brother of yours a lot like you?"

I swirl what's left of the beer in the bottom of the bottle and consider her question. "Vincent is a couple of years older than me. I think he might've hit thirty this year." I make a face. "Anyway, he's more of a troublemaker than I am."

"Oh, really?" Navie grins. "Is that possible?"

"Yes, really," I say with a shake of my head. "While I've always pulled questionable behavior, like Tad's stupid gas cans, Vincent pulled questionable-er behavior. He was always in trouble from doing stupid shit … until he had Sawyer."

Navie's features soften. "That's sweet."

"I mean, he didn't really have a choice, being a single dad and all. But he really pulled a one-eighty." I chuckle at the thought of my brother, the one who absolutely did not give a shit about anything, beaming at Sawyer the first time he rode a bike with no training wheels. "He's a good dad. Nah, he's a great fucking dad."

She grins. "That's awesome."

"It'll be nice to have him back around for a few days. I miss him, you know?"

She turns away and grabs a pop out of the cooler. "I do know, actually. Not that I have a great relationship with my family and I *did* move here to be away from them, but loneliness is a real thing. Sometimes that leads to really stupid mistakes." She makes a face. "But my friend Dylan just moved to town, so hopefully that'll help me stay sane."

Ding! Ding! Ding!

"Dylan? New boyfriend?" I ask as if I don't already know the answer.

"Nope. She's a girl I've known my whole life. Probably the only friend I have—friend who's a girl," she adds for my benefit. She unscrews her drink. "She's staying with me for a few days until her rental is vacant."

"That sounds … fun." Other adjectives are on the tip of my tongue, but I let them go because I'm not supposed to know her.

"It will be."

"What brought her here?" I tip my bottle back. I'm not sure if I want to know who stole her pots and pans or not, but I have to try. It's the only way to know who's on the right side of life.

Navie watches me take my drink with a heavy dose of curiosity. I'm not sure if she thinks I'm prying, which I am, or if she thinks I'm interested in hearing more about Dylan, which I also am, but she's clearly warring over how to answer this question.

I'm not surprised. Navie is fiercely private about her life outside of Crave, but she opens up to me more than anyone, I think. Her laughter is usually free, her heart warm and genuine, but she keeps stuff about herself kind of locked up tight. I'm good with that, normally. But if someone is stealing her cookware, that's an issue. I just want her to know I'm here for her.

She throws her sandwich tray in the trash and faces me with a resolution that makes me a little nervous. "She wanted to get a fresh start anyway …"

"And …"

She closes her eyes.

My stomach twists.

"And I was dating Logan and it—"

"Whoa," I say, my eyeballs about popping out of my head. "Logan. *Logan?* Logan, the guy I threw out of here, what, six months ago? For fighting with Machlan? For fighting *me*? The complete douche?"

She sighs. "That would be him."

"Navie. Really?"

I think back to the night that Logan challenged Machlan over Hadley. It was ugly. And bloody. And my fist hurt for a week afterward. He's a good for nothing and can't even take a punch the right way, let alone know how to treat a woman.

She winces as she looks at me. "Please don't tell Machlan."

"Why did you think that was a good idea?" I ask. "I mean, come on, Navie. You've seen him in action. You've seen him in here, drunk off his ass, acting like a fool. He's nowhere near good enough for you."

"Thanks." She grins sheepishly. "I know. I do. Or I did. Whatever. I just ran into him at Peaches one night when I was picking up takeout, and he apologized for that whole night, and I … I guess I was lonely, and things just … happened. But not anymore." She shakes her head. "We're done, and Dylan is here and ready to swoop in and take my mind off it in case I succumb to some kind of asshole withdrawal."

"You were that beat up about him that your friend had to move here to keep you company?"

"No." She rolls her eyes. "Just perfect timing. Dylan's pretty stressed out and wanted to kind of get away from everything. She tells herself I need her to justify it in her own mind, but I'm fine. You know that."

I raise a brow to silently challenge that idea. Navie may always pretend she's fine, but I have doubts. She's strong as hell. She's smart. She's capable. But she's a human being with weaknesses like the rest of us, much to her chagrin.

Her answer is to stick her tongue out at me.

"Logan?" I ask again.

"Shut up, Peck." She shakes her head again. "Not my best decision, I'll agree, but it was okay for a while."

I tip my bottle toward her. "I'm gonna doubt that."

"My heart is a little tender, okay? I'd appreciate a bit of pity."

I watch her over the lip of the bottle as I down the rest of my beer. I set it on the bar and knock it with the back of my hand. It sails down the smooth bar top and falls into the trashcan at the end with a satisfying *clink!*

"I should eat the rest of that sandwich," Navie says. "Eating out is going to get expensive, and I don't have that kind of expendable income. Heck, I don't have a lot of non-expendable income."

"Why don't you just cook?"

"Mind ya business, Peck." She sticks her tongue out again as she pulls a stack of napkins off the shelf behind her.

I climb off the bar. Taking my hat off, I run my fingers through my blond hair. That was a warning not to press, and I want to respect her request, but I also want to make sure she understands why I was pressing.

"Do you need anything, Navie?"

Her eyes fly to mine as she sets the napkins on the bar. "Why did you ask me that?"

"I don't know. Seems like a fair thing to ask a friend."

"Yes. I'm fine. Thanks for asking, *friend.*" She smiles before looking down at the napkins. "The world needs more men like you."

"Convince Molly of that."

She looks up and laughs. "I'm never gonna understand your infatuation with her. Never."

"And I'm never gonna understand why you'd even breathe the same air as Logan." I signal goodbye and head to the door. "Add my drink to my tab. And that twenty for the gas unless you accidentally forget. That's cool too."

"Goodbye, Peck."

I keep my head down to avoid the sun as I step back outside. I can completely understand why Dylan called *me* a jackass now. She thinks

I'm Logan. *Navie and Logan?* Makes me sick. That's not even being lonely. That's being ... stupid.

A grin splits my cheeks as I imagine the look on Dylan's face when she realizes her mistake. A chuckle rumbles past my lips as I consider the reaction of that little spitfire when that happens because it will. Linton is too small of a town for it not to.

Trudging along the sidewalk, my mind goes to the text I got from Nana earlier about coming over for dinner. I told her I'd be by, partly because I love fried chicken and partly because I can't tell her no.

But as I climb in my car, I do some quick math. I can be at Nana's in ten minutes, and she's expecting me in about twenty. I start to take off when I see Navie's car tucked in behind Crave.

"I've been late before," I grumble and head the opposite way of Nana's.

THREE

Dylan

"THAT HURTS."

I wince. My little toe that's silently screaming for assistance is swollen. It's a shade of red like it's been slapped ... or taken a sucker punch from the corner of my suitcase, which is what actually happened.

"Darn thing," I groan. Hobbling over to the sofa, I collapse against a pile of pillows. There's one covered in pink sequins, and another that's a soft, bright yellow that looks like it's been crocheted. Next to that is my personal favorite—a blue, almost water-like design that evokes serenity.

Usually. My throbbing toe kind of supersedes the Zen.

Navie's apartment is small but cute as a button. There's an abstract painting of what I think is a farm over the couch, and a lime green and gray rug that stretches across the living room. A diffuser sits on the little round table in the area that's probably pitched as a dining room slash breakfast nook.

I hold my toe and work it back and forth. The pain burns at first and slowly subsides as I tend to it. Sinking back into the pillows, I fill my lungs with oxygen. They inflate … effortlessly, which is a surprise.

There has been a tightness in my chest for as long as I can remember.

Stress, the doctor said. *What in your life is stressing you this much, Ms. Snow?*

Oh, I don't know. Maybe that it's falling apart.

I sat on the examination table—an appointment I only made because Navie made me swear I would go—and looked at him blankly. Wouldn't it be an easier question to answer if he asked me what isn't causing me stress?

Surely, this was normal. That's what I kept telling Navie. Doesn't everyone walk around with pain in their shoulders and their chest squeezed so tight that they can barely breathe at least twice a week? Aren't panic attacks normal when your boyfriend leaves you for his ex-fiancée and your mother basically makes you earn her love?

Apparently not. And this whole breathing easy thing is everything they said it would be. It's definitely something I could get used to.

Closing my eyes, I feel the muscles in my body give in. The tightness that's become second nature starts to relax when my phone rings.

"Crap," I say, eyeing the contents of my suitcase strewn around the room.

I hop up and dig through the clothes that will get me through until the moving truck delivers the rest of my stuff. Finally, under a tee shirt with a pair of lips painted on the front, I spy the phone.

"Hey," I say, testing my weight on my toe.

"You doing okay?" Navie asks.

"Yup. It's been a very eventful afternoon."

She sighs. "That worries me."

Laughing, I retake my spot on the couch. "Don't be worried. It's fine. My toe isn't broken, and Logan was effectively put in his place."

"What did you do, Dylan?"

I twirl a strand of hair around my finger and smile. "I might have gotten bored, and I might have just happened to see a sign for Dave's

Farm Stand or whatever it is. And then maybe I wanted to see if he had any produce—"

"You did not."

"*Or* I remembered that you said Logan worked out there sometimes and helped Dave, whoever he is, work on trucks and farm … shit. So I took a look." I shrug. "I can't help it that fate decided Logan and I should meet. He was just standing there, so-to-speak, when I arrived."

"Fate didn't decide that. You did," she deadpans.

"I'd rather be karma than fate. Anyway, I did my greatest Best Friend Fuck You speech, and he promised to stay away from you and bring back your pots and pans. I think that's a total win. You can thank me later."

I pluck at the hem of my shirt. How nice would it be to be karma? To have the powers of justice and fairness? That might be better than endless tacos.

A girl can dream.

"You know," Navie says, "I don't even think I want the shit back. I'd rather just forget he exists at all."

"I've had those."

"Had those what?"

"Those guys you wish didn't exist." I drop the edge of my shirt. "Case in point: Charlie. I'd rather forget that I was left after committing a year to a relationship because he realized that he didn't love me —that he couldn't possibly love me because he truly loves Vanessa." I sigh. "Or take this one guy I dated once. Super cute. Looked hygienic. Paid for dinner and let me pick some movies. But there was this one night," I say, feeling my stomach rumble as the memory comes back to me. "I got up in the middle of the night to pee and legit stepped in his urine. The dude sprayed all over the floor, and it was on my foot."

Navie makes a gagging noise, and I try not to throw up in my mouth.

"I wish I could forget they both exist," I say, fighting off a shiver.

"I bet you do. That's how I feel about Logan. I didn't even really like him. I'm just pissed off he took my kitchen utensils and then ghosted me. He was just a stupid fling. I don't know what I saw in him in the first place."

Logan's face flutters through my mind. His bright blue eyes and almost shy, yet mischievous smile light a bubble of excitement in my stomach.

I snort. "I do," I say before I can catch myself.

"What?"

"I saw him. He's cute, Navie."

"Dylan …"

"I mean, he's an asshole," I say, getting to my feet. "We know that. But it's not hard to see why you took him up on whatever offer he threw down."

She groans. "He's not *that* cute. I have guys in the bar every night cuter than him."

"Then I think it's time that I accompany you to work."

"Not tonight," she says. "Machlan just left, and I'm here alone. I can't protect the men from you."

"Ha. Ha. Ha. See ya when you get home."

"Adios."

I end the call and toss my phone onto the couch. The apartment is ridiculously quiet—even quieter than my apartment in Indiana. There are no neighbors fighting or talk shows seeping through the walls. Heck, there's not even the smell of burnt pizza. Everything is just … still.

It's very Navie, very calm-in-the-storm. She always has a way of doing that. Riots and chaos can be going on, and Navie is the one in the middle doing yoga.

We met on the first day of kindergarten and bonded over chocolate pudding as finger paint. We were virtually inseparable until she left to come here.

I was devastated when she left, but I understood. If my family is difficult, hers is toxic. Seeing her so happy and adjusted here makes the months I spent without her okay. I'm just glad to be here with her, my only real friend, now too.

I study the length and try to guess how many steps it would take to get from one to the other when a movement catches my eye outside the window. I slink over to the curtain.

Logan walks up to the front door with a big box in his hand.

"Victory is mine," I whisper as I reach for the door handle. I yank it open. "Well, hello there."

He grins over the top of the box. His teeth are white and straight, his hat pulled down over his forehead.

"I was going to leave this here," he says, tapping on a box of pots and pans.

He's the enemy, Dylan. Be strong.

He shoves the box toward me. "Since you opened the door, here you go."

I take the box and set it inside. I should flash him a tight smile and close the door, but I'm only human. Besides, I'm not the queen of karma, so I should probably have manners.

For karma's sake.

"I'm happy to see you *bringing those by*," I say, clearing my throat. "Even though they aren't her old ones, they'll do."

"I couldn't find the old ones."

"Pawned them."

He fights a laugh. "I'm doing the best I can here, okay?"

I lean against the doorframe and take him in. He's so disarming with his blond hair poking out the sides of his cap and tall, lanky frame. And no man should have lashes that long. It's just not fair.

But it is proof that everyone is a disappointment. I've speculated for years that no one actually cares about other people anymore, and this Logan thing proves it. By looking at him, you'd think he was the kind boy-next-door type when, in reality, he's a hedonistic jerk. It's very disappointing.

It's either that, or I set my standards way too high.

Like top of the ozone layer too high.

"Navie will appreciate you being a man about this after all," I say.

"Yup. Logan is a real winner."

I arch my brow. "Third person? Really?"

"I didn't take the pots and pans, Dylan," he says with a sigh.

"Then what happened to them? A burglar broke in and ignored the television and her computer and the cookie jar of cash that probably holds thirty bucks, but still? Not plausible, Logan. But why you'd want them, I don't know. Was it to get back at her in a way she'd think about every day? Is that it? Are you so in love with her—"

"With Navie?"

"Obviously."

He laughs. "No. She's like my sister."

My brain scrambles. I open my mouth, but nothing comes out. Forcing a swallow, I eye him carefully. "I have a lot of questions as to why you'd sleep with someone who's like your sister and then steal from her, but I'm not sure I want the answers."

"Good," he says, leaning forward. "Because if I start giving you answers, you're gonna feel really stupid, and I don't want to see your pretty little face all scrunched up in embarrassment."

"Don't flirt with me."

He shrugs, the corner of his lips tugging to the sky.

He's lit from behind by the setting sun and a sky full of vibrant rays. It's like he's the center of a painting, the star of a poster from some Hollywood romantic comedy, and I can barely take it.

I have to look away.

And berate myself for thinking this about a guy who screwed over my friend.

"I forgot your Jack," he says. "I can bring it by later. Thinking maybe you need it."

"Nah, I'm good, Chef Boyardee. I shouldn't drink anyway. Drinking puts me in all my feels, and that's not the place for a sane girl to be."

"You mean you're sane?" he teases.

I level my gaze with his and try not to laugh. "Yup. You don't even want to see me really mad."

"Does smoke come out of your ears and everything?"

"Yup."

We both struggle to keep a straight face. In seconds, we're laughing.

The sound of our voices mixing together sets a too-comfortable ambiance on Navie's front porch. It shouldn't be this easy to be friendly with Logan, and I shouldn't be questioning how he could possibly be such a jerk to Navie, but I am.

I'm a traitor.

A traitor who can't quit talking.

"Did you get that truck done?" I ask.

"Yup. And I paid the guy back for the gas. Just mentioning that so you don't think I'm a thief."

"But you are. You know, pots and pans."

He takes his hat off and scratches the top of his head. "But I brought the pans back and paid for the gas. So maybe I'm a good thief like the good witch in the Wizard of Oz."

"She was still a witch," I say.

"But pretty in that pink dress. It was pink, right? It's been a while."

He moves to put the hat back on. The air comes alive with his cologne. It's aromatic with an aquatic, slightly woody hint that barrels through my veins and makes my brain foggy.

Glancing at his watch, he frowns. "I gotta be hitting the road."

"Hot date?"

He stuffs his hands in his pockets and grins. "Yup."

My stomach flip flops as I take a step back toward the door. The logical part of my brain tells me that this is a good thing—that he'll be leaving Navie alone—but the female part of my brain, the one that favors charisma and looks over sensible actions, is kind of sad.

"My date tonight makes the best cheeseball in the world. She puts extra bacon in it just for me, and word on the street is that she made fried chicken. *It's the best*," he adds. His eyes twinkle as he describes the night waiting for him.

"Good. I need to get going too," I say, jamming a finger behind me. "I have to, you know ... make sure all of my stuff is ready to move and all that."

"Where ya movin'?"

"I'm renting a house on Vine Street. Just waiting on the tenants to get out. They were supposed to be out last week, but the landlord had a hard time getting them to go, so now I have to wait."

He nods. "Cool. Well, if you need anything done around there, I know people who'll work for cheap."

"Thanks."

"Now I gotta get going, or Nana will be pissed."

"Nana?" I say as he heads down the sidewalk. "What kind of name is that?"

He smiles before climbing in his truck. The engine starts before he rolls the window down.

"Don't forget to give Navie the pots and pans," he says.

"I will."

"And if you get a hankering for fried chicken, I know a grandma who loves to feed people. It's one of Nana's best recipes."

My mouth drops open. "You just ghosted my best friend, and you're inviting me to dinner? With your grandmother, no less."

Even though I'm quietly thrilled Nana is his grandmother and not some exotic beauty, I feign indifference.

"Sorry," he says, revving his engine. "I forgot about all that ghosting thing."

"You're a bastard, Logan."

His laughter is loud as he backs down the driveway. He waves from the street before his tires bark as he pulls away.

I go back inside and close the door behind me. Venturing into the kitchen, I spy a shirt slung over the back of a chair. Navie tossed Logan's shirt there this morning as she complained about not being able to make breakfast.

Glancing back at the door, I try to imagine Logan screwing Navie over like that.

It's hard to imagine him being such a dick. He seems so ... I grin before I can even get the words into a coherent thought.

"Face the facts," I say as I pick up the shirt. "He's a troll like Navie said."

I toss the shirt into the trash can.

And force myself not to take it back out.

FOUR

Dylan

"I AM AN ADULT, for heaven's sake."

Glancing at the pile of paperwork in front of me—bills that need paid, papers that need my signature, and a budget that I need to peruse to remind myself of its existence—I do the logical thing: I fall back on the floor, sending papers flying in the air, and think happy thoughts.

Happy thoughts that, by definition, don't include adultish things.

"I need a grown-up," I moan.

I think back to my last birthday, the one where I turned twenty-nine, and how I thought this would be the year I got myself together. The year I felt like I knew how to handle all the things. Life. Paperwork. Insurance.

Instead, I'm camping out on Navie's couch at two in the morning while she's at work, and I'm killing time. I don't even have my own place yet and am living out of a suitcase and a duffel bag.

I might never reach adult status when it comes to all the things.

I gasp as the front door pushes open. The only available weapon close by is a tube of mascara. I grab it and hold it in front of me as Navie walks in.

"You scared the shit out of me," I say, blowing out a breath.

"Sorry. I just live here." She shoots me a tired smile before dropping her purse on the table. "And what were you going to do with that?" One of her fingers makes a slow circle in the air as it points to the mascara in my hand.

I drop it.

"Um, maybe poke the intruder in the eye," I offer with a sheepish shrug. "That's a solid plan. Right?"

She nods like I'm crazy. "Sure. Or you could've smothered him in all those papers. What on earth are you doing?"

Grabbing the closest paper to me, I take a look at it. "Sorting my life."

"I hope it's going better than it looks."

"It is. Kind of." I peruse the financial data on the paper I'm holding. "According to this, I'm doing great at living on a budget. Well, except for this one little line item."

"Eating out?"

"Kind of. I call it the HAS Line," I say.

"Has? Like, you *has to have it*?"

"Kind of again. It stands for Hungry Angry Sad. It's where I put all the things I buy when I'm hangry, mad, or sad. It's *quite the line*," I cringe. "I've heard of stress eating. Who knew stress shopping was a thing? Because it is, and this HAS Line proves it. I mean, who spends two hundred dollars, give or take, on gourmet ice cream delivery? Me. That's who."

"Hey, I'm not going to judge you over ice cream. But I will take a little offense to the fact you didn't bring any of it here."

I laugh. "Don't say that. I'll order some and that HAS Line will double next month. I mean, do you like pistachio coconut or brambleberry pecan?"

Navie giggles. "Neither. Right now, I just want to save enough money to cook at home without using the microwave."

"Oh!" I bounce to my feet. "I helped you with that today. Can't help my damn self, but I did help you."

Navie gives me a worried look while she unwraps her hair from a bun on the top of her head. Then she slips her arms into her shirt, shimmies around, and then tosses her bra toward the closet that houses the tiniest washer and dryer known to man.

"There," she says. "I can think now." She slumps into a chair with lavender padding and looks at me. "What did you do?"

I smack my lips together with a little shrug and turn my eyes toward the big box by the door. She follows my gaze.

Her head falls to the side as she looks at me again.

"What?" I ask.

"I'm afraid to ask."

"Afraid to ask what? I got your pots and pans back." I sit on the sofa. "You can say thank you. That's the socially acceptable reply."

"You didn't buy that, did you?"

"Nope. *Logan did.*"

I'm unsure if the sigh that comes from her mouth is in disbelief or frustration. She rests the back of her head against the chair and watches me carefully.

"What exactly did you say to him?" she asks.

"Nothing that I feel sorry for."

She chuckles. "I'm not sure that you've felt sorry for anything you've ever said in your life."

"I wouldn't have said it if I thought I'd feel bad about it."

"So …"

I pull my legs up on the couch. "I just told him what a jerk he was and the least he could do was return your stuff. I must've been very convincing because he took the money he got from pawning your stuff it and bought you a new set."

She cringes.

I smile widely.

She cringes harder. "You're a pistol," she says.

I'm not sure she means that as a compliment, but I definitely take it as one. "Thanks. I think so too. Why do you always underestimate me?"

"I don't know, but I really did this time. I mean, Logan isn't a cupcake, if you know what I'm saying. He doesn't bend to people's will very often."

I imagine him throwing punches and sweating all over the place. *Dayum.*

"It's just hard to believe he succumbed to your ... tactics," she says.

"Well, I don't really like the word threaten because it sounds so harsh. But I guess you could say that I kind of threatened him—in a very ladylike manner, of course."

She presses her lips together and nods. "*Ladylike.* I'm sure."

"It was," I insist. "I don't even think I cursed. And I didn't suggest the removal of any body parts either. Ladylike. Boom."

She laughs, wiping her hands down her face. "I bet he didn't know what to do with you."

"I didn't know what to do with him," I admit. "I expected him to be cocky and just completely disgusting, but ... he wasn't."

I pull my knees to my chest and think of Logan's smile. He wasn't any of the things I thought he'd be. He was sort of kind, actually, and not quiet, per se, but polite. He definitely let me say my piece—even if I didn't give him much leeway to talk.

Still, he wasn't the manwhore I braced myself to encounter.

Navie screws her face up as though she can't understand my thought process. "He wasn't?"

I look at her like I'm missing something. She looks at me like she's awaiting an explanation.

"No, he wasn't. And I feel bad for saying that because he ghosted you, *and* he's a thief," I say. "He's completely the enemy, and I get it. I'm with ya, sister. But he was ... nice. Although I'm sure it was an act," I add.

"Interesting."

I shrug. "Or not." I bite the end of a fingernail and contemplate a way to change the subject. Luckily, she does it for me.

"You look comfy," she says.

"I am. Considering we're sharing about six hundred square feet of space, I'm rather cozy." I pick up the yellow pillow and toss it side to side. "I love what you've done with the place."

She laughs. "Shut up."

"I mean it," I say, laughing too. "I actually took a couple of mental notes about how you use mirrors to make the rooms feel bigger, and the use of plants to make it feel more outdoorsy or something. I don't know what it is, but I like it."

"We'll have fun decorating your house. When does your stuff get here?"

"A couple of days. The moving guy left me a text today that they're a couple of days behind, which works out perfectly since I don't have my house yet. And I don't start work at the bank for a couple of weeks, so it should be enough time to get semi-settled before I start work."

A bolt of excitement tears through me as I think about my new place. There's so much hope in a new house—a place free of negative vibes. I've needed this for a long time, probably longer than I even realize. Navie has been saying it for years.

"Have you heard from your mom?" she asks.

My spirits sink as I avert my eyes from Navie. My heart is still sore, my feelings tender about leaving my family behind. It was definitely by choice because I made the decision to go, but I wish it didn't have to be this way.

"Yes," I say. "She texted me yesterday and asked if I made it. I said I had, and I haven't heard from her since."

I attempt to keep my voice void of any emotion, shielding Navie from the hurt I feel at my mom's antiseptic behavior toward me. But she's Navie. She hears it. She's seen it. She's walked every frustrated moment alongside me and has been angry on my behalf many times.

"I'm sorry, Dylan." The words come out thick and heavy.

"It's okay," I say past a lump in my throat. "She'll call when she needs something—when there's an opportunity to earn her love."

Navie reaches out and places her hand on my thigh. She gives it a gentle squeeze. "I wish I could say something to make this easier, but I know I can't."

"Yeah, you can't. It's just one of those things we can't do anything about. People choose where they spend their energy, and my brother and sister are that place for my mom. They get her love even though they're massive fuckups. I have to prove my worth. It's okay. It's just how it is."

Navie's palm lifts from my leg, and suddenly, I feel very alone again.

She's been the only person in my life that I've been able to talk freely with about my relationship with my family. Everyone else assumes there's something wrong with you if things with your parents and siblings aren't perfect. They don't stop to consider that maybe you're the one wanting and trying to have a great situation while the others don't. And maybe it has nothing to do with you.

I force a swallow.

"You deserve a great life, Dylan," Navie says. "You should have people around who make you laugh and help you when you're sick and are present in your life every day, not just when it benefits them."

"That's what I want. I mean, it's not asking for too much to want to see me as a human being and not just as some … tool to helping them get what they want, right?"

"Of course not."

"Then why does that feel selfish sometimes?"

I frown. The vulnerability of talking about this feels as if I'm bleeding right in front of Navie, and I loathe it. The back of my neck tightens as I war with myself whether to shut this conversation down while I can or to open up to the one person who gets me.

"It feels selfish because that's what society tells us to think, and it's bullshit," she says. "You don't have to take the gas out of your tank to fill everyone else up. You're allowed to keep some of your energy and spirit for yourself."

She's right—or I hope she's right, anyway. My tank is so empty I can hear it rattle, and it's because it can't run on empty promises.

I need help bailing Reed out of jail. I know you just got your bonus at work. You don't mind helping your family, do you?

Koty's electricity is going to get turned off. I'm sorry it'll cost you all your play money again this month, but you need to do this for your sister. She's going to look for a job next week. She'd do it for you.

I spent the last of my savings to take Koty for a spa day. Poor girl was so upset about the divorce and all that I just needed to perk her up. Now I can't pay my cable bill. There's nothing to do here but watch television. I can see depression right around the corner. Unless, of course, you're going to help me out.

I sigh.

It was one thing after another. If I said no to any of it, despite the fact that Reed will just get thrown back in jail again in a couple of weeks and Koty wouldn't bother giving me a drink of water if I were dying of thirst, then I get the silent treatment. It's the same treatment I get if I need help. But, on the contrary, if I jump when they need me, I get invited to family cookouts. I have to fight for my place in that family. And I'm tired of it.

"I just hate feeling like this—like me doing something for me, setting some actual boundaries, isn't okay. Like, I know it makes sense. I do. I need to be able to live and grow and not exist for them. But last night when I laid here and closed my eyes, I felt this twist in my gut, and I started second-guessing everything again."

"Don't."

She gets off the chair and takes the three steps to me. She nudges me with her hip until I scoot over and she can drop beside me.

A lump grows in my throat as she looks at me with the kindest eyes.

"Listen, Dylan. You weren't put onto this planet to be Reed's clean-up crew. Your brother is a grown ass man, and he chooses over and over again to screw up his life. It's not your problem anymore. Heck, it never was."

"I know."

My admission must lack enough gusto for Navie to believe it because she continues.

31

"And Koty is a decent person," she says about my sister. "And I hate that her husband left her and the kids behind, but you can't be expected to foot the damn bill for their lives. At some point, she has to grow up and take care of things herself. And even if you say no, they should still love you. It's bullshit how they treat you. I don't know how you took it this long."

I settle my gaze on a mirror facing me on the opposite wall. It's an odd picture—me sitting with Navie on her couch when I was in my own home just a few days ago. It's almost hard to believe the reflection is true.

But it is.

I don't want to think too much about it. If I do, the tightness in my chest will be back. And the headaches. And ... *No. Stop, Snow. New place. New start. New me.*

"Okay," I say, getting up and finding my computer. "Honey and jam ice cream, or should we try the whiskey and pecan?"

Navie shakes her head.

"Right," I say. "Both."

Click!

FIVE

Peck

"I THINK IT'S A GREAT IDEA."

Machlan looks at me from the other side of the bar. The look on his face is fairly unreadable. It could be that he's pretending my suggestion is terrible. But there's a remote chance he's contemplating my proposal for a new weekend activity at Crave with the seriousness it deserves. A small chance, but a chance nonetheless.

"Peck," he begins. "Shut up."

"Think about it," I say, not shocked he reverted to dismissing my moment of brilliance. "Move the pool tables to the side and add a giant bull right in the center and let people ride it. I saw this thing once where—"

"Pretty sure that's a violation of my insurance policy."

"Then your policy is a pussy." I tear at the label on my beer. "What about a wet T-shirt contest?"

"I think Hadley would find the idea of women dancing on top of bars with their T-shirts soaked so everyone can see their nipples kind of in bad taste."

"Karaoke?"

Machlan tips his head back and looks at the ceiling.

"Fine," I say. "Belly shots. It's a tried-and-true way to increase revenue. I mean, I don't have facts to back that up, but I just don't know how you can go wrong with it."

"Peck ..."

I shrug. "I didn't want to have to go there, but you're shooting down everything I fire your way." Leaning against the bar, the edge digging into my ribs, I level my eyes with his. "If you want to do it and take all the credit, I'm fine with that. I know you like everyone to think you're the genius."

"Who's a genius?" Navie comes out of nowhere. Her purse flies under the bar with a thud. She looks at me, then at Machlan, and then back to me. "Cleary, it's neither of you two."

"Hey," I say, leaning back and clutching at my heart. "That wounds me."

Machlan rolls his eyes at my antics. "I mentioned how I'd like to shake things up on the weekends, and Boy Genius here came up with some ideas that would do one of three things: get my insurance cancelled, have Hadley leave me, or turn the place into a porn club."

Navie twists her lips. "Tell me more about the last one."

"See?" I yelp as I sit up. "Belly shots are the answer, Mach. Fuck it. I'm taking the credit for this."

Navie laughs as she swipes a piece of hair off her forehead. "You know, I could've guessed where that idea came from without anyone telling me."

"Because it's genius, and you equate me with genius things, right?" I ask.

"Something like that." She and Machlan exchange a grin. "So let's keep thinking of ideas—in case there's a gelatin shortage or something," she adds, looking my way, "and see what happens. In the meantime, does anyone know how to treat a burn?"

She grabs her wrist and winces. There's a red welt across her skin that looks like it hurts like hell.

"What did you do?" Machlan asks.

"Burned it frying a hamburger. I mean, I don't cook for a couple of weeks and then try to fry a hamburger, which I do here all the time, and apparently forget how."

A glimmer of happiness shines in her eyes, and it hits me right in the chest. There's a weight off her shoulders. I doubt it's the pots and pans specifically, but probably more like she thinks things are put to bed with Logan. That makes me happy—even if I had to pretend to be him and get guilted into buying him out of trouble.

How did that even happen?

"You're welcome," I say before tipping the rest of my beer back.

"For what?" Navie asks.

"For being me, I guess."

Ignoring the confused looks of my friends, I send the bottle careening down the bar. It flies into the trashcan at the end.

"Butter," I say.

"What the fuck are you talking about?" Machlan asks.

"Butter on burns." I shrug. "I read that once. Or heard it. Or something. You put butter on burns to make them better."

Machlan chuckles. "That's not true."

"It is."

"It isn't. What's the science behind that?" He crosses his arms over his chest, enjoying a situation where he thinks he has the answer. "Butter is a fat. Fat would keep the heat inside the burn. It's counterintuitive."

He has a point. Damn it.

"While you take that up with the interwebs," I say, "I'm going to figure out how to make you money."

I have no clue what I'm going to do, but what I'm *not* going to do is sit here and have Machlan prove me wrong. It's not that I was *guaranteeing* butter would work. I was just *suggesting* it, and I'm not giving him the opportunity to flaunt his *minor* victory over my head.

I look around Crave. There are a few people in the back. Pool balls are being racked up as they chat over the table.

"Hey," I call back there. "Question—what would you guys like to see in here on weekends?"

"What are you doing?" Machlan asks.

I look over my shoulder. "I'm taking a survey of your five patrons—myself not included."

"People don't know what they want. You just have to give it to them," Machlan says.

I smirk. "Pretty sure that's illegal in all fifty states."

Navie laughs, jabbing Machlan in the ribs, as I turn back to the pool players.

"So?" I ask.

"Cheaper drinks," one of them suggests.

Machlan snorts behind me.

"What else?" I ask.

The blonde puts a pool stick between her boobs and grins. "How about you strip teasing on top of the bar?"

"That I can do," I say.

I turn to face Machlan. His eyes are narrowed.

"Don't," he says.

"The people want it. A good businessman delivers what the people want." I glance over my shoulder. Again. "You want it, right?"

"Do I ever," Blondie says.

I shrug. "See?"

"I think we give him a shot," Navie offers. "I mean, it could really—"

"Peck," Machlan shouts as I leap onto the bar.

Staying a few feet away from him so he can't reach out and swipe my legs out from under me—been there, done that—I plant my boot-clad feet shoulder width apart. I'm not expecting the country song that pulses out of the speakers.

"Get it," Navie shouts over the beat.

Laughing, I start with a roll of my body. I don't have a damn clue how you're actually supposed to do this. I just get up here from time to time to get a rise out of Machlan because it pisses him off ... and hopefully to get a little attention from Molly if she's around.

A whistle screams through the air from Blondie as I lift the edge of my diesel truck logo shirt. I spin my hat around backward, the music just starting to feed into my blood when it shuts off.

"Down, Peck," Machlan barks.

"Don't blame me if you go broke," I shout back to him.

The bar is flooded with light. The front door open, and Dylan steps inside.

My stomach flip flops at the sight of her.

She has on the same cutoffs that she had on the day she ripped my ass at Dave's. A T-shirt falls easily off one shoulder. It has a rainbow across the front.

Her eyes scan the bar, lighting up when she sees Navie. I stand still —both unable and afraid to move.

"Hey, Navie," she chirps. The door closes behind her. She makes her way across the room toward the bar. "Thought I'd check this place out tonight ..." Her voice falls as her gaze lands on me. "What are you doing here?"

I gulp.

I'm not sure how to play this off ... and in front of Navie, no less. I look at my friend and spy a quirked brow.

"I'm volunteering to host a strip tease event on Saturday nights," I say. "Want a preview?"

"Get. Down," Machlan says. Again.

Dylan presses her lips together. Still, there's a hint of a smile that makes me grin. I don't know what it is about her refusal to be nice to me that's so amusing, but it is.

"I can't believe they let you in here," she says.

"Why wouldn't we?" Navie asks.

I bow my head as I hop to the floor. The soles of my boots squeak against the concrete. If I look up, I'll see the equivalent of a rainbow-shirt wearing iceberg get plowed by a few *Titantic*-esque truths that are probably going to hurt.

Me.

That's who it's going to hurt. Because she's going to blame me for not telling her, and her fingernail poking my chest hurts like a mother-fucker.

Dylan pops her hip, a hand finding the bend right above it. Her eyes are glued to me as she sighs. "Well, at least he returned what he stole."

"Good thing we don't kick him out over not paying for shit," Machlan says, heading toward the storeroom. "Fucker always has a tab."

"I pay it off every month," I yell at him.

I turn slowly back around to see Navie and Dylan looking at me. Dylan looks defiant, as usual, but Navie's something else. Curious, maybe.

"I didn't know you guys knew each other," Navie says.

Dylan raises a brow. "I told you I met him yesterday."

"Huh. I must've missed that."

My heart starts to pick up its pace as I feel the impending bomb drop hovering overhead. "I'm going to head out."

"You want me to add your beer to your tab?" Navie asks.

Dylan's jaw drops. "How can you be so nice to him? I mean, I know he brought everything back and all that, but seriously, Navie. Be mad. Be angry." She balls her fists up and shakes them in front of her. "Stand up for yourself, girlfriend. Don't let him ghost you and then just pop back up with that stupid charm and cute smile."

Navie cocks her head to the side. I smile sheepishly.

"Tab. Yup," I say, walking backward toward the door.

"See ya later, Peck," Navie says.

My foot halts midstep as the realization I've been waiting to hit Dylan flushes over her face. Her eyes widen before they narrow. The apples of her cheeks turn the prettiest shade of pink as she starts putting pieces of things together.

I retreat again, quicker this time—

"Stop," Dylan demands.

Navie comes around the bar, a white bar towel fisted in her hand. "What's happening here?"

"Who is that?" Dylan asks, pointing at me.

"I really gotta go," I say.

"What's his name?" Dylan looks at me. "What's your name?"

"Little late to be asking that now, isn't it?" I rotate my hat around again, pulling it snugly down as far as I can.

"You're Logan. Right?" Dylan watches me intently. "Tell me your Logan, or I'm going to flip tables."

"What are you talking about?" Navie asks, laughing at her friend. "That's not Logan. That's Peck."

Dylan lets out a little shriek as she flies in a half-circle to face Navie. "What are you talking about? That's not your cute best friend here ... until I moved here. Now I'm your cute best friend here. *Anyway*, that's Logan. The jerkface that ghosted you!"

Navie's laugh fills with confusion. "No, it's not. That's Peck. Why on Earth would you think ..." Her voice trails off. A lightbulb goes off as all the pieces in a puzzle are snapped together in her brain.

"Yeah ...." I mumble.

"Peck," Navie warns.

"Don't *Peck* me. I didn't do anything wrong."

"The hell you didn't," Dylan interjects. "You let me think you were Logan. You brought Logan's pots and pans ... or Navie's pots and pans that you—I mean, Logan—stole ... Ugh. This is giving me a headache."

Both of them watch me for a reaction. Navie is mildly entertained, but Dylan looks mostly shocked. If I had the balls to laugh at her pretty little face scrunched up in horror, I would. *Buuuut* I don't. Not even close.

I shuffle my feet, unsure if I should get another beer or run before I get poked in the chest again.

"That skillet was a good one, right?" I ask.

It's a stupid thing to say, but this is a stupid situation. Maybe the stupidest situation I've ever been in, and with Walker, Lance, and Machlan Gibson as cousins, I've been in a whole lot of them. So that says something.

Navie's features soften. "You bought those? For real?"

"Yeah."

"Both of you hush," Dylan says. She moves her weight from one foot to the other. "You aren't Logan. You're Peck."

"Yup," I say. "I'm pretty sure we've made that clear—ouch!"

She slaps my bicep. The sound echoes through the bar, catching the attention of Machlan as he reappears. I plead silently for him to help me. He laughs instead and disappears once again into the storeroom.

Fucker.

"What's that for?" I ask, rubbing my arm.

"Why didn't you tell me?"

"You never asked," I say. "And you didn't give me a chance."

"Bullshit."

"Bullshit what?" I say with a chuckle. "I was under a damn truck, and here you come roasting me for all this stuff, and I finally was like, 'Okay. I'll be the bad guy if it'll make you stop talking.'"

She gasps.

"Only because you were confusing the hell outta me. I had work to do, and you were accusing me of being some asshole that ghosted my friend." I blow out a breath. "So now that you know I'm not Logan—thank fuck—we can move on. Right? Are we friends here?"

No one answers. It's like they're stunned silent.

"Also," I add since they're being quiet. "I'm still the cute best friend here. I won't relinquish that title."

Still ... nothing.

I slide my hat on backward again. "I'm going to figure out who is going to feed me tonight. Good night, ladies."

"I heard Sienna made Walker chicken noodle soup today," Machlan calls as he comes out of the storeroom again.

I jam my finger in the air as if to say, "Gotcha," and head for the door.

SIX

Peck

"IF YOU'RE such a crack mechanic, why haven't you fixed this yet?" Walker walks across the parking lot of Crank and wipes his face with a purple bandana. There's a smear of grease along his eyebrow that makes him look a little like a pirate. "How does it take this damn long to take an oil pan off a machine?"

"Simple. Some genius told me not to use penetrating oil because it's for pussies. Could've had it fixed in ten minutes otherwise."

"Ten minutes, my ass."

"Okay, maybe twelve," I joke. "But … watch and learn, Captain."

I smack the final bolt with a hammer to loosen it the rest of the way —hopefully—and then grab the wrench. A few twists, and it's off. The oil, thick and black, splashes into the tray underneath.

"Annnd done—the hard way, I'll point out," I say. "Which was stupid and a huge waste of time, but you're paying me by the hour, so what do I really care?"

Walker's arms are smeared with grease too as he crosses them over his burly chest. He's as big as a damn house and strong as an ox too.

Regardless of how menacing he looks or assholish he sounds, he's one of the best people I know. And now that he has Sienna Landry living with him—and on the verge of marriage, if I'm guessing, and I'd have to be guessing because Walker doesn't talk about those kinds of things —his edges are getting a little softer too.

I wouldn't tell him that, though. Soft edges or not, he could still kill me.

"That's a good point," he says, jamming the bandana in his back pocket. "Maybe I oughta pay you a salary. Then I could just give you a list of things to do every day and not give a shit how long it takes you to do it."

"Maybe I'd quit."

He snorts. "I've tried to get rid of you for years. Ain't got ya to leave yet."

We exchange a smile because he's right, and we both know it. I'd never leave him, and he'd never let me anyway. Somehow, our dynamic gets shit done. Four or five mechanic shops have tried to open in Linton in the past handful of years, but they close down fast every time. No one can compete with Crank because we don't steal our customers' money and actually give a damn about our work. It's not exactly a cutting-edge business model, but it works. Well.

"I'm gonna grab some lunch," he says. "I'll be back in an hour or so."

"Where ya going?"

"Home. Sienna made this beef thing her sister sent her the recipe for."

My ears perk up. "Oooh. Tell her to save me some. I'll be by for dinner."

"Fucking hell, Peck. She's my girlfriend. Not yours."

"Clearly," I say, rolling my eyes. "But she likes cooking for me too. As friends. As *family*."

He heads to his truck. "If I didn't need ya around here, I might strangle ya."

I laugh as I get back to the tractor. Satisfied that the oil is doing its thing, I head underneath the back end to check on a bearing. The gravel bites in my back as I get situated under the machine.

No matter how many rocks I pick out of my hair or how scraped up my skin gets, I'd never trade this job for anything in the world. Every project is like a puzzle I can solve. I know I can. And when I do take something broken and repair it, it gives me a high. When a farmer calls and asks Walker to send me to a field to get his equipment back on track, it maybe even gives me a purpose.

There's nothing like it.

There's nothing like knowing you're useful, that you're good at something. That someone needs you around ... even if it's for something as ordinary as fixing equipment.

I check the bearings and make sure they're good. Climbing out from under the tractor, I watch a car pull into the parking lot. It's a blue compact car with a cute little brunette in the driver's seat.

Leaning against the tractor, I grin as Dylan steps out of the car.

"I'm Peck," I call out. "Just thought I'd start everything off right this time."

She grins. "I got that. Thanks."

"What are you doing here?"

"I came to see you."

I press off the tractor.

She's so darn pretty.

I take her in as she approaches and realize I'm not even looking at her physical traits. I'm smiling at the possibility of what's going to come from her mouth. Despite her jazzing me, bantering back and forth with her and having her give as good as she gets is entertaining.

I chuckle.

"What?" she asks.

"Nothing. What's up? Need to blame me for some other deviant's mistakes?"

"Ha-ha. No."

I rub a hand down the side of my face. "Then are you coming to blindside guilt me into making a purchase for some random housewares that really have nothing to do with me?"

She drops her chin and looks at me through her lashes. "Really, Peck?"

"Ah, that's a good sign! You're using my real name."

She tries not to laugh but fails. Finally, she gives in, and the sweet sound billows across the parking lot.

A truck honks as it passes, and I wave without looking at who it is.

"Your real name can't be Peck," she says.

"And why can't it?"

The idea that maybe she's just offended me flitters across her face. "Well, I guess it can. It just doesn't seem like a proper first name. That's all."

"Is there such a thing as a proper first name these days? You've got kids named after space dust and fruit and cartoon characters. I don't think Peck is that crazy, to be honest."

She grins. "I dated a guy once—well, I don't know if you could say I dated him, if you know what I mean. But anyway, his name was Prince. His actual God-given name was Prince. Who does that?"

I mumble something. What? I'm not sure. I'm too busy trying to shove off this idea of her going at it with some dude named Prince.

"Your name is Dylan," I tease, rerouting my brain away from the guy I've decided I dislike. "What kind of name is that for a girl?"

"Hey, now. That was my grandma's name."

I jab at her with my elbow as I start to walk away from her. "I'm just kidding."

She follows me across the parking lot, sidestepping the mud puddles. Her nose crinkles as she touches the water with the side of her foot.

I get to the door of Crank before her and pull it open. Watching her try to get by the last two holes—the deepest ones in the lot—will be the highlight of my day. She bites her lip as if calculating quantum physics as she studies the possibility of hopping between them.

"Um, you could go around them," I suggest. "Or walk through them like I did."

"Ew. No."

"It's water. It's not gonna kill you."

CRAZY

"It's mud and oil and … stuff." She sighs. "And I'm not going around them. This is my path, and I'm bending it to suit me."

"Well, if you could bend it a little faster, that'd be great. All the air conditioning is going outside."

She puts her hands on her hips. "You could shut the door."

"And you could just walk through the damn puddle."

Firing me a last playful glare, she tries to hop over the last two holes. Her shirt glues to her body as she bounces, her hair shifting around her shoulders. It's playful and fun and fucking sexy, and I'm not prepared when she loses her balance. Her flip-flop must get wet because she slides to the side, her legs splitting apart into a wide stance, and she grabs my arm to steady herself.

Her hands wrap around my bicep. They're small and dainty, but her grip is strong. I flex without thinking, and her eyes light up.

She looks up at me, her lips parted. My throat goes dry as I try to keep myself unaffected—or at least something other than grabbing her and kissing that look off her face.

"Should've walked around it," she says softly. She releases my arm and tucks a strand of hair behind her ear. "Okay. Let's go in before the electric bill is outrageous."

"After you."

She darts in around me, taking a wide berth so we don't touch. The door closes behind me.

"It's so quiet in here," she comments. "I expected it to be loud."

"Walker is on lunch, or it would be. The tools are pretty noisy."

She forces a swallow. "So I hate doing this. It pains me, really. But … I wanted to say I'm sorry for … kind of … screwing up everything with Logan and you and all that mess. And I wanted to thank you for buying Navie those pans. You didn't have to do that."

"Yeah, I did. You would've come looking for me if I hadn't."

"So you bought them so you wouldn't have to see me again?"

There's a twinge of a challenge in her voice. It sends me into overdrive.

"No," I say. "Not at all. I mean, yes. I did buy them so I wouldn't

45

have to see you *like that* again. Damn, girl. You can be scary. But I don't mind seeing you *like this*."

The corner of her lips twitch, but a smile doesn't come.

I lean against the window that overlooks the shop bay. "Fine. I kind of like seeing you when you're not pissed, okay? Does that make you happy?"

She grins. "Yup. Thanks."

She walks around the lobby and takes in the magazines, sample tires in the corner, and candy machines. She wants to say something, but I don't know what it is.

Guilt. It could be guilt. Maybe she's feeling bad about me buying stuff out of pocket for the stuff for Navie.

It has to be.

I consider letting her feel bad but can't. There's no way in the world I wouldn't help Navie out after that asshole took her stuff.

"Just so you know," I say, "I would've bought all that for Navie without your guilt trip had I known."

She looks at me over her shoulder.

"I would've. Really," I insist. "Navie's my buddy. I had no clue she was dating Logan at all, or I would've convinced her not to—which is why I didn't know. She didn't tell any of us." I suck in a breath. "Probably a good thing because Machlan would've killed him."

Dylan turns to face me. "He's your cousin, right?"

"Yup. Him and his brothers, Lance—a teacher—and Walker. He owns this place. And they have a sister, Blaire, who's an attorney in Chicago."

"Machlan seemed really nice last night."

It's a statement. Not a question. An observation that lingers in the air for me to pick up and take off with.

"He is," I say.

"You guys take care of Navie, huh?"

I shrug. "Yeah. I mean, that's what you do, isn't it? Take care of your friends?"

She twists her lips before looking at the floor. "That's what's supposed to happen. I'm glad she found you guys."

My chest starts to ache, and the discomfort propels me to move. I press off the window and busy myself with repositioning my hat on my head.

Her tone bothers me, but I don't know her well enough to ask her about it. I don't want to pry. I hate when people try to pry things out of me.

"Well," I tell her. "Now you've found us too, and if you can manage not to be mean, maybe we can—"

"Mean? I wasn't mean," she says, cutting me off. The spark is back in her eyes. Funny that it makes the pain in my chest evaporate too. "I was being … defensive of my friend. *Our friend.*"

"Fine. But you owe me for your defensiveness."

She pulls her hair on top of her hand. An elastic comes from her wrist, and in two seconds flat, she's piled her hair into some messy looking bundle. I wonder vaguely if that's what it looks like when she gets out of bed.

"How about this?" she says. "You come to Navie's tonight, and I'll cook the two of you dinner in your cookware."

Even if I wanted to say no, which I don't, I couldn't. There's no way to say no to a woman who looks like that when she's inviting you to dinner. Plus, I kind of like bantering with her. Plus plus, I love not having to find food on my own.

"I really can't turn down dinner," I say. "Especially when I'm already so invested in it."

"Great. See you tonight. At … six?"

"I don't get out of here until about five thirty, so how about seven? That way, I can shower first."

She starts to crack some comment. I can see it on the tip of her tongue. But she laughs instead, nods, and head for the door. "See ya at seven."

She leaves a trail of orange-scented air behind her.

SEVEN

Dylan

"THAT'S REALLY GOOD, DYLAN." Navie gives her finger a final lick. "Like, really good."

"Why, thank you."

I give the spaghetti sauce a final stir and then switch off the heat.

My grandma's recipe called for homemade red sauce, but I used jarred. She's probably rolling over in her grave right about now, but there's not a lot I can do about it. Inviting Peck over for dinner just shot out of my mouth without any forward thought, and I wasn't prepared to spend six hours watching a pot simmer.

That's insane. But it makes the best sauce for people who care about those things. People like my nonna. Not people like me.

"It was really nice of you to offer to cook dinner for Peck," Navie says.

I've been her friend too long to miss the hint of humor in her voice. It's not just humor. That would be one thing. It's a tease, a prod of some sort that has me rolling my eyes.

"Well, I felt like a dick." I pick up the spoon I used to stir the sauce

48

and give it a good lick. "Besides, he's your friend. Since I'm going to be living here too, it makes sense for me to make friends."

"Uh-huh."

I turn away and lick the spoon again.

She's crazy. The invitation I extended to Peck was merely to make up for my miscalculations about his identity. And I do need friends here. It can't hurt to be acquaintances with a guy who can change tires, anyway, can it? Seems super logical to me.

"I'd go with friends with benefits, if I were you," she says.

The spoon hits the spoon rest with a thud. "Navie."

"What?" she asks, pressing a hand to her chest like she's taken aback by my rather forceful use of her name. "What are you Navie-ing me for?"

"Stop it."

"Stop what?"

"Stop insinuating I'm trying to get laid or something." My cheeks turn the same shade as the sauce. I pop open the oven and bend to retrieve the meatballs. If she comments on my red face, I'll claim it was from the heat. "I'm righting wrongs over here, not … lining up dongs."

Navie snorts so loud I look to make sure she's not choking.

"Besides," I continue, "dealing with some guy, no matter how hot he is, is the absolute last thing I need to be doing right now."

Thoughts of Charlie threaten to blitzkrieg their way into my brain. I jumped into that too fast. There were probably signs he wasn't ready for a relationship, and I ignored them. I wanted his attention. I craved his love. The problem was that he wasn't in a space to give me either because he was still in love with Vanessa.

I force those thoughts out of my mind with every bit of mental energy I can gather.

I sit the meatballs on the counter before flipping the sauce back on. One by one, I lay them into the pool of tomato-y deliciousness.

Navie takes a slice of mozzarella off the plate beside me and nibbles on the end. "Can I give you one tip?"

"No."

"Wrong answer." She bites off the end of the cheese. "There's this girl named Molly McCarter. Peck says he's in love with her, but he's not," she says. "He just *thinks* he is. He couldn't possibly be in love with that rat, and she's definitely not in love with him—or so says the chain of men who have escorted her out of Crave every night last week."

I cover the meatballs with a lid and try to reason a woman would blow a guy like Peck off if she knew he was into her. I'd bet double or nothing on my HAS budget that his body is rock hard under all those car company T-shirts. And he's so damn funny and sweet and kind—so far, anyway. I suppose he could, theoretically, not be her type, but I don't know a woman who wouldn't die over him.

Except me. Because I'm not into the idea of competing for another man's affection.

Nope.

"I don't care who he loves," I say. "Or who loves him. I'm just your cutest best friend making dinner for you and your ex-cutest best friend."

Navie laughs, plucking another chunk of mozzarella off the plate. "I'm going to go change my shirt before dinner. This one smells like fingernail polish remover."

She traipses across the room, mouth full of cheese, her head bobbing side to side. As soon as she's gone, I slink against the cabinets.

I hope this was a good idea. It felt like it at the time, and it's not like it feels like it's a bad idea now, exactly. Navie's leap to Peck's love life is just a little jarring.

Sure, he's adorable with a heavy dose of subtle sexiness that's pretty incredible. But he also seems like really good friendship material. He can take a joke. His patience runs deep. Quite frankly, he's the kind of guy I should make friends with.

If he's in love with someone else, won't that make it easier? He'll friend-zone me right from the start.

I press off the cabinet as the doorbell rings.

"Grab that, Dyl. Please," Navie calls out from her bedroom.

I suck in a deep breath and make my way to the door. I tug it open.

"Heya, Dylan."

Peck smiles brightly on the other side of the doorway. Clean jeans stretch down his long legs, and he's traded a diesel company's shirt in for an eighties rock band. A blue baseball hat with white stitched L.A. sits on his head.

"Hey, Peck." I step to the side so he can walk in. "How are ya?"

My voice is too high. It's like my brain worries that Peck could somehow telepathically know I was just mulling over his love life and feels embarrassed. Either he doesn't pick up on it, or he's too well-mannered to point it out.

"Great. Something smells good in here," he says.

"I just threw a little spaghetti and meatballs together. Easy supper, you know?"

"That sounds like it would be a big pain in the ass to make, actually."

I grin. "Well, not true, but I'm happy to play along. You should be *so* grateful I went to all this trouble to make a pain in the ass dinner for you."

The blues of his eyes match his hat. I can see it as he moves toward the window. The light makes his irises shine, blending different shades of aqua together.

"Let's be honest," he says. "This isn't for me. It's for you."

"What's for me?"

"This dinner. It's an apology dinner because you have guilt." He turns on his heel and looks at me. A giant smirk lights up his face. "As you should."

I gasp. "I have no such thing ... Well, not much," I admit. "But I'm not making you dinner out of guilt."

"Huh."

I try to glare at him but can't quite get it just right because of his stupid smirk. My efforts are saved by Navie.

She flings her bedroom door open with a flourish before striding into the room with not just a new shirt but also different jeans and sneakers too.

The ones she wears at work.

I give her a look she pretends not to see.

"Hey, Peck. Welcome to my humble abode," she says, holding her arms out to the sides like a game show host. "I wish I could stay and have dinner with you guys, but Machlan just called and said he needs me to come in. Who am I to say no to the boss?"

Peck raises a brow. "You. Every damn time you work."

"Well, he really seemed like he needed me this time."

"I'm sure he did," I deadpan. "You're a terrible liar, Navie."

Her eyes sparkle with mischief as she gently pushes Peck out of the way. "I'll see you two later."

The door closes with a loud wumpth.

My eyes flick to Peck's. I have no idea what he's going to say now about being stuck here with just me. I'm not sure what I even have to say about this because I was not prepared. Not that this is anything to prepare for. It's just an apology dinner between two potential friends. No big deal.

My stomach ripples as his lips part, and the easiest smile ever is shot my way. Immediately, tension I didn't know I had melts away from my shoulders, and I sink into a smile of my own.

"I'm glad she's gone," he says.

My mouth goes dry. "Why?"

"Have you ever seen how much that girl can eat? Now that she's gone, that just means more meatballs for me." He winks as he walks by me and into the kitchen area. "Tell me you made garlic bread."

A laugh topples from my lips. "I did."

He takes a plate off the table. "Can I fill my plate?"

"Sure."

He busies himself with the pasta and garlic bread. "What did you do today? Accost any other unsuspecting guys about crimes they didn't commit?"

"Are you ever going to let me live that down?" I take a plate and begin filling it too.

"Nope."

We finish getting our dinner in silence. The only sound in the apartment is the silverware clamoring against our plates as we load up with spaghetti.

In a few moments, we sit across from each other at the table. Peck removes his hat and hangs it on the back of his chair. His hair sticks up wildly as though he put the hat on it while it was still wet. I have to force myself to look away.

I clear my throat. "So you asked what I did today. I actually got a call from the landlord at my new digs. He said I can get the keys tomorrow."

It's the best redirection I can come up with.

"Cool. Vine Street, right?" he asks.

"Yup," I say, trying to hide how impressed I am that he remembered that. "Just passed that house with the big balcony on the second floor. Man, I'd love to have one of those one day. It reminds me of *Gone with the Wind* or something. So romantic. Anyway, it's perfect timing because my stuff is coming tomorrow too. Finally, something is working out."

I slice a corner of meatball and shove it in my mouth to keep from talking. Peck doesn't fill the void, though. He sits in his chair and watches me chew.

"What?" I say through a mouthful of meatball.

"Nothing."

"Come on." I squeeze the bite that's still too big to swallow healthfully down my throat. "What?"

"Does it ever occur to you to breathe when you're talking? Or do you just worry about that if you pass out from oxygen deprivation?"

I take the napkin beside my plate and throw it at him. He laughs as he easily dodges the flimsy paper product.

"I have a lot to say. A lot of *passion*," I joke.

"Do you?"

"I do."

He takes a sip of the ice water on the table, and I realize I had beer in the fridge.

"Hey! Don't drink that." I scoot my chair back and jump up.

"Did you poison it, and now feel bad?"

"You're *so* funny," I say, the words mixed with both sarcasm and a laugh.

I grab a bottle of beer that Navie said he'd drink and open it. As I carry it to the table, I narrow my eyes. "Now I regret being this nice to you."

"Now I regret teasing you," he says as he takes it. "Thanks, Dylan."

"You're welcome, Peck." I get seated again. Spinning a forkful of pasta around, I feel him watching me across the table. "What's the story behind your name, anyway? Surely, your parents didn't just love the name Peck."

"What's not to love about my name?"

I drop my fork. "Come on. Were you never teased? No one ever called you peckerhead?"

He laughs, setting the bottle on the table. "A few times, I guess. Mostly by Machlan, come to think of it." He grins. "But the name Peck is actually a nickname."

"Aha! I knew it."

"Want a cupcake?"

"I always want a cupcake."

He shakes his head.

"What's it mean?" I ask. "Is it short for peckerhead then?"

"Uh, no. My grandfather gave it to me. Legend has it that I was four years old, and we were in Crank. Crank was Pop's shop originally. He left it to my Uncle Ed—Walker, Machlan, Lance, and Blaire's dad. He was my mom's brother. And then when he died, it went to Walker."

I've only had a few conversations with Peck over the past couple of days, but I've never seen him this serious. The joke that's always *right there*, waiting to come out is nowhere to be found.

My instinct is to reach out and put my hand on his or touch him on the shoulder because there's pain there. Or emotion. Or something. But I don't know him well enough to do that, and it feels like it would be intrusive somehow.

So I intrude a different way. Because I can't help myself.

"Does that bother you?" I ask.

"What?"

"That your Pop's shop is Walker's?"

He shakes his head. "No. It's how things go. What was Pop gonna do? Leave it to my mom?" The end of that sentence gets scoffed with sarcasm, the final words halting. It's as if he has to spit them out. "Anyway," he says, swallowing hard, "it doesn't bother me. But I do like working there. Sometimes, I'll see something that reminds me of Pop or even Uncle Ed. And Walker and I have had some damn good times in there."

A grin splits his cheeks as he takes another long swig of his beer.

"So the nickname …?" I push.

"Oh, yeah. So Pop had me in the shop because I loved anything with an engine. Still do. I'd beg him to take me. Nana says I used to call up there and tell him she needed him so he'd come home, and then I could get him to take me back with him."

I laugh. The picture in my mind is so sweet—a cherub-faced blond baby crying for his grandpa. "That's awesome and very manipulative of you."

"Right? And apparently one of those days, he was working on a truck. He couldn't figure out what was wrong with it or whatever, and I kept saying 'peck, peck, peck.' I kept doing it and leaning toward the truck and finally Pop heard what I was getting at. There was a knock in the engine," he says with a shit-eating grin. "I didn't know how to say that, so I just replicated the pecking sound I heard."

"Oh, my gosh. That's so adorable."

The apples of his cheeks turn red. His brows pull together, and he slides his phone out of his pocket. With a finger hovered over the screen, he looks up at me. "I need to answer this. I know it's really rude, but this is the only call I *have* to take."

"Yeah. Sure. Go ahead."

"Hey, Nana," he says into the device. He nods once, twice, and then three times. "No. No, no, no. Don't do that." He sighs. "Don't. I'll … I'll be right there. Just sit still, for the love of God, and don't touch anything." His eyes find me. They're defeated. "Love you too."

My spirits fall as I realize he's leaving.

"I hope everything is okay," I tell him.

"I hate this because your cooking is awesome, and I didn't quite mind bantering with you either." He smiles. "But my nana has mixed up all her meds. She had a heart attack not that long ago, and I need to get over there and re-sort her pills before she kills herself."

The affinity he has for her melts me from the inside out. Even the way he talks about her—as if she's the best thing ever—makes me wish I could tag along and meet the woman who makes a man like him care for her that much.

"Go," I say. "It's fine. Honest."

We both get to our feet quietly. Peck bumps the table as he gets his hat off the back of the chair and the silverware clatters together. The sound feels hollow, and I realize how empty this room is going to feel in a few minutes.

"I'm really sorry about this, Dylan."

"Don't be. I tell you what. I'll bring you lunch tomorrow. Leftovers, though. Nothing fancy."

His face lights up. "I'll tell you what. To make up for this, I'll help you move in tomorrow."

"No," I say, flabbergasted at the offer. "Everyone hates moving. I'll just be cleaning tomorrow mostly anyway."

He heads to the door. "I'm a great cleaning guy. Okay, that's not true." He chuckles. "But you have to let me help, or else I'll feel really …"

"Guilty. You'll feel guilty." I fist pump in the air. "Thank your nana for turning the tides my way."

He pulls the door open and laughs. "Vine Street. Just passed Gone with the Wind. Right?"

"You don't have to do this," I say, following him a couple of steps out of the apartment.

He faces me head-on. It doesn't feel awkward like it can sometimes when a guy is leaving after dinner. It feels like I've known him forever. Yet when I think about it, I really know nothing about him. I have the comfort level with Peck to ask him whatever I want—for him to offer to help me move—but have all these questions I'm curious to have answered.

So odd.

And so great too.

"Thank you for dinner," he says softly. "It was delicious, and I look forward to eating more of it tomorrow."

With a final simple smile, he turns the corner and is gone. And even though I'm now on my own for the evening, I don't feel alone. My heart is full, and my soul is ... content.

If this is any indication of what it's like to be around Navie and her friends—potentially my friends—I just might be okay.

EIGHT

Peck

"THERE IT IS," I say, passing the house with the balcony.

I pull up Dylan's driveway and hop out of the truck. My boots dig into the soft lawn on the side of the gravel driveway leading up to a cute little house. It's pale blue with dark blue shutters that could use a good coat of paint. There are flower bushes—roses, maybe—underneath the front windows, but they've seen better days.

Despite needing a little sprucing up, the place isn't bad. The roof looks solid. The windows look like they're in good shape, and it even has a small attached garage.

Dylan's car is pulled up to the open garage door.

"Hello?" I call out.

Taking a quick gander around, I don't see her.

I stand in the middle of the driveway and breathe in the clean air in hopes it settles me a bit. I've fought myself all morning not to get here too early. After I drank my coffee slowly, I took the longest shower of my life, then checked on Nana, left Vincent a voicemail, and did a quick scope of Crank to ensure Walker didn't need me.

Not that it would've mattered if he did. It just killed time.

Leaving early last night was both a good thing and a bad thing. Good because Nana royally screwed up her meds. If I hadn't shown up, lord knows what would've happened. It was bad, too, because I kept wondering if it would be kosher to show back up at Navie's.

Dylan is just ... cool. Easy to talk to. Pretty to look at. Funny as hell. Wanting to spend more time with her isn't the craziest thing I've ever had to justify.

I head up the driveway and enter the garage.

"Dylan?"

The bay where you'd logically park a car is half-filled with trash. Flies buzz the white and black bags that are piled mostly on the far side. I head farther into the room and climb two block stairs and give a door a little knock.

"Who is it?" her voice calls from the other side.

"Peck."

"Come in," she says.

The handle is loose as I twist it. The hinges squeal as I push the door open and enter the kitchen.

Dylan is standing at a bar that separates the kitchen from an eating area. Her bright pink shirt and yellow sunglasses tucked in the front don't match the frown on her face.

"Hey," I say. "What's going on?"

She gives me a sound that I wouldn't quite call a laugh. "Peck ... This place is ..."

I look around. The kitchen is old but workable. The flooring is intact but outdated. The ceiling sports popcorn from the seventies, but many houses here do.

"It's solid. And we can fix anything you don't like," I offer.

Biting her bottom lip, she nods. "Go look in there." She motions toward a doorway across from her.

I take a peek inside.

Animal hair is thick on the floor—so thick, in fact, that it almost makes a second carpet. There's fur on top of a dresser that was left behind. The unmistakable odor of cat piss is present, and I'm sure it'd be worse if the window wasn't open.

"Yeah …" I turn to face Dylan. "That's rough."

"It's like that in the laundry room, and the living room isn't much better." Her shoulders fall. "I'm allergic to cats. Like, allergic-allergic. Like, allergic like I shouldn't be in here at all, probably."

"What happens to you? You aren't going to die or anything, right?"

Her lips twist almost into a smile. "No. I'm not gonna die. But I probably will break out into hives, and my lips will blow up like balloons."

There's fear in her eyes that's overkill over a bunch of swollen lips.

"Let's go outside," I say.

She looks around the room, gnawing on her bottom lip again.

I give her the look Walker gives me when he's tired of my shit. "Come on."

Her feet don't move very fast, but she winds up at the door to the garage. I hold it open as she passes through and follow her into the driveway.

"I can go get one of those carpet shampooer things," I offer. "Or we can rip it out and put something else down."

She presses her palms on her forehead. "I don't think I can do that on a rental."

"Well, I'm pretty damn sure the landlord can't do this to you either."

"I can't even think," she says, squeezing her eyes shut. "I'm bamboozled by this."

"Did your landlord not even check it before he gave you the keys?"

"I don't know," she wines, dropping her hands. "I think he did. He told me they left a little mess, but I was so anxious to get the place that I told him not to worry about it." She gazes at the house. "I'm screwed, Peck. I don't know what I can do. Cat … stuff, whatever it is that I'm allergic to, embeds itself in the fibers of a house."

I think she's going to cry. Her bottom lip goes between her teeth again, and she works it back and forth. Her green eyes stay wide open like she's afraid to blink or tears will fall down her cheeks.

My stomach twists into a knot. I don't know what to do. This isn't my department. I'm great at executing plans but coming up with them —especially for other people—is someone else's job.

"Well ..." I jam my hands in my pockets. "I'm sure you can get out of the contract. I mean, you haven't even moved in. Who is your landlord?"

"Mark Billingsley."

"Want me to talk to him?" I offer.

"It's not just that. I mean, what am I going to do? My stuff is coming in a pod thing soon, and I have nowhere to even put it now. I could fill Navie's entire apartment with my stuff."

She kicks a pebble around the driveway. Her shoulders are tense. Each kick is a little harder until I'm afraid that if she aims wrong, she'll put out a window with the rock.

"Are there storage units around?" she asks.

I shake my head. "Closest one I know of is about forty-five minutes away."

"That'll be convenient." She sighs as if the weight of the world is on her shoulders. "I need to find a place to rent."

My brain goes into overdrive. There aren't a lot of vacant houses around Linton because most people never leave once they get here. The houses I know are rentals are occupied, and most of them are owned by a guy out of Chicago who has the personality of a wounded badger.

Dylan looks down and scratches a place on her calf. "Flea bite."

I walk a circle trying to rack my brain for something to solve her problem when I spy the leftovers she brought me for lunch. The smell and warmth of walking into Navie's last night stuck with me all night. So did the conversation with Dylan.

All night, I wished I could've stayed. It was like hanging out with Walker's girl, Sienna, or Machlan's girlfriend, Hadley. Being around both of them feels like being with family. Like I can say or do anything without it being held over my head—in a bad way, anyway. My family roasts me for years over every stupid thing. At least I know they care.

Dylan is like that. But more ... exciting.

"Hey," I say, turning to face her.

Her eyes lift to mine. "Yeah?"

"I have an idea."

"Please tell me you just thought of a place to rent for cheap that isn't filled with animal fur."

"Maybe I have."

She perks up. "Really?"

"Maybe …"

This could be a terrible idea. It's *probably* a terrible idea.

I try to talk myself out of saying what I'm about to say because … well, because of a lot of things. Because of that old saying not to fix what's not broken. Because she's so pretty. Because it would be an invasion of my personal space, and I'd be asking her to do it so I can't even get mad when it happens.

Don't do it, Peck …

"So I know a one bedroom, one bath," I say in a rush before I start listening to myself. "Not that big, really, but enough room to move. Not big enough for all your stuff, but there's a big barn out back where you could keep your stuff until you can figure out what to do with it."

I grit my teeth as she happily receives this information.

"You do? Peck! That's great. Where is it? Is it available? Who do I call?"

"It's available. It's just out of town on the other side. Near Bluebird Hill."

"I saw a sign for that. It's some kind of outdoors area or something?"

I nod. "That's it."

She looks at the house and then back at me. "Do you know how much the rent is? I was paying four hundred dollars a month for this place, and that was about the top of what I can do."

"I think it's less."

"That would be perfect." She scratches her leg again. "Who do I call?"

Rocking back on my heels, I look at the ground. "Me."

She sighs in frustration. "Don't mess with me, Peck. I seriously need to find something."

"And I seriously have a room you could stay in."

I look up at her. There are equal parts of hope and suspicion in those green orbs, but I get it. I feel the same way.

A part of me is excited at the thought of having her around to joke with for a few days. But a part the same size is worried this might be all kinds of fucked up. But now that I've already spilled the beans, I have to ride it out.

"I can't stay with you," she says.

"Should I take that personally?"

"No," she says with a grin. "But I barely know you. It would be super careless to move in with you."

"I was using the words 'stay with me' because it sounds way less permanent than 'move in with me,'" I say. "I don't mean forever. I just mean while you figure this out."

Her face falls. "This isn't your problem."

"I'm aware of that. But if someone has a need and you can supply the fix, you should. I have a room and a bathroom that never gets used. And a big ole barn out back that's pretty much empty. You're looking for both those things." I smirk. "Or you can pile your things in Navie's apartment, and the two of you can sleep outside. Up to you."

She narrows her eyes. "Are you serious-serious?"

"As serious as I'm gonna get."

"Do you sleepwalk?" she asks.

"Um, I don't think so."

"Do you eat a lot of beans?"

I laugh. "You're gross."

"I lived with a guy once that loved them, but they didn't love him back, and I'd rather not do that again if I have the choice."

"Well, then, I'll explicitly ask for no beans, no guacamole when I go to Peaches and get Mexican."

Her brow furrows. "Peaches for Mexican? That makes no sense."

"Tell me about it."

She rubs her forehead again as she walks in a small circle. She stops to look at the house before turning on her heel and facing me again.

"I guess it won't hurt anything since you're in love with Molly," she says.

My head spins with that announcement. *Molly? What the fuck does she have to do with anything, and how does she even know about her?*

"What? What do you know about Molly?"

"That you love her."

She says it carefully, testing the sound of the words in the air. Each syllable is enunciated, broken out by a thoughtful tongue.

Leaning back, she waits for my response. It's one I don't want to give her.

Molly and my feelings toward her are complicated.

She's been a constant in my life—more so than anyone even knows. I don't bother to explain it to them because it's none of their business, for one. And, for two, they already have their mind made up about her.

She's not easy to get along with. There are things about her that even I don't love. But underneath her attitude is a person who needs someone to care about her. I promised her one day a long time ago that I would always give a shit.

It's a promise I won't break.

"I have things to do today, you know," I tease.

"I'm calling bullshit because you planned on helping me today."

"And now I'm not and could go by Crank and help Walker rip a tranny out of a SUV. Or go check on Nana or have a drink at Crave."

"At this time of day?" she asks.

"Are you judging me?"

"Maybe." Her cheeks split with a smile. "What's the rent?"

"Whatever you want to pay. Honestly, the room is just sitting there."

"Four hundred a month then. That's what I was going to pay here."

I laugh. "Yeah. No. How about we just talk about it later? See how you like it and how it works out?"

She wants to argue with me, but she can't. I'm her only option, and I'm not upset about that.

"Fine," she says with a grin. "I would love to *stay with you* for a while."

I look at the sky and sigh. "Like you're doing me some big favor."

"Oh, but I am," she says cheekily.

"Only if you cook a lot. Can we add that to your rent? Like you have to make dinner when you can so I don't have to go find it every night."

She laughs. "You never cook?"

"Never. If I can't get Nana to make something, I go to one of my cousins' houses. If they're not making food, I just go buy it somewhere."

"That's a waste."

"It was. Now I have you."

We exchange a smile.

The air between us picks up, and a gentle breeze carries the scent of cat pee our way. We both make a sour face.

"Let's get out of here," I say.

"I need to talk to Mark and get my security deposit back."

I head to my truck. "Follow me. We'll take care of that together in case Mark has anything to say. Then we can head to my house." I pop open the door when I'm stopped by Dylan's voice.

"Hey, Peck."

"Yeah?"

She smiles. "Thanks for this. All of it."

"Yeah. Of course."

There's more she wants to say, but she doesn't. She climbs in her car instead.

It's for the best. I need to figure out what the fuck just happened anyway.

NINE

Dylan

"IF I HAD KNOWN you were a hoarder, I wouldn't have invited you to come here," Peck says. He wipes his brow with the back of his head. "If I see another box labeled 'Not Sure' …"

He leans against the wall of the barn. My things, in boxes laden with my generalized description of the contents, are stacked in a neat row behind him. His jeans are dusty. Bits of cardboard are stuck to his faded blue T-shirt and dot the top of his baseball hat.

We've worked to unload the shipping container for the past hour. Luckily, I had my personal things—clothes I wear often, dishes, toiletries, and the like—clearly labeled, and we took those inside his house. The rest we stuck in his barn until I can find a permanent housing solution.

"At least I'm honest," I say. "I happened to look inside your kitchen cabinets, and I'm not sure you're sure you know what's in there either."

"Of course, I do. Kitchen stuff."

"And these boxes have my stuff."

A laugh sits on the tip of his tongue. "Two totally different things, Dyl."

"Not really," I say, trying to ignore the slip of a nickname. "Kitchen stuff means those items go in the kitchen. My stuff means it goes with me. Basically, it's the same thing."

I brush a strand of hair off my forehead. Peck watches me like he has all the time in the world and doesn't have anywhere else to be.

I've noticed this is a thing with him. When he's with you or talking to you, he's *with you* or *talking to you*. It would be unnerving except for the fact that he seems like he cares.

Or at least has enough manners to pretend really well.

Really well.

Well enough that I'm convinced he could reiterate the gist of any conversation we've had thus far.

Who does that?

"I was in a hurry, okay?" I say. "And low on boxes. So a box might have some candle holders, a piece to a blender I used to have, some coffee pods, and a Christmas ornament. How would you have labeled that?"

"Trash."

I gasp. "You did not just call my life's treasures trash."

"No," he says, his blue eyes sparkling. "I called some random shit you just rattled off trash. But if the candle holders were made outta gold or something or if the ornament had your dog's paw print from its first Christmas with ya, then that's obviously not trash."

"Dog's paw prints?"

He shrugs. "I don't know. Don't people do that?"

"Yeah. With their kids' fingerprints," I say with a laugh.

"I bet people do it with their dogs too."

"Maybe. Doubt it, though. Wouldn't the paint get stuck in their fur or something?"

He shoves off the wall and walks by me with a grin. "You think too much. Come on. Let's go get a drink."

I follow him out the barn. The late afternoon sun teases the horizon, painting the sky with colorful rays, and the crickets begin to sing their ode to the day. It's so peaceful here. It's unlike any other place I've ever been.

Just like its owner.

Peck is a few feet ahead of me. I happily remain a few steps behind. Today has been a whirlwind. When I woke up this morning, there was no way I thought that I would be bunking with Peck by the end of the night. I would've said I would've been way too nervous to share a house with a man at all, let alone one I barely know.

But I'm not.

I don't know how to feel about that yet.

He stops at the steps leading up to the back porch. "You comin' or what?"

"You walk too fast."

His smile touches his eyes. Leaning against the rail, he waits on me to catch up.

I stop next to him. A warm breeze trickles over my skin, bringing the scent of pines and freshly cut grass with it. It smells like a candle you'd buy with hopes that it would take you back to a vacation or a moment in time when you had no worries in the world. It's *that* smell.

He climbs the stairs after me, giving me plenty of room.

"That's all your stuff, right?" he asks.

"Yeah. The rental company will be by tomorrow to pick up the empty storage container."

The back porch squeaks as I step on it. A grill sits to my right and a porch swing to my left. Some type of orange lily grows in a pot at the end, stretching toward the setting sun.

We step inside the house, and Peck flips on a light. He washes his hands and then busies himself with pouring two glasses of lemonade. I take his spot at the sink.

"Thank you," I tell him. "You didn't have to do this."

He glances at me over his shoulder. "You're welcome."

"I want you to know that I won't take this for granted. I'll be on the lookout for a place on my own starting tomorrow. I won't wear out my welcome."

I dry off my hands before taking a glass from him.

He moves around the kitchen, wiping off the counters as I sip my lemonade. The kitchen is on the small side anyway but looks even smaller with him in it. It's not that he's huge—I'd guess he's right at six foot or so—but he fills out a space somehow. I'm not mad about watching his muscles flex and ripple as he moves.

Not mad at all.

The sweet drink quenches my thirst as I watch him tidy up. Everything he does, he does with intent. It's like tying up the garbage bag is an important project he's taking on, and he's doing it with care. There's a quality about that I find soothing in a strange way.

He tosses a sponge in the sink. "So ..."

"So ..."

I set my drink on the table.

What happens now? I have no idea.

This isn't like sharing a space with Navie or another friend. This is Peck Ward, a guy I've known a few days but somehow trust implicitly. Even if Navie didn't already know him and adore him, I think I would've. Or maybe it's because of their friendship that ours is so easy. It's as if I've known him for a long time. And through Navie, I guess I have. I've heard so many stories about this man, stories that have made me laugh until I cried. Through the tales, I picked up that he's been in Navie's corner since she arrived in Linton.

Maybe he's in mine too.

There's a kindness in his eyes that settles all the anxiety I think I should be feeling. But I'm not. At all. How could you feel nervous when he's so nice?

I bet they said that about serial killers too.

It hits me that this is the modern day, grown-up version of getting in the car with a stranger. Only, instead of a car, it's a house. And instead of a puppy, it's puppy dog eyes.

I'm probably dead.

My mouth opens to ramble something random, something to take up the space between us until I can figure out how to dart out of here before he carves me up with a knife, when he laughs.

"What?" I ask instead.

"What are you thinking?"

"Why? Can you read my mind?"

He snorts. "No, thank God. I have a feeling that inside your mind is a scary place."

I pick up a saltshaker from the table. If nothing else, I could wield it at him and give myself a couple of seconds to run if this goes awry.

"You know what else would be a scary place?" I ask.

"Inside one of your boxes?"

"Very funny. I was thinking something more like ..." I toss the shaker in the air. Surprisingly, I catch it with the same hand. But I have no time to celebrate how cool that probably looked. I have work to do. "Soundproof rooms. Trunks of cars. Barns with power tools."

His brows pull together.

He's even cuter when he's serious.

Damn it.

"You got something you wanna tell me, Dylan?"

"Not if you don't have anything you wanna tell me, Peck. If that's even your real name."

A light bulb goes off over his head, and he begins to laugh. Humor dances across his face, his hand dragging the jawline that's speckled with the day's stubble.

"You're having second thoughts, aren't you?" he asks.

"No," I say too quickly. "I mean, not really. You know ... totally am."

My lips smack together. I toss the shaker again, but this time it lands on the floor in front of me. "Shit," I mumble as I bend to scoop it up.

"You don't think I pressured you into this, right? Because I'm not that guy, and if I did or said something that made you—"

"No." I shake my head fervently. Heat tinges my cheeks as I feel very, very silly. "I'm just nervous, I guess. I'm sorry for acting like a weirdo."

"Why are you nervous?"

It's an honest question. He stands tall, facing me completely as if to demonstrate his openness.

A lump settles in my throat. "I just get a little enthusiastic some-times and was worried that maybe I jumped into this too soon. I mean, I don't really even know you."

"You were kind of quick to accept my offer." He tosses me a wink. "I'm kidding."

"I'm not. One time, I told someone I liked kids and, the next thing I knew, I had a part-time job at a daycare watching a bunch of babies for minimum wage. And then I tried to quit, and they wouldn't let me and …" I sigh. "I can get in over my head fast."

He walks across the kitchen, his jeans showing off a set of thighs that were probably crafted by the hands of God, if I were guessing, and picks up his lemonade. The longer it takes him to down the lemonade, the antsier I get.

Finally, he drops his glass in the sinks and smiles. "If you don't want to stay here, I get it. Although I might bitch—meaning I will—about packing your shit up again, I'll do it. A woman should never stay anywhere she's not comfortable."

"It's not that, Peck, I am comfortable with you—here, I mean," I say, correcting my misspeak. Because although the first part is true, it sounds weird. Like I mean it more than I do.

"Good."

"Everything just happened so fast that when I had a second to look up, I realized you could be a serial killer, and all I had was this salt-shaker." I set it on the counter.

"And what were you gonna do with that?"

"Hit you in the eyeball."

His laugh is quick and loud and, even though I know it's at me, I laugh too.

"I might just cancel my home security with you around, Hawkeye," he chuckles. "A saltshaker? Really?"

"It's all I had."

"Just a helpful hint—knives are in that drawer," he says, pointing behind me. "Unless you have some super skill I don't know about, they'll come in handier than a damn saltshaker."

He crosses his arms over his chest. The veins flex in his forearms beneath nicks and scrapes and scars. I look away before I get distracted in a very real way.

"Tell you what," he says. "I'll give you two minutes to ask me anything you want before we leave."

"Leave? What do you mean, leave? Where are we going?"

"One minute, fifty seconds."

I grin. "What's your name?"

"Wesley."

"Aha! I knew it!"

"You knew what?" He laughs.

"Your name wasn't Peck."

"I told you it wasn't Peck, genius," he teases. "I just didn't tell you what it was."

"Why?"

He shrugs. "No one calls me that. Sometimes, I forget my name isn't Peck."

"Wesley, huh? What's your middle name?"

"Chapman. Wesley Chapman Ward."

I ponder that. It's a very strong name and reminds me of a pastor in the Old West that would shoot you with his six-shooter if you acted up.

"I like it," I say.

"Well, good, because there's not a damn thing I can do about it." He looks at his watch. "Anything else? Or are you sure I'm not a murderer?"

I raise a brow. "Well, I'm fairly certain you're not. Wesley sounds much more good guy than bad buy."

"And you're pinning your safety on that? My name?"

No, I'm pinning it on that smile.

"Yeah. You got a problem with that?"

"Nope. Your life." He grins. "Now come on. We have somewhere to be."

"Where are we going?"

"Somewhere."

"Unless that's the name of an actual place, that's a cop-out."

He laughs and heads for the door. "Come on, Hawkeye."

"I'm not dressed to go anywhere," I say, looking at my dirty shirt and shorts. "I'm not presentable."

The light fills the room as he pulls the door open. He stops with his hand on the knob and looks at me. He grins. "There's not a damn thing wrong with how you look. Now come on before dinner gets cold."

He bows his head and heads out the door. I follow, my cheeks aching from the smile on my face.

TEN

Peck

"HERE WE ARE," I say.

My truck rolls to a stop next to Nana's rose bushes. I cut the engine and take a deep breath.

Although I've never lived in the white house with black shutters, it's the place I think of when someone says the word "home." It's where I'd go if I had a bike wreck—or a car accident as I grew up. This is the place for pot roast on Sunday afternoons, and where my cousins and I would gather to watch baseball games or fighting events because she'd fix us so much food we couldn't eat it all. Christmases have always been held here, and the lawn has hosted more Easter egg hunts than any place I've ever been. Even now that we're all in our late twenties and early thirties, we still hunt candy-filled eggs each spring just because it makes Nana happy.

And maybe us.

I look over my shoulder and see Dylan looking at me.

"Why do you look nervous?" she asks.

"I'm not."

"Liar."

Either I'm way too easy to read, or she's making a stab in the dark, but she's not altogether wrong.

I've never done this. Sure, I've watched my cousins bring girls to Nana's house dozens of times, but I've never walked through her door with a woman. It's always felt like a big deal to me. Like bringing a lady to meet the most important person in my life would be the moment I knew I'd found the person for me.

Yet here I am, sitting in the driveway with a girl I barely know.

I just invited her to tag along like I was heading to Carlson's Bakery or something. I blurted it out before thinking it through before-hand—something Walker and Sienna say I need to do more often.

Clearly, they're right.

Dylan leans against the door, squaring her shoulders to me. "Just because I'm staying at your house for a while doesn't mean you have to cart me all over the world with you." Her eyes glint with mischief. "I mean, unless you think I'm gonna steal your stuff while you're gone or something."

I laugh. "I have a history with you that makes me believe you're anti-theft. Plus, you have this vigilante justice thing going on—ouch!" I say as she takes a swipe at my shoulder.

She laughs too. "Honestly, though. I can see you're having second thoughts about bringing me here. I can just sit in the car. I'm totally cool with that."

I consider for a split second backing down the driveaway and heading toward Carlson's after all, but the longer I take in her button nose and the spray of freckles across her cheeks, the more I kind of want to take her into Nana's with me.

She's just a friend. It's not like I'm taking a girlfriend.

Totally different thing.

I think.

"Come on," I tell her as I pop open my door. "Let's go."

"Peck ..."

"If you don't come on, there won't be any food left, and I'm not gonna feel bad that I'm stuffed and you're starving."

ADRIANA LOCKE

The passenger's door squeaks as she pushes it open. The metal clinks as she swings it shut. I stand at the front of my truck and wait on her.

She rounds the corner, shaking her shirt. "You could've at least let me clean up."

I could've. But something tells me Nana will like her just fine the way she is.

"Nah," I say.

"This will be a terrible first impression."

"Don't worry," I say as we head toward the back door. "You'll never get the honor of being the worst impression anyone has ever made on Nana. That goes to a girl Vincent brought here in high school. In a bikini." I laugh at the memory of Nana's reaction. "I think she was a little drunk too."

Dylan's eyes go wide. "What? Drunk and naked? Was he out of his mind?"

"I'm not sure Vincent was ever in his right mind back in those days."

I pause at the ramp leading up to the back door. Dylan eyes me carefully with a smidgen of trepidation in her eyes as she walks slowly up the wooden planks. I follow, gazing at a trail of dirt down her right side. It bends at the curve of her hip and slides down the back of her shorts.

Focus, Peck.

"Hey," I tell her as we get to the top.

She turns and looks at me. My chest rises and falls so quickly that I'm aware of it. So many things are running through my mind, and I can't sort them all. Especially knowing Nana has undoubtedly seen us by now and is waiting on us to come in—probably loaded with a hundred questions and even more presumptions.

"I should've warned you before now," I say. "But, um, this is kind of a new thing for me, and I don't know what Nana's going to say or think or … whatever."

I take in her rosy cheeks and the soft curve of her lips. I'd be damn proud to walk in there with her hand in mine. It would thrill Nana to death. Probably literally. I make a mental note to be this sure of the woman I do take to meet my grandma someday.

Dylan sticks her tongue in her cheek. "So what you're saying is that she's going to think we're screwing?"

I cough like I've been knocked in the gut. And in the balls. They both ache like a motherfucker.

She laughs at my reaction, grabbing my shoulder as I sputter. The contact doesn't help. At all.

Cringing, I take a step back.

"Please behave," I almost beg.

"Define behave."

"Why do you have to make everything hard?"

She fights back a laugh as I realize the innuendo she just ran with. "I make things hard. Good to know."

The inside of my cheek burns as I bite down on it.

"Sorry." She clears her throat. "So I should make it clear that we aren't screwing?"

"Can we not talk about us screwing on my grandmother's back porch?"

She spies my discomfort like the little troublemaker she is. My attempt at adjusting myself doesn't go by unnoticed. She doesn't even pretend to have missed it.

"Oh, so we are screwing? I thought we weren't?"

My lips part when a tapping sound rings out from the sliding glass door behind Dylan. Nana stands on the other side, her face lit up.

This is gonna be fun.

Giving Dylan a narrowed eye, I venture past her—being careful not to touch her—and slide open the door.

"Hey, Nana," I say as unaffectedly as I can.

"Well, hello to you too."

Her smile is too bright. Way too bright. *Shit.*

"I didn't know you were bringing a girlfriend," she says. The happiness in her voice can't be mistaken.

I look at Dylan. She looks at me. And smirks.

She's getting way too much enjoyment out of this.

"Nana," I say, forcing down the lump in my throat. "This is *my friend that's a girl named* Dylan."

The emphasis is lost on my grandma. She doesn't even hear it. She blocks it out like she does when Machlan tells her that cake for breakfast is bad for her blood sugar.

"Dylan, it is a pleasure to have you over for dinner," she says, taking in my friend. "Please, come in. Have a seat. Make yourself at home, dear."

Dylan saunters by me, bumping me in the side with her shoulder. "I think she likes me," she whispers.

"Behave," I mutter. But if she hears me, she ignores me.

Par for the effing course.

"Look at this kitchen," Dylan says as she climbs on a barstool. "It's so lovely."

"Why, thank you. My husband had this redone for me the year before he passed away. I'd like to update it a little, but I don't quite have the heart."

"Well, I happen to love it." Dylan smiles genuinely at my nana. "It feels like a kitchen should, you know? All warm and cozy."

My grandmother beams.

I lean against the wall completely forgotten as this little mischief-maker wins over Nana. A chuckle passes my lips as I wonder what Nana would think if she heard the shit that usually comes out of Dylan's mouth.

Dylan hops off the bar and gets into a discussion with Nana about cookie jars. I couldn't chime in even if I wanted to. The sight of the woman who's been like a semi-comfortable nail in the bottom of my foot chatting it up with my silver-haired grandma like they're the best of friends is enough to make my head spin.

"You could put them up there," Dylan says as she points at the top of a cabinet. "We could put some ivy around them or little lights, and it would be so fun. I think that would be so cute."

Nana's smile splits her cheeks. "You think like I used to think, back when I could do things for myself. It's hard once you become dependent on everyone else."

"Oh, stop that." I tug open the refrigerator. "It's not like you're dependent on anyone. I have to fight ya to let me help you most days," I say. I peer behind the wall of butter containers that hold various leftovers. "Has Lance been here?"

"Yes. He was here today. Why?" Nana asks.

"Because he ate the rest of my cheeseball." The door closes with a thud. "I'm gonna kick his as—butt."

Nana gives me a stern look. "Just do it before Sunday dinner. I refuse to get in the middle of your cheeseball wars."

Dylan laughs. "You fight over cheeseballs?"

"Um, yeah," I say. "If you'd had her cheeseball, you'd get it, Hawkeye."

"Stop calling me that." She sits across from me. "Or else I'll call you something … Wesley."

Our lips upturn at the same time.

"You two lovebirds are too cute together," Nana says.

Dylan's eyes fill with amusement. "We aren't actually lovebirds."

"Oh, don't start with me," Nana says.

"What?" Dylan laughs. "We're not. We're …"

Her voice drags off as the humor in her features starts to fade. She sticks her hands under the table as she looks at me for help.

"We're friends, Nana," I say. "You know Navie, right? This is her friend."

"I'm old, but I'm not stupid," Nana says. She runs a hand through the air like she's silencing us. "You two can call it what you want, but I know. I'm not blind." She walks to a cabinet. Bending over, she reaches for a tray and almost falls.

I spring out of my seat and grab onto her. "Whoa, there. You okay?"

"Yes." She pats my hand on her arm. "These cabinets are just so deep. I get dizzy when I bend over and dig around for what I need."

"Hey," Dylan says. "I saw a thing in the store the other day. You can attach these little trays that slide in and out of your cabinets so you don't have to dig around."

Nana leans against the counter. "Oh, that would be wonderful. Can we do that, Peck?"

"Sure."

Dylan adjusts her weight from one foot to the other. "You know, I don't want to interject myself into a situation that's not mine to be in … but, um, I'd be happy to come over and help you with those and to rearrange the cookie jars. I mean, if you want. I don't start work for a while …" Her cheeks flush. "I'm doing that talking without breathing thing again, aren't I?"

I wish I had a funny comment in my back pocket to whip out. That or something to redirect everyone's attention from the fact that Dylan is looking at me. But I got nothing. This woman doesn't know my nana from Adam, yet here she is offering her time and thoughts and energy five minutes after saying hello. Like I would or Walker or Sienna. *Like family.*

"You would do that for me?" Nana asks.

Dylan nods. "Sure. Of course." She then turns to me, looking … contrite. "If I overstepped, I'm sorry," Dylan says quietly when I fail to respond.

My tongue is tied up, twisted around as I take in what's happening. Dylan being so sweet to my grandmother, and Nana thrilled to have someone take an interest in something she values.

"You didn't overstep," I tell her. "Not at all."

My throat is lined with cotton as I try to force a swallow down the narrowed tubes. I wish I could reach for her and give her a hug, but that would be out of line.

Because she's my friend.

And Nana seems to have forgotten that too.

"I'd love to spend time with you," Nana says. "It would just thrill me. I was afraid I'd be dead and gone before Peck was going to settle down. It's like he thinks I'm gonna live forever."

"Well, that's because you are," I deadpan.

"And again, Nana," Dylan says, testing out the name, "I'm not Peck's girlfriend." She looks at me with a weighted stare. "I'm sure whoever gets that title will be deserving of it, but it's not me."

"Well, it should be," Nana says, smacking me on the chest before going into a speech about how if I don't hurry up, she'll never get to see my children.

I don't want to have this conversation with Nana at all, let alone in front of Dylan.

It's not that I'm against getting married or having a family or even having a steady girlfriend. I'm not. I even like the concept and see it work well for other people. I just don't think it will work for me. Not really.

Sure, I've dated a little here and there. I'm never alone if I don't want to be. But hopping from bed to bed like Lance did before he met Mariah isn't that appealing, and dedicating yourself to a relationship you think might work out over time is such a drain when it doesn't work out. Because do relationships ever really work out?

It's so much work to care about someone on that kind of level just to see them walk away. Because that's what people do. They walk away. Even if they love you now, even if they gave birth to you, they'll take off for the next thing when it comes. It's the story of my life. Besides Nana, Molly McCarter has been the most consistent person in my life when it comes to women, and we've never been … anything.

I look up into Dylan's face. She eyes me carefully like she can see through me. It's a little unnerving.

Nana sits in her rocking chair that faces the kitchen from the living room. She cringes as she gets settled.

"Where are you from, Dylan?" Nana asks.

"Indiana. I was born in Detroit, though. We moved when I was little—six or seven, I think—so I don't remember much about it there."

"What brought you to Linton?"

"Well, I suppose I looked up one day and realized I wasn't where I was supposed to be." She looks up at me and gives me the shyest smile. "I needed some space. New friends. To be closer to Navie because she gets me."

My chest fills with a warmth that almost burns. "I can't imagine anyone not loving your fuzzy personality," I tease.

"Believe it or not, I can be a little too ... fiery ... for some people," she says with a wink.

"Yeah, well, every group of friends needs a firecracker."

She laughs, tucking a strand of hair behind her ear.

"You know what I think?" Nana asks.

We both look at her. She rocks gently back and forth, a look of pure contentment on her face. "I think every firecracker needs someone to light their fuse for them to really glow." She scoots to the end of her chair before hoisting herself up to her feet. "Now, who's ready for dinner?"

My gaze catches Dylan's somewhere over the middle of the island. Slowly, our faces break into a smile as something is shared during the quiet exchange. Whatever it is, it ends with Dylan's bright laughter.

Dylan stands. "Can I help you get it ready, Nana?"

"I'd love that," she says.

They work side by side, Nana telling war stories from the kitchen as Dylan listens intently. They laugh like old friends as they plan the changes for the kitchen. I don't think they even notice when I get up and slip out the back door.

Planting my hands on the railing, I look at the dark sky. Stars are sprinkled above and shine down like Christmas lights twinkling softly.

I fill my lungs with air and blow it out in one long, steady gush.

My head is filled with so many thoughts. There's a fullness in my chest that I can't ease either. Seeing Dylan here—being so sweet to Nana and so damn pretty with a layer of orneriness just under the surface—is so confusing.

Mostly because I like it.

And I think I could probably get used to it, if I wanted to.

"Easy, Peck," I whisper. "Don't get in over your head here."

Because I'm not. Yet. But I might be on my way if I don't catch myself now.

ELEVEN

Dylan

"OH, SCREW IT."

I rip the blankets off me. Blowing out a breath, I kick until my feet are on top of the sheets. The room is cool and dark and quiet enough to fall into a peaceful sleep.

Except I can't. Closing my eyes just makes things worse.

My brain is too busy to let me rest. It's like a squirrel has taken up residence inside my head. It's bouncing from one topic to the other, replaying the events of tonight over and over again.

I can't shake the feeling in my stomach—the one I get every time I think about Peck and Nana and dinner in her little kitchen. Nana asking me questions like she really wanted to get to know me threw me for a loop. Sure, she did it because she thought I was Peck's girlfriend, but still. She asked.

A soft laugh breaks the stillness around me as I recall Peck's reaction to her assumption. He was so adorable as he tried to make it clear we aren't dating.

Because we're not.

I flex my toes and then point them. Back and forth, they go as I try to distract myself from my new landlord. That's easier said than done. He's taken up most of my brainpower since we got home, and I can't seem to shake it. Or him. Or whatever this is that's ruining my sleep.

Peck is an anomaly, an unexpected layering of a man who is so much more than he appears. At first glance, he's your typical good ole boy. An adorable class clown type that can't be serious if he tried.

But that's not all he is. Navie is a good judge of character, so I always knew he'd be a good and kind person. If she trusts him, I do too.

But seeing him care for his nana … how attentive he was, how gentle. And then how he quickly offered me a place to stay when he didn't have to.

I've gotten glimpses of more, and I can't help but wonder what else there is to see when it comes to Peck Ward.

"Ugh," I groan. I grab my phone and fire a text to Navie.

ME: Can't sleep. Tell me a story.

NAVIE: I watched two men have an arm-wrestling contest tonight at Crave, and the loser ended up with a broken arm. I heard the snap and everything.

ME: That's disgusting.

NAVIE: Tell me about it. Why can't you sleep?

ME: Don't know. New place, maybe?

. . .

84

NAVIE: Probably. I need to finish picking up the bar so I can go home. Call me tomorrow?

ME: Ok. Be careful.

NAVIE: Yes, Mom.

I TOSS my phone on the nightstand.

Looking around the room in the muted light from the moon streaming through the window, I can make out the barn in the distance. Everything I own, except for what fits in my suitcase in the corner, is in that barn. In cardboard boxes. Probably getting trampled by mice.

What has my life become?

I never really cared to have some deep connection with a person or a place. That's probably because I never have felt that way about anything besides Navie. But I didn't expect to be almost thirty and basically starting over. I have nothing to show for my life up until now except for a wariness about life.

That's sad. Even I know that.

My legs swing to the side of the bed. I get up and stretch before heading to the bedroom door. It opens quietly as I step into the hallway that extends off the kitchen. I make my way down the little corridor that holds the bedroom I'm staying in and a separate bathroom.

My bare feet smack against the hardwood floors as I make my way into the kitchen. There's a light on above the stove but no sign of Peck. He said he had some things to do when we got home, and even though I waited around to see him again, I finally took a shower and went to bed.

I pull open the refrigerator and try not to laugh at the contents. There's a tub of butter, a gallon of milk that I'm fairly certain is expired by the date printed on the container, a couple of takeout cartons, and a few bottles of water.

After making a note to go to the grocery store for necessities, I take a bottle of water and close the door.

The drink is cool as it trickles down my throat. I gaze out the window over the sink at the barn in the distance. The yard looks like it falls on the far side of it, and I wonder if there's a lake or something back there.

I'm mid-daydream about swimming in the lake I might have just made up when a sound causes me to jump. I spin around and

My

Mouth

Drops

Open.

Holy effing shit.

"Sorry," Peck says. "I … um …" He forces a swallow as he takes in my body barely covered in a pair of short shorts and a tank top. "Guess I need to remember I'm not here alone anymore, huh?"

Not if it stops you from walking around like that.

A white towel is tied around his waist. It sits just below his belly button—low enough to show off the top of the lines etched into his sides.

His body is thick and strong, his skin tanned to perfection. His stomach is cut into hard, muscled squares, and his shoulders are broad. The line from his neck down to his shoulders is enough to make my mouth water.

The corner of his lips turns up.

"Oh," I say, clearing my throat. "Yeah. Um, I guess I need to do that too. Remember I'm not here alone anymore. I mean, I've never been here alone, but you know what I mean."

My cheeks flush as he chuckles.

"Right. Learning curve," he says.

He saunters past me like we do this every night. Like he's not displaying a body that looks handcrafted by God himself.

He rummages around in a cabinet. I watch his back flex and his muscles move. The towel dips to the lowest part of his back, and the way his sides taper down is incredible.

I think my brain might explode.

Sure, Peck is good looking. I'd bet any girl he's ever met has a crush on him. There's nothing to not like. But does anyone realize just how hot this man is because, if they do, how is there not a woman here permanently?

He turns around with a box of cookies in his hand. The simple smile on his face matched with the layers of sexiness below is a complicated vision. Add in that he's crushing on someone else and I'm his renter for a while, and that leaves me in a conundrum.

"Want one?" he asks.

Definitely.

I shake my head and try to gather myself. "No, I better not."

"Suit yourself." He takes a cookie and shoves it in his mouth. "I have a thing about snacking at night. I can't sleep if I haven't had a bedtime snack."

I drink in his body again. "I like bedtime snacks." *Stop talking.*

He flashes me a puzzled look before sitting the box on the table. "So are you a night owl or just can't sleep?"

"I can usually sleep anytime, anywhere. It's probably because this is a new place and all."

He nods. "Well, you didn't really have a chance to settle in. We kind of unloaded your stuff and then went to Nana's. I probably should've left you alone to get situated a bit."

"Oh, no," I say. "I enjoyed meeting your grandmother. I'm glad you took me."

He gets a glass out of a cabinet. He opens the refrigerator and takes out the milk. His nose wrinkles after he unscrews the cap. "That's spoiled."

"I thought so. I'll go to the store tomorrow."

The milk hits the trash with a thud. "I can go. I just usually don't bother because it's just me, and I don't eat here a lot."

"Is there a reason behind that?" I ask.

"Behind what?"

"You not eating here?"

He shrugs. "I don't know. I just ..." He shifts his weight. "If I tell you something, you won't laugh at me?"

"I'll do my best."

"Which means you will." He grins.

"Which means I'll do my best. Try me."

Stop. Talking. Dylan.

Luckily, he takes my words at face value and doesn't read into the innuendo. I grab a seat at the table partly because my legs are a little weak and partly because it gives me a better vantage point.

He leans against the counter, his hair wet from the shower. Like me, he's barefoot. I couldn't paint a more delicious picture if I tried.

Still, something in his eyes mutes the vision. I brace myself for what he might say.

"When I was a little kid, I was alone a lot," he says. "Nana and Pops babysat me most of the time when I was a really little kid, but once I was six or seven, I was in school and stayed with my parents more. Theoretically, anyway. They were usually gone."

"So, you were home by yourself?"

"Most of the time." His face sobers. "I remember coming home and making myself a plate of tortilla chips and cheese and watching television. And all these families on the sitcoms had big meals together, and I always thought how great that would be—to come home and sit down and have someone ask you about your day. To be there every single day."

My chest tugs. I can just imagine this blue-eyed, angel-haired little boy sitting alone waiting. It breaks my heart. How could his parents leave him like that?

"I guess now I just ... I still like that idea. And because I have no one here, I go to Walker's or Lance's."

"Why don't you have anyone here?" I ask softly. "I mean, I'm one-hundred percent sure you could have a girlfriend if you wanted one."

He shrugs. "Probably. I guess I could."

"So why don't you?"

"You're pushy, you know that?"

"I think you've known that since the day we met."

He laughs. "I think you're right."

I wait for him to answer my question. When he doesn't, I press on. "So?" I ask.

"So what?"

"So what's your story? Why is a guy like you single?"

I pull my legs up on the chair. His eyes whip to my legs as I draw them up. My body heats from the weight of his gaze, and I try not to melt into the chair.

He looks up at me. "Why is a girl like you single?"

"Well, to be honest, I had a boyfriend not too long ago."

"What happened to him?"

"He left me for the woman he was engaged to before." My insides twist as I remember the phone call when he delivered the news that he was not, in fact, coming back to Indiana. That he was staying in Wisconsin with "the love of his life." "He loved her first, and I can't compete with that."

Peck walks across the room and sits across from me. The scent of his body wash caresses me as he gets situated. Every cell in my body responds, becoming fully awake at his presence.

"That guy must've been an idiot," Peck says.

"I'll agree to that." I give him a small smile. "So I answered you. Now, you answer me."

He leans back in the chair. His body is long and lean as he looks at me over the bundle of bananas in the center of the table.

"I don't know, really," he says carefully. "I guess I've never made it far enough with a woman to ask her to move in."

"Does this mean you and I have made it farther than you and anyone else?" I tease. "I'm so honored."

He snorts, clearly amused at my take on the situation. "We'll be starting a family soon."

I think about that. "I've never really been dead-set on having a family."

"Why?"

"Because my family is … a hassle. It doesn't sound terrible to think about only having to take care of myself for a change. I sort of shunned all deep relationships for most of my life because it felt too exhausting to have to manage them." I think about my relationship with Charlie and how I kind of forgot that for a minute. "But then I met Charlie, and it felt manageable to me for the first time. Probably because he was on the rebound, and I didn't know it, so he was telling me all the sweet and precious things." I laugh at myself. "And then he was on 'a business trip' which means a secret trip to reconcile with his ex. Then it wasn't so manageable anymore."

"He fucking what?" He shakes his head. "He's an asshole, Dylan. Didn't deserve you."

"Yeah, well, what's done is done." I shrug. "And I'm tired of competing for people's affection."

Peck considers this. "Well, I always wanted a family of my own."

"So why don't you have one?"

He looks down and fiddles with his fingernail. There's a long pause. I don't think he's going to answer me when he finally lifts his gaze.

"Kind of like you, I guess. I'm not sure I can manage it," he says.

"You're built for something like that," I tell him. "I've seen you with your nana. You're a family guy."

He grins. "Well, that's the thing. I am a family guy. If I were to get married, I'd be married forever. But people …" He blows out a breath. "You know, people come and go these days. They don't commit to anything. It's like they're married because a big party sounds fun and then they get a wild hair up their ass, and they're on to the next thing six months later."

"Not if it's love," I say. "If you love someone, you can't live without them. That's what they say, anyway. That's what I told myself when Charlie left me. He loved her first, and that's where his love was always rooted. I can't fight that. True love always … finds a way."

His brows rise, and I think he's going to laugh, but he doesn't. Instead, he leans forward. "Does it, though? Does love always find a way? Or does it sometimes go unanswered?"

The question is fired in the tenderest of ways. It's not a rhetorical thought; he wants an answer.

I lean forward too. Across the small square table, we look at each other. His eyes are so blue, so pure, that I could fall into them and never find my way back out.

"Can you really, truly love someone who doesn't love you back?" I ask softly.

He raises his shoulders but doesn't answer as if he's expecting me to continue with my thought.

"Love should be based on mutual respect. A healthy love, anyway," I say, thinking as I go. "I'm not sure you can be in love with someone who doesn't open themselves up to you in the same way. Maybe you can love them, but not be *in love* with them. Those are two different things."

He rises slowly, tightening his towel as he stands. I get to my feet too. We stand face to face, which is entirely too close considering he's wearing practically nothing and looking delicious. The playfulness I usually see in his eyes vanishes, and an intensity takes its place. It steals my breath.

I want to kiss him. I want to reach up and take his stubbled face in my hands and touch my lips to his, pressing my body against his.

He steps toward me, his body angling ever so slightly to mine. I think he's going to reach for me.

His weight shifts, his fingers flexing. At the last second, he runs a hand down his cheek.

My body falls. I exhale with more force than necessary, but the breath I've been holding burns.

"I'm going to head to bed," he says. "Feel free to watch television or whatever. I sleep like a rock. It won't bother me."

"Thanks," I say, forcing a swallow down my throat. I feel as though I've been dismissed, yet not. His stare stays on my face, not once moving down my body.

He walks by me but stops at the door. He looks at me over his shoulder, but there isn't enough light to read his expression.

I stand in the middle of his kitchen, holding my breath. I don't know what I want him to say, but he doesn't say anything. He just gives me a smile and disappears into the night.

TWELVE

Peck

"WENT BY NANA'S THIS MORNING," Walker says. He blows across the top of his coffee.

The early morning sun floods the open bay of Crank. I turn my back to the light and try to focus on the truck in front of me. It's futile. I know it. And by the look on Walker's face, he knows it too.

Fucker.

"Oh, yeah?" I ask.

"Yeah. Sienna made her some blueberry muffins, so I dropped 'em off."

"Send me any?"

His hand drops to his side. Coffee sloshes to the dirty garage floor. "For fuck's sake, Peck."

"But she knows I love them."

He shoots me a glare. "Anyway, Nana said you brought your girlfriend over last night."

The wrench I'm holding drops to the floor. It sends a pinging sound through the bay.

"So Nana's not crazy. Got it," Walker jokes. "Anything you wanna share?"

"There's nothing to share. I told Nana that." I pick up the wrench. "Can't I just take someone by for dinner?"

"No."

It's my turn to glare.

I go back to the fuel filter in front of me. It's an easy job that I've done ten million times in my life. But for some strange, green-eyed reason, it's taking me a lot longer than necessary today.

This is why you think before you speak. Or act. Or invite some woman you've been too interested in from the moment she marched her cute little ass your way and demanded you go buy cookware to your nana's. If you just jump into shit, you end up in the kitchen in the middle of the night ready to kiss the hell out of her.

Part of me thinks I just should've done it. I'm fairly certain she would've been receptive. But what if I'm reading her wrong? What if she's just really thankful that I bailed her out of her situation? Besides, it's just asking for trouble in the one place I don't want it: home.

"So ... who was it?" Walker asks.

"When did you become such a nosy bastard?"

He slurps his coffee just to annoy me.

"Dylan," I say with a sigh.

"Okay. Wait. Dylan. Is that a girl? Or ..."

"Yes, Dylan is a girl, you fucker."

He holds his hands up. "Fine. I'd have been cool with it either way." He takes another quieter drink. "Who is she?"

I work on the filter and don't look up. Maybe he'll get the hint. "Navie's friend."

"And ...?"

"Oh, good lord." I blow out a breath and stand. Facing Walker, I hold my hands out to the sides. "Can we make this quick? Someone is paying me to do a bunch of shit, and it won't matter that you've wasted my fucking time today, he'll be a dick at the end of the day if I don't get enough done."

Walker grins. "He sounds like an asshole."

"He is."

"Better humor him them."

I shake my head.

"I'm sorry that I'm a little shocked. I mean, you took a girl to Nana's. That's some big shit right there, Peck."

"It's not," I insist, ignoring the stupid twist in my stomach. "She's just a friend of Navie's who needed a place to stay. So I offered her a room until she finds something—"

"She's living with you?"

I watch the realization settle over his features. It starts as shock and ends somewhere around confusion mixed with complete and utter entertainment.

Sliding my hat around backward, I look at him. "What's it to you?"

"Is she hot?"

"Damn it, Walker."

"She is. She fucking is, isn't she?" He laughs, his big ass chest shaking as he humors himself with my life.

I don't dare tell him how hot she is. Or that I couldn't sleep last night knowing she was in my house. Or that I had to get up extra early this morning to take care of myself in the shower so I didn't walk around needing to jack off all damn day.

But it's not just that. Hell, I've been with other women over the course of my life, and I've not felt this way about any of them. I want to talk to her. Hear her laugh. Listen to her tease me. Answer questions that she poses that make me uncomfortable.

What is that? What kind of voodoo bullshit is that?

"When do we get to meet her?" Walker asks.

I go back to the filter. "Whenever you run into her," I say, cranking on the equipment a little too hard.

"So she's not coming to Sunday dinner at Nana's?"

"She could be gone by Sunday, Walker. She's not living with me forever. She had a rental on Vine Street that was full of cat hair. Like piss and fur everywhere, man."

"There's nothing worse than cat piss," Walker says.

"Right?And she's really allergic. Like, very allergic. So, she's just landing at my place until she can find a place to rent. How hard is that to understand?"

My teeth grind together as I think about the day she'll leave. I have no idea why, but the idea already sucks balls.

"I know a place out on Longs Chapel Road," Walker says. "You know MaryAnn that comes in here with the van that has the bad transmission?"

"Yeah."

"She and Mike just moved. I ran into him the other day at Goodman's gas station. He got a promotion, and they moved over to Merom. Anyway, that house they lived in out there was a rental."

He's being helpful. I know that. But something about that information just pisses me off.

"I'll tell her," I bite out.

Walker busies himself sorting a couple of deliveries. I work on the filter and what to do about Dylan.

My chest rises and falls as I think about her. She's dangerous. I feel the fire every time I'm around her. It's like I've drunk a fifth of whiskey. My insides are squeamish, my body heated, and all I want to do is enjoy myself.

That's what she feels like. A fifth of whiskey.

While I'm all about imbibing from time to time, one thing is always true: when it wears off, you feel like absolute shit. And that's what this will feel like too when she moves on.

Actually, I bet watching her leave feels worse than a hangover. I bet it hurts like hell.

"You know," Walker says, his voice falling over his shoulder, "it's okay to like her."

I smack the wrench off the frame of the truck. "What are you talking about?"

My annoyance must be palpable because Walker drops the sheet of paper in his hand. He turns around and raises a brow.

I wipe my hands down my jeans. A trail of grease stretches down the denim, and while that usually drives me crazy because it'll get all over everything by the end of the day, I barely notice.

"She's staying with me," I say. Again. "There's nothing to get all nuts about."

His arms cross over his chest. "That right there is you calling me a dumb fuck."

"What?" I ask, exasperated. "What the hell are you talking about?"

"You saying there's nothing between you two is calling me a dumb fuck because I'm not fucking blind, Peck. Neither is Nana."

"Nana just wants us all to get married and have babies so she doesn't have to worry about us anymore."

He considers this. "Okay. That's probably true. But she does have some fifth sense about shit, and she says you and Dylan are together."

"It's sixth sense, not fifth sense, and she just likes her because she volunteered to help her rearrange her kitchen," I say.

It's a lie. A bald-faced fib that I hope gets Walker to back off.

But it doesn't. That would be too easy.

Walker's face remains blank for a long time. Then a slow smile stretches across his cheeks. "I get it."

"You get what?"

"You feel like you're cheating on Molly McCarter."

What the fuck?

"I do not," I say with a sigh. "This has nothing to do with her."

"How could it not? You're the one saying you're gonna marry her one day."

"And I would if she'd marry me."

Walker shakes his head. "I don't get ya."

"Good."

He drops his arms in a frustrated huff. "If I could knock some sense in you, I would."

Despite his pushiness and the way he needles me, he wants the best for me. He'd never say that. He'd pretend he doesn't care for the most part. But he does care, and that's what this is all about.

I sigh. "Look, since we're pretending to be a bunch of gossiping girls right now, I'll play along so this can be over."

"I take offense at you calling me a girl."

"Don't care." I grab a rag off the wall and wipe my hands off.

CRAZY

"Dylan is a great girl. I like her. She's funny, and nice, and yes, she's hot. And pretty. And she's not staying with me. I don't even know if she's staying in Linton for long."

"You could ask her."

I toss the rag in the trash. "You're right. I could. But it's none of my business. She wants a relationship about as bad as I do."

"So she's scared to like someone who might be a decent person and like her back too? Got it."

My eyes roll so hard that I'm afraid they might get stuck.

Walker laughs. "I got it. I know what to do."

"Oh, I can't wait to hear this."

"I'm going to find a hitwoman and put a mark on Molly."

"What does Molly have to do with anything?"

He raises a brow.

I blow out a breath. "Would I marry Molly? Yes. If she loved me, I'd marry her right now. But she doesn't love me," I say. The words burn my throat as I say them. "She doesn't love me like that. I'm not sure she'll ever love someone like that. But at least I'd protect her."

"She needs protecting from herself is what she needs."

My jaw clenches again.

I turn away from my cousin and walk outside. The fresh air hits me in the face, the breeze stronger than it was when I got here an hour ago.

I inhale a large breath, and something in the air reminds me of wet paint. Just like that, my mind is taken back to a night many years ago.

Tap! Tap!

I look out the window. A little girl with messy pigtails is on the other side of the glass. Her eyes are filled with tears. Her lip is split. And as soon as I lift the window open, she starts to cry.

"Can I come inside, Peck? Please? I need to hide for a little bit."

My chest burns as I turn around. Walker is watching me from beside the truck.

"You okay?" he asks.

"Fine."

"Good. Old Man Jacobsen called. His tractor is sitting out by the highway. Thinks he got some bad gas. Can you go out and help him?"

I nod and start out toward my truck.

"Peck," Walker calls out.

I grab the door handle and swing it open.

"You're a good guy." He grins. "And if you tell a damn soul I said that, I'll call you a liar."

I smirk. "I'm a good guy, huh? Is that why it bothers you so much that your girlfriend loves me?"

He throws something in his hand my way. It whizzes by my head and sails across the street.

Chuckling, I climb in the cab as he flips me off. I give him a little wave before throwing a little gravel with my tires before hitting the road.

THIRTEEN

Dylan

"I'M REALLY EXCITED to get started." I smile at Joanie Phillips, my new boss at Linton Bank and Trust. "I'll see you soon."

Joanie shakes my hand. "We are so excited to have you on board. I think you're going to be an excellent fit here."

"Me too."

I turn to leave the bank when Joanie calls me back.

"Oh, Dylan. There's one more thing." She pulls her eyeglasses to the bridge of her nose and peers at a piece of paper in her hand. "When you were hired, you didn't have your address yet. Do you happen to have that?"

"I do. Well," I say, "I have a temporary one. The rental I was going to use didn't pan out, but I'm staying with a friend."

Peck's face rushes through my mind, and I have to fight to keep my smile professional and not giddy. I take the pen she offers and scribble down Peck's address.

"You know," Joanie says. "I know where there's a rental. A friend of my daughter's is moving to Merom, and their house is a rental. Her husband got a promotion."

"That's nice."

"They're such good people. I'm happy things are turning around for them. Anyway," she says, bringing herself back on topic. "I can get you the landlord's information if you're interested."

"Oh, um, yeah. Absolutely. That would be great."

She winks. "Perfect. I'll see you next week. And if I get that info beforehand, I'll call."

"Thanks again."

I slip outside. My steps should be much lighter after the meeting with Joanie. Not only did it go swimmingly, but she also offered me a dollar an hour more if I would get my notary certification, which I have no problem doing. Even though I struggle with budgeting myself, I've always loved working with money. I've worked in a bank my entire life. Joanie seems wonderful.

And she knows where there's a house for me.

I press my lips together and make my way toward Navie's car. The thought of leaving Peck's house so soon should be exciting. I'll be back to good, creating the new life I came here for. Except … it's not exciting. Or good. Or welcome.

It's annoying.

Listening to him get ready this morning, smelling his cologne in the house after he left, and seeing his coffee cup in the sink and toast crumbs on the counter should be annoying too, but it's not. There's something very satisfying about it. And honestly, I want more of that. It's not that I can't live alone because I can, and I've always kind of loved it. But this feels … different.

Maybe the house won't work out. I won't be that disappointed.

"Hey," I say as I climb into Navie's car. "Thanks for waiting."

"How'd it go?"

"Oh, great. Um, she offered me a little raise already. Can't beat that."

"Look at you go," Navie says. She pulls the car out onto the street.

"So we got your groceries. We met the lady at the bank. Do you need to do anything else before I take you home?"

She pilots the car around a pothole and then takes a right-hand turn. Her hair is freshly cut with new pink streaks from root to tip.

"You didn't have to come with me," I tell her. "I could've done this alone."

"I know. But I haven't seen much of you since you left me for Peck." She grins. "But I can't say I blame you for that."

"I didn't leave you for him. I didn't have a place to put my stuff, and you don't want to walk around me on your couch forever."

She shrugs as if she wouldn't mind. Truth be told, she probably wouldn't. But that doesn't mean it would've been the right choice.

"So ... how are things going with you and Mr. Ward?" she asks.

The lines etched into his skin last night reappear as if they were waiting on an invitation. I squirm in my seat.

"Fine. Things are fine," I say.

She snickers. "I bet they are."

"What's that supposed to mean?"

"It means I've seen the man before. Shirtless, even. I know him, Dyl. What I don't know," she says, turning onto the long road that leads to Peck's house, "is how you refrain from jumping his bones."

I laugh at her crude language. "It's not that hard to control myself."

"You're a better woman than me."

"Then why didn't you hook up with him?" I ask.

She considers this. "Well, I would've. Trust me. But somehow our relationship became very brother and sister, and it just never had the opportunity to become sexual in nature." She looks at me smugly out of the corner of her eye. "But if you venture into that arena, I want every single delicious detail."

My stomach flip flops at the idea. It's hard enough to think about Peck. I haven't had to see him face to face after our late-night kitchen meeting last night.

All day long, I've thought about him. And how serious he was. And how I thought, and maybe even hoped, he was going to kiss me.

Following that thought is the worry that things will be different between us today.

I hope not.

That would be a shame.

Navie pulls the car up Peck's driveway and turns it off beside Peck's truck. She pops the trunk as I climb out. We meet behind the car and load up the grocery bags and carry them inside.

"Thanks for coming with me today," I tell her.

She nods, taking in the kitchen.

"What?" I ask.

"Just seeing how he lives." She turns in a circle. "I'm weirdly impressed. It's so clean."

I giggle as I sort through the purchases from the grocery store. "He is clean. And pretty damn organized, to be honest. I mean, this place could use a woman's touch, for sure, but it's not even close to some of the bachelor pads I've seen in my life."

Navie grins. "Maybe you could put a little touch on this place."

"Why? I'll be leaving soon."

The door opens, and Peck walks in. He gives Navie a little wave and then sets his sights on me. His head bows as he searches my eyes.

There's a minuscule amount of awkwardness hanging in the air between us. If there's anything in life that I don't want, it's for things to be weird with Peck.

"Don't," I say.

"Don't what?"

"Don't ask me what I'm making for dinner." I hold up two packets of hamburger. "I'll cook with you, but not for you. At least not every night," I say, correcting myself.

He laughs. "I can deal with that."

Navie giggles and heads for the door. "You two are adorable together." She stops at the doorway. "You should come to Crave tonight, Dylan."

I glance at Peck. He's watching me carefully.

"Okay," I say slowly. "Um, what time?"

Navie's grin gets wider. "Whenever. The fun usually gets started around nine thirty or so. Wouldn't you say, Peck?"

"Yup. That's usually when I get there," he says with a rogue grin. "Talked to Machlan today?"

"Why?" Navie asks.

"Just getting a feeling as to his temperament today. Wondering what I can get away with."

Navie laughs, turning her attention to me. She jams a thumb in Peck's direction. "And he calls me a troublemaker."

"So nine thirty?" I ask.

"Does that work for you? I mean, you can come whenever, but it'll be pretty quiet before then," she says.

"Yup. That's fine. I have no plans. Obviously," I tell her.

She gives me a thumbs-up before opening the door and walking out. Somehow, the room gets smaller without her. When it's just Peck and me together.

"I got groceries," I say, stating the obvious. But it seems like as good of an icebreaker as any. "I don't know what you like, so I got the basics."

He takes an apple out of a bag and tosses it in the air. He catches it easily. "I like about anything. But you didn't have to do this. I could've got groceries. I should've, huh?"

A ripple of uncertainty passes through his eyes.

"No," I insist. "It's not your job to feed me. I actually enjoy grocery shopping. Is that weird?"

"Does this have anything to do with that Have Line thing?"

I laugh. "It's HAS Line, and sometimes it does. But I like to buy food even when I'm not angry or sad." I take out a jar of peanut butter and set it on the table. "I think it's a control thing, to be honest."

"Control of the menu?"

"No. More like that I have my shit together. I can buy groceries. There was a time in my life, my late teens, when I couldn't just walk in the kitchen and get an apple. Things were hard. And now that I can go and buy whatever I want—within reason, of course—it feels good. I think that's why I like it."

He moves across the room until he's standing next to me. I swear that having him this close messes with the electricity in my brain because everything misfires. All I can smell is the scent of his cologne. All I can feel is the electricity sizzling between us. All I can taste is that almost-kiss last night.

Damn it.

Lifting the packages of meat, he carries them to the fridge. "I will tell you a little secret."

That you regret not kissing me too?

"What's that?" I ask, holding my breath. He's not going to mention not kissing me, that I know, but as long as he doesn't answer, there's hope.

"I'm actually a decent cook." He shuts the refrigerator door. "At least, I think I am. No one else may like it, but I do."

"And you're telling me this because you're fixing dinner for me tonight?" I tease. "You sweet thing."

He laughs. "Not tonight. I need time to consider the menu. Besides, we're going to Crave tonight, and I don't want to have to rush dinner. Perfection takes time." He winks.

I try to play off his charm. It would be really easy to dance a little jig, but I don't. Because I'm an adult. Ish.

"*We* are going to Crank?" I ask. "Together? I mean, that's great, but I just didn't expect you to go with me."

"Yeah, well, it'd be good for you to meet the townsfolk." He winks. "And Navie told you to come tonight. On Friday. At nine thirty. When the place goes a little bonkers, usually."

"Hey, it sounds fun."

"Oh, it is." He leans against the wall and smiles. "But you're gonna need a bodyguard."

"Are you volunteering for the job, Wesley?"

He scowls, making me laugh. I toss a tub of butter his way. He catches it and puts it in the fridge.

"I had one of those," he says.

"Sue me for not trusting it." I take out a box of crackers. "What time do we leave?"

"Well, I think it's probably best to get there earlier than nine thirty. But I need to run a couple of errands first. So maybe we meet there around eight? Kind of break the place in first?

"That sounds good. I need some time to get cleaned up."

"I think you look great."

I ignore the look in his eye *and* the riot inside me. He's being kind. Period. Nothing more.

"Well, thank you, but I need a shower and to change," I say.

He glances at his watch. "I need to run a part out to a farm for a tractor and then swing by Nana's and ... okay, really, I need to go see if she saved me one of Sienna's blueberry muffins. But I also need to make sure someone visited her today. It was Lance's turn, but he called earlier. He and Mariah had something come up with the baby they're supposed to be adopting, so I said I'd go over."

"Go. Tell her hello from me. I can meet you at the bar later," I offer.

He nods. "Sounds good. Just shoot me a text when you're on your way over, and I'll make sure I leave. It'll be my diversion. Sometimes I get over there, and it's hard to leave."

"Gotcha. I'm just gonna put the rest of this away. I mostly got staples since you were kind of lacking, well, everything."

He eyes the food on the table. "Want me to help?"

I do. Not because I need it, but because I want to keep him around. But there's no way I'd stop Peck from going to Nana's. She's such an amazing woman that it's no wonder Peck and his cousins look after her. I'm almost envious that I won't get to see her. Although, turning up two days in a row would definitely get her started on the relationship train again.

Not going there.

"Nope. I got it. Have fun," I say.

He grins. "Okay. Tomorrow, I'm cooking for you," he says, pointing a finger my way.

"Deal."

He flashes me a final killer smile before disappearing outside.

I walk to the window and watch him get in his truck. He looks like he doesn't have a care in the world.

"That's what I need to do," I say, dragging myself away from the window. "I need to have less cares in the world."

My phone rings on the table. I look at the caller's name on the screen. I reach over and silence the call from my mom.

"Starting now."

FOURTEEN

Dylan

"WHO KNEW there were this many people in this town?"

My voice is drowned out by a large truck with huge tailpipes. They're so big that I'm pretty sure I could crawl into one of them and hide in the event of a zombie invasion.

Trucks line the street outside Crave. There are a few cars here and there, but it's by far and large trucks. Big ones. Loud ones. Dirty ones.

I run a hand down the front of my coral-colored faux-silk shirt. Way too much thought went into choosing my outfit to go to some small-town bar. I even went as far as taking selfies in the fullest-length mirror I could find in Peck's house and scrutinizing them that way. The winner was the pinky-orange shirt that skims my curves and makes my breasts look like they exist. Paired with a pair of denim shorts and some strappy wedges, I don't look too I-got-dressed-out-of-a-suitcase.

I don't think.

"It's just a bar with friends," I whisper as I pull open the door to Crave.

Surprisingly, it's not too packed. The building is long and narrow with a couple of pool tables in the back. A bulletin board lines the front wall, and a long bar extends down the right side. Christmas lights hang above a mirror behind the bar, showcasing the bottles of liquor and random signs that seem to have been hung haphazardly on the glass.

Patrons fill the booths dotted along the wall parallel to the bar. Others take their chance with darts and pool sticks in the back. Navie makes a drink for one of the men sitting at the bar. Her head falls back as she laughs at something he said.

Peck is nowhere to be seen.

I suck in a breath and head her way.

"Hey," she says as I approach. "Where's Peck?"

"I'm not sure. He said he'd meet me here." I get situated on a stool. "Um, how are things tonight?"

Navie laughs. "Relax, Dyl. You look like you're ready to go in for a root canal."

"I do not."

She shakes her head and hands me a beer. Hoisting a finger in the air to a woman at the end, she leans in. "Have fun. Meet people. This place is a lot of fun if you let it be."

"I'll try."

She grins, letting out a little laugh. "I gotta work. But I'll check on you in a bit." She scoots down the bar to the woman with the red bandana wrapped around her head.

I take a sip of my beer, giving a forced smile to the man sitting three chairs down. He tips his bottle my way before turning back to the television he can't possibly hear hanging above the coolers.

"Hey, roomie." Peck's voice is inches away from my ear. It makes me jump. He chuckles, taking the seat next to me. "Sorry it took so long. My brother showed up at Nana's, so I got sidetracked. I haven't seen him or his boy in a long time."

"You didn't have to leave for me," I say. "Do you need to go back?"

"Nah. He was getting Sawyer ready for bed. I told him to come up here, but I think he was looking forward to a low-key night."

"I get that."

Peck grins, and I think the whole place lights up.

My chest burns with some unnamed emotion as he takes off his black baseball hat and runs a hand through his hair. The air is kissed by the scent of his cologne. My view is blessed by the sight of him in a plain white T-shirt. He moves to accept a beer from Navie, and I can almost see the lines of his body move under the cotton.

"So," he says, pausing to take a drink. "What do you think?"

That you are delicious.

"Um, yeah." I fight to remember the question. "I, yeah. I think this place is nice."

He laughs at my confusion. "This place is not nice, Hawkeye. But you get two points for being polite."

"It is," I insist, a laugh in my voice. "I like it. It feels homey. Homier than the last time I was here." I cringe internally because I have no idea where I was going with that, and now I sound like a fool. "You know what I mean." Even though he doesn't. He can't. I don't even know.

His brows raise, pulling up the corners of his lips into a grin as he takes a drink.

"Look at you two. My two cute best friends," Navie says.

I glance up to see her standing beside Machlan.

My mouth goes dry. His short dark hair is styled in a way that looks like he just got out of bed and rolled with it. Tattoos dot his skin, and a wicked smile toys on his lips.

Shit.

"I don't think we've actually met," Machlan says to me. "I'm Machlan."

"I'm Dylan."

"Like I told you," Navie says, "she's my best friend. Besides you, Peck, of course," she says with an exasperation that makes us all laugh.

I press my lips together, feeling my cheeks heat. Why in the world was Navie dating a douchebag named Logan if she had such gorgeous best friends and co-workers? Clearly, she had better options.

I'm looking at them. And the night has just started.

Her eyes perk up, and I know some shit is about to be stirred. I grip the sides of my chairs as I silently plead with her not to do whatever it is she's about to do. She grins.

"Hey, Mach. Did you know Dylan and Peck are living together?" she says.

"I did not," Machlan says, looking at Peck. "Why didn't you mention that?"

"Oh, I don't know. Maybe because it's none of your fucking business?"

"He's renting me rent a room," I say. "It's not a big deal."

Machlan's attention lands on me. I shift in my seat under the weight of his gaze.

"Dylan, with all due respect—a woman who looks like you is living with Peck. It's a big fucking deal."

He flashes me a grin that would probably melt weaker individuals. But as Peck opens his mouth to fire something back at his cousin, I decide to intervene.

"Well, thank you for what I'm taking as a compliment," I say. "I'll be sure to keep you posted on any other 'big fucking deals,' should they happen."

Peck bursts out into laughter. "That's gold."

"Coming," Navie shouts down the bar. She taps the wood in front of me with her knuckle and grins. "Please don't get into any trouble tonight. I don't really have the money to bail you out." She winks. "Come on, Machlan." She grabs his arm and pulls him down the bar with her.

Peck toys with the label on his bottle and looks at me from the corner of his eye. "So ..."

"So ..."

We grin at the same time.

"Machlan is an asshole," Peck says. "Just kind of ignore what he said."

"No way. He said I was cute. I'm not ignoring that."

Peck's grin turns into a smirk. "He said you were hot. Not cute."

His lips twist around like he's not sure what to say next. I'm not sure either. I'm not sure I can talk because my temperature just spiked to a million degrees. But if I don't say something and just sit here in all my feels, this could get weird.

"Well," I say, "I'm okay with him thinking that too. It's not bad for the ego to think a guy finds you attractive."

"He's not wrong, you know."

Our gazes collide in the small space between our bodies. His smirk digs in deeper, pulling mine along with it.

The room gets hotter. His cologne stronger. My shirt feels like its plastered to my skin as I let Peck Ward taunt me with his eyes.

Dear lord.

He leans toward me. I'm not sure if it's to whisper something he doesn't want to be heard or if it's … something else. But as I bend toward him, ready to accept either thing, the music overhead changes, and the bar erupts with chants of Peck's name.

"Can you excuse me for one second?" He grins. "I'm being beckoned."

Pulling back, he shoves a hand up in the air. The crowd roars loader.

The iconic song by Ginuwine that has absolutely nothing to do with a pony pulses through the building. Peck downs the rest of his beer and then hops up on the top of the bar.

My heart pounds in my chest as I watch him roll his hips as he plants his feet on the bar. He looks down, his hat over his forehead and hiding his face.

He pops an invisible collar. Cheers erupt from the back of the room. He lifts the hem of his shirt just enough to show a sliver of skin, and I wonder if this happens regularly. If it is, where the hell have I been?

I get situated in my chair and watch as he grabs the bill of his hat with one hand and his junk with the other. He thrusts his hips forward a couple of times before twisting his hat on backward. His eyes find mine immediately, and he grins.

Raising a brow, I grin back. He laughs. I can't hear it over the roar of the music, but I wish I could.

He dances down the bar, gyrating and rolling with the beat. A whistle breaks out through a lull in the lyrics, and Peck tugs on the neckline of his shirt. His hips tilted forward, hat on backward, tongue sticking out of his mouth makes me *crazy*.

I can only imagine him doing that in that stupid white towel. Or less.

Knowing how hard his body is was one thing. Now I have to know that he can move the damn thing? Having knowledge of both of those delicious pieces and not being able to partake in them shouldn't happen. It's not fair.

I squeeze my thighs together as Peck dances back down the bar. He stops in front of me, towering over my perch in the chair.

"Not bad," I mouth.

He points in my direction and then bends his finger, curling it for me to join him.

I lean back. "What? No," I say, shaking my head.

His grin grows wider. He squats down, extending a hand my way.

The crowd loves this, goading me to join him. Blood roars through my veins as he looks at me with a sexiness that I'm not even sure he realizes he possesses.

"Peck ..."

He reaches forward and takes my hand. His palm is hot and sweaty and such a turn-on that all resistance melts. I climb onto the top of the bar, ignoring Navie's shocked face a few feet away, and stand next to Peck.

My brain gives up trying to process the sensations ripping through me at the speed of sound. It switches on autopilot as my endorphins take over.

Peck's eyes are glued to me as he turns me to face him. I can feel the heat off his body.

The song hits the chorus. Peck puts a hand on my shoulder, leans back, and pops his hips toward me.

"Come on, Dylan," Navie yells behind me. She's seen me dance before. I'm not great at it, but I've danced a time or two on top of a bar.

I take a deep breath. *Go big or go home.* I shake my head. *Don't think of home. Home is him in the kitchen with a towel. Think of this.*

With a teasing little shrug of my shoulders, I turn away from him. He dances up against me as I sit back and shake my ass against him.

A muffled groan hits my ear as his hands plant on my hips. We move together, in sync, his solid build up against me. His fingertips dig into my skin, slipping beneath the hem of my shirt and touching my body. My head rests against his chest.

The lights are hot as I breathe in the scent of his sweat mixed with his cologne and try to not lose all control.

He takes my arm and throws it behind me, over his neck. My fingers touch the dampness of his skin. He rolls against me. I press back. We move in a circle and end up facing the other way.

The crowd roars as I bend forward and shake my ass his way. He bites his lip for effect, making me laugh, before pulling me against him once again.

"Damn, Dyl," he whispers in my ear. But I'm not sure if I'm supposed to hear it. Instead, I look at him over my shoulder and wink.

"That's enough," Machlan shouts.

It's only now that I hear the crowd. I'd forgotten they were there.

It takes everything I have to press away from his body.

The crowd boos as we separate.

The back of my shirt is damp from his body, and the eyes of the crowd suddenly feel heavier than before. I look at Peck. His hat is skewed on his head, his cheeks pink from the dance. An effortlessly sexy smile breaks out across his face, and I forget all about the crowd.

"That was awesome," he says. He doesn't wait for my reaction. Instead, he hops down as the song comes to an end and takes my hand again. I give it to him without hesitation and let him help me down.

Our breathing is ragged as I stand in front of him. Someone walks behind him and claps him on the shoulder, making some comment that I don't quite register.

His eyes are so blue, the color of the angry sea, as he looks down at me. A mixture of confidence and vulnerability dances across his face as he watches me for my reaction.

"You don't dance too bad," I say.

"You either."

I bite my lip to keep from smiling a big, lopsided grin. My hand is still encapsulated by his when he looks down at them.

"Guess I could let you go now," he jokes.

"I mean, you can," I say. "Or just keep me close in case your fans want an encore."

His eyes light up. "Maybe I can instigate them into it."

"I have a feeling you could do that with very little effort."

He raises our interlocked fingers between us. We both watch as he separates our hands.

The energy between us thickens, preparing for the next interaction. The trouble is, I don't know what I want that to be.

I mean, I do know. I want him to pick me up and set me on the bar and grind against me again. That's the hedonistic answer. That's the response of a woman who hasn't felt this light and amazing in a very, very long time.

But the responsible woman knows that the longer I encourage physical contact with this glorious man, the more it will make things harder in the long run.

Like the next time I run into him half-naked in the dark.

I shiver. "I, um, I need to use the ladies' room."

He nods. "It's over there." He points at a sign next to the pool tables. "Want me to walk with you?"

"I got it."

"Okay."

I dip my chin. As I make my way through the crowd, surrounded by bodies and laughter, I feel … exposed. Vulnerable. *Defenseless.*

"It's time to build up some walls," I mutter. "Before I find myself a mess. Again."

FIFTEEN

Peck

I FLOP DOWN ON A BARSTOOL. My heart thumps in my chest as if I just ran a marathon. Sweat dots my brow, and I wipe it off with the tail end of my shirt.

What the fuck just happened?

The smile on my face and throb in my balls will both stick around for a while. As a matter of fact, I doubt either will ease up until I figure out how to deal with Ms. Dylan Snow.

I can still feel her skin in my hands—the smooth curve of her hip. The warmth of her body and the way it molded to my palms.

Motherfucking hell.

I look toward the bathrooms but don't see her. I have a half a notion to go back there, but there's really no reason to. Except that I crave that feeling—the one where every cell in my body feels alive when I'm next to her.

"That was some show you put on up there tonight," Navie says.

She slides a beer my way. Propping her elbows on the bar, she rests her chin in her hands. She's getting comfortable. It's her way of letting me know she's not going anywhere until I humor her. I usually do, but tonight, I kind of don't want to talk. It feels like it would spoil it somehow even though I don't know what "it" is.

"What?" I tip the drink back. It spills down my throat. The cool liquid splashes into my stomach, soothing the riot in my overheated veins a bit.

"You know what," Navie scoffs. "What the hell was that? I mean, I loved it. I think it's epically great. But ... you know ... what's it mean?"

I shrug.

She sighs. "Come on, Peck."

The bottle hits the bar top with a thud. "I don't know what it means. I was just fucking around. But ..." I look for Dylan again. "I'm not mad about it."

"It looked like you were pretty damn happy about it, if you ask me."

The corner of the label is nicked. I pick at it instead of looking at her.

I suppose it's obvious that I am *pretty damn happy about it*. How would anyone not be dancing with Dylan and having her enjoy it and not be *pretty damn happy about it*?

I probably need to reel that in a little bit.

"See?" I ask. "That's the thing. I didn't ask you."

I tip the bottle back and forth. The rattle is a nice distraction from the pressure of Navie's interrogation.

"Well, for what it's worth," she says, standing tall. "I think the two of you together are magic."

Magic. A smile plays against my lips.

I don't know what she means by that, exactly, but I know being around Dylan feels a little like magic. Special. Easy. Like something—anything—could happen at any given moment. And having her dance with me tonight—a stupid tradition I started years ago—was *epically great*, as she put it.

But magical? That's not even a real thing.

"Hey, bartender! I need another drink," someone shouts from the other end of the bar.

Navie's face falls. "I'll catch you later. But this conversation isn't over, pal." She starts to turn but pauses to give someone a penetrating glare over my shoulder before she walks away.

I don't have to guess who she's looking at.

A hand squeezes my arm. I turn around and see a pair of whiskey-colored eyes looking back at me.

"Having fun?" Molly asks. She bats her eyelashes my way to hide the irritation behind them. "It looked like you were too happy to make an ass out of yourself up there."

I search Molly's eyes for some thread of warmth, for some inkling that she's in a good place tonight, but there's nothing besides a vacant abyss that I've looked into time and time again over the years. The only emotion in the midst of the light brown orbs is a sadness that is as constant as the little mole beneath her right eye.

That's what pulls me in, what weakens me, every time she pulls one of her stunts. And that's what this is, make no mistake about it. She saw Dylan and me, and she's not happy about it.

Good for her.

Because tonight, for the first time maybe ever, I like how I'm feeling a whole hell of a lot more than I care about her being pissed off.

"I didn't see you come in," I say.

She squeezes my arm one last time before letting her hand fall to her side. "Yeah, well, I just got here a few minutes ago. Long enough to see your little performance."

The question she didn't ask, the one about Dylan, hangs in the air. She doesn't want to lower herself to ask who she is, but she's not about to leave before finding out.

It's her modus operandi, the way she operates. She strings me along just enough to think there might be a chance between us someday, and for the most part, I go with it. I tell people I love her—and I might. I care about her a whole hell of a lot, even if she isn't the nicest person sometimes. But I see what Molly does and who she is. I know her better than anyone. And I know it's driving her absolutely crazy to see me enjoy myself with someone else.

"Who are you here with?" I ask.

"My sister. She's talking to some guy outside." She blows a strand of hair out of her eyes. "I didn't want to wait out there like a third wheel or something."

"Can I buy you a drink?"

She flashes me a half-smile. "No. I'm fine."

She *is* fine. She's just pissed, but I'm on too much of a high to really worry about it too much.

I take a long drink. Molly stands beside me and watches like she expects me to swallow and then explain all the things she wants to know. I would if that would make her go away, but it won't. Not a chance.

I start to get up to go find Dylan and talk her into getting a burger somewhere else when she slides up next to me.

"Hey," Dylan says. Her smile falters as she assesses the situation. "Am I interrupting something?"

Molly's hand goes to my shoulder. "Oh, no. You aren't interrupting," she says sweetly. "I was just talking to Peck." She runs a fingertip down my arm.

Dylan watches Molly's antics. "Oh. Okay. Don't mind me."

I expect her to leave, but to my amusement, she doesn't. She sits on the stool to my right. I can't fight a chuckle as Dylan stands her ground against a woman most women avoid.

Molly bristles to my left. "Who are you again?" she asks Dylan.

"Molly …" I warn under my breath. I hear the edge in her voice that indicates she's about to get out of hand.

Shaking my arm out from under her hand, I sigh. "Molly, don't you need to go find Megan?"

"No. Megan's a big girl. She'll be fine," she says.

"It's nice to meet you, Molly," Dylan says. There's an emphasis of her name—a confirmation that she's put a few things together. Namely, that this is the person she's heard about me *being in love with*.

Shit.

"I'm Dylan Snow," she says.

"I've never seen you before."

"No. No, you haven't. I'm new to town." Dylan lets her gaze drop to mine. She's hesitant, careful even, as she picks her eyes back up and looks at Molly. "I've heard a lot about you."

Molly laughs. "I'm sure you have."

Dylan takes a step back. Her posture is more rigid, her jaw set firmer than before. Still, a practiced smile is on her face.

"Peck," she says, "I'm going to head on out. I've had enough excitement for one day. See you at home."

I cringe as I look at Molly out of the corner of my eye. Her brows shoot to the ceiling. She grabs my forearm instinctively as she recovers from the shock of Dylan's words.

"You didn't mention a roommate," Molly coos beside me. "Is this your cousin or something?"

"Nope. Not a cousin," I say. *That would make a lot of thoughts incestuous.*

"Oh."

I should say something. I should at least try to explain the situation to Molly and get her to go find Megan and do whatever it is she does on Friday nights.

But I don't.

I don't say a word because there's a hint of misbehavior in Dylan's eyes that I kind of want to see play out. She has the situation under control.

"No, we aren't cousins," Dylan says with a laugh. "That would make things … weird."

"That would make a lot of things really weird," I agree.

Our eyes meet in the space between us. Even though we aren't touching, we're close enough to kickstart the buzz I feel when we're together. I want to reach out and touch her—even if it's the top of her hand.

She searches me for an answer to a question I'm not privy to. But the longer she looks, the more my stomach clenches. Because what if I don't have the answer? Or what if she doesn't like the one she finds?

"As Peck's closest and oldest friend—" Molly begins but is cut off by Machlan.

"Yeah, that's my title," Machlan says. He wipes the bar in front of us. "It's definitely not yours." He flips Molly a disgusted look before venturing away.

Molly ignores him much the same way she ignores everyone. "Peck and I have been friends since we were children. Isn't that right? We've spent many nights together, curled up in his room, watching the sunrise—"

"Molly, I—"

"Why do you wear this hat?" Molly interrupts me. She takes off my hat and runs her fingers through my hair. "I love the red one with the blue socks on the front better. It brings out the blue in your eyes. I wish you hadn't lost the one with the fish on it. It was *so you*."

I duck out from underneath her hand and take my hat back from her. I shove it on my head. "Molly, stop."

"What?" she asks, a tinge of hurt in her voice. "Am I not allowed to play with your hair anymore?"

I roll my eyes.

Dylan laughs, getting to her feet. "Peck, tonight has been … real." She glances over my head at Molly. She laughs again and lets her gaze fall back to me. "See ya later."

She gives me a final smile, one that's laced with annoyance, and walks right out of the bar as if she owns the damn place.

I'm still watching the door when Molly sits down beside me in the chair Dylan just vacated.

"What the hell was that?" Molly asks.

I drag my eyes back to her. "Just stop. You don't care. You just want—"

"I always care. You know that."

Her eyes soften as her entire face shifts to something more vulnerable. It's true—she's vulnerable. But not in the way she's playing me right now.

"Molly, just stop it. Please."

"Why are you being mean to me?" she asks.

"I'm not being mean to you."

She takes my beer and downs half of it. Her bracelets clamor against the bar as she sets the bottle back down. Without Dylan around, there is no touching my shoulder or batting her lashes. Why? *There's no audience.*

"I'm not being mean to you," I repeat, "but don't do that. It's not cool."

"Don't do what? Don't put that girl in her place? She was making a fool out of you, Peck."

I glare at her. "No. You know what just happened? She made a fool out of you."

Her jaw drops.

"Why do you do this to yourself?" I ask her. "Damn it. You're better than this, Molly. You don't have to go up to some woman who's done nothing to you and be a jerk."

"First of all, I wasn't a jerk."

I slow blink in response.

"Second, she did do something to me."

"What? What could she have possibly done to you?" I pause, waiting for an answer that doesn't come. "She had the audacity to have fun with me in your presence? Is that what she did?"

"Peck …"

Navie slides me another beer. A bit of the liquid sloshes out on the bar. I'd normally grab a napkin and clean it up, but I don't. My head hurts too bad, my body too pulled to a place outside this establishment to care.

Instead, I take a long, slow drink before turning my attention back to Molly.

"Dylan is nice. You could've made a friend there," I tell her.

"I don't want to be her friend."

"Good, because it's probably not going to happen now."

"Good, because I don't care." She crosses her arms over her chest. "She's not right for you."

A chuckle passes my lips, but it's not one of humor. It's filled with years of frustration at a woman who refuses to see the light. Any light.

Anything besides the darkness that's surrounded her for the past twenty-six years.

"I like Dylan," I tell Molly. "She's funny and sweet and …"

Her face falls.

I sigh. She's going to play this card until it can't be played anymore. The longer I sit here, the more I want to leave. To go home. To see Dylan and make sure she's not fucked up by this little show Molly's put on. She's not used to her antics and might not write them off like everyone else does.

"Molly, I need to get going."

"Are you going to see her?"

"Well, we live together."

A look of panic settles on her face. It's a fear for herself, not for me. She's never really cared about me.

This is not a revelation. I've known this stinging fact about her my entire life. I've always just been unsure that she was able to care about anyone, like maybe that part of her is broken. I've never blamed her for that, considering the reason behind the nights we've spent together over the years. Reasons I'd still go to prison for if the police hadn't taken care of it already.

I take Molly in—the feel of her hand on my arm, the smell of her perfume dancing through the air. The pull of her gaze trying to bring me back into her world.

Usually, those things matter. They're so familiar, and I worry that if I don't have them, my life will be off-balance. That or someone else will be in my place and hurt her.

But tonight, things are … different.

It's not her touch I crave, and the strength of her perfume is strangling out the remnants of Dylan's on my shirt, and that alone annoys me. The eyes I want to be looking into—the ones I want to be checking to make sure they're okay—aren't whiskey colored. They're the prettiest shade of green there ever was.

I let the rest of the alcohol flow down my throat. "Molly," I say, motioning to Navie that I'm leaving, "have a good night, okay?"

"Peck." My name comes out in a rush as she reaches for my arm. "I'm sorry," she says.

She bites her bottom lip, waiting to see if I'll cave. I always do.

"I just sort of lose my mind when I'm triggered, and it's been a bad night," she says. "Then I come in here and see you and her and … I just love you, you know?"

Dylan's words on love, which have stayed with me since she said them, come barreling back. *Can you really, truly love someone who doesn't love you back? Love should be based on mutual respect. A healthy love, anyway.* Molly doesn't respect me. She's happy to have me on the periphery, someone she uses when needed. But she doesn't want me or love me.

And maybe, just maybe, love isn't what I feel for her either.

"Good night, Molly," I say again.

A streak of panic flashes across her face. I give her the best smile I can manage before I walk out. And for once, I'm walking away from her. And it feels just fine.

SIXTEEN

Dylan

"WELL, this isn't going to work."

I take out the last shirt from my suitcase and lay it flat on the bed. The remnants of the wardrobe I packed to last me a few days until my rental was ready stare back at me from the top of Peck's black guest room blanket.

My options for work at the bank are more limited than I realized. It's fancier than the bank in Indiana, and I don't think I have enough pieces to really stretch my wardrobe longer than six days or so.

I try to focus on my clothing predicament and not the other one— the one prickling at the back of my brain. It's must easier to worry about the logistics of getting clothes out of the barn, or getting a dresser, or moving into the rental Joanie might have information about rather than thinking about what Peck is doing with Molly right now.

Sitting on the bed, the mattress dipping with my weight, I blow out a breath.

It's none of my business what Peck is doing. None at all. Tonight was just us goofing off and having some fun. So what if I felt more alive on that bar with him than I might ever have before? It didn't mean anything. *To him.*

"Damn you," I whisper.

Despite the words toppling from my mouth, I smile. The man just gets better and better the more I see of him.

I can still feel his hands on my body and the weight of his gaze. His cologne still clings to my hair. I close my eyes and can almost put myself back on that bar with his body behind mine—nothing mattering except our movements to that song. I've never done anything so ... sensual in my life. Not with any other boyfriends over the years. Not even with Charlie and I dated him for a year and a half.

No, this was different. Crazy in the best way. Real, raw, and electric.

But when I open my eyes, I'm forced back to reality.

And Molly.

A knock on the door gets my attention. I look up. My heart skips a beat as I see Peck standing in the doorway. I didn't hear him come in, but there he stands with one arm gripping the top of the doorframe.

"Hey," I say. "What are you doing back so early?"

His muscles flex as he grips the door tighter before releasing it. His hand drops to his side. The light from the hallway billows around him, making him look taller and broodier than he is.

I stand so that I'm not at a disadvantage.

"Did you have fun tonight?" he asks, ignoring my question. He moseys through the room, his bare feet slapping against the hardwood.

I hesitate. Did I have fun? With him, yes. But if he means all-around, including the last piece where I watched a girl Navie and Machlan hate, a girl Peck loves fawn all over him to stake her claim, then no. Not so much. They have history. Something that no amount of dancing on a bar can compete with. At least, unlike with Charlie, I was warned up front and knew I needed to pull back.

He reads my uncertainty. "I'm sorry about Molly," he says.

"Don't apologize for her. She's a big girl. She knows what she's doing."

"You're right," he groans. "She does know *exactly* what she's doing."

We face each other a safe distance apart. I wonder why he doesn't come closer—if he's fighting the same pull to me that I'm struggling with over him.

There's a chance I'll never be able to be around him now and not feel this tingle, this need to be in his orbit. I'm not sure how all of this will work if I can't shake that.

"Can I ask you a question?" I ask.

"Sure."

"Is she always this …" I search for the right word. "Aggressive?"

"Believe it or not, she can be just as indifferent."

He shoves his hands in his pockets. The waistband of his jeans dips, and I have to fight myself not to stare.

"Can I ask you another question?" I ask.

"Yeah."

"Why do you like her?"

His eyes fire immediately. It's like he was prepared for this question. His lips part, and I know I'm going to be given some spiel that he gives everyone about Molly. But that answer—that canned response—isn't what I'm after.

I hold up a finger. "Whatever you're going to say, don't say it."

"But I'm just tryin' to answer the question you asked."

"I want you to answer it," I say, picking up a shirt and folding it. "But I want you to think about it first."

He makes a face like he's confused.

"You're going to give me some practiced answer, and that's not the answer to the question I asked." I plop the shirt by the pillow. Turning around, I look at him directly. "I want to know why you like her for real."

His hands slip out of his pockets, and he watches me curiously. A sober look filters his features. He looks around the room, meandering slowly until he ends at the window. Leaning against the wall, he stares into the night.

"I didn't mean to offend you," I say softly.

"It's fine. It's just that no one has really asked me that before."

"Really? No one?" It occurs to me that maybe it's not my place to ask. "I'm sorry if I'm overstepping my bounds here—"

"You're not."

He doesn't move. His body faces away from me as he stands there with his shoulder against the wall like he has all night to talk about this.

I sit on the edge of the bed. My stomach spirals with a flutter of nerves as I try to figure out what he's thinking.

He bites his bottom lip as his gaze drifts out the window again.

"I just ..." I stammer. "I just don't understand. Clearly, you like her —even by your own admission. So there has to be something you see in her that justifies it. Not that it has to be justifiable to like someone. You can like people just because you do."

I suck in a hasty breath.

His lip pops free of his teeth. His face becomes completely passive. It's like he relaxes right in front of me.

The wrinkles on his forehead smoothen as his shoulders fall, and I wonder how I didn't realize how stressed he looked before.

"It's hard to explain," he says softly. "It's ... complicated."

"I think that's pretty normal," I offer. "I mean, I can't really think of a relationship that I've ever had that's not been complicated. Once emotions get involved, everything sort of tangles up."

"Yeah ..."

An awkward silence settles over us. The easiness that we usually enjoy is tainted somehow by the discussion of Molly.

"I told you about Charlie," I say. "Not everyone understood our relationship, and I was fine with that."

"What was your relationship with him like?"

"Good," I say, picking up another shirt. "Mostly. We were together for about eighteen months. Navie really never understood our couple-dom, and my mom hated him. But she hates anyone who takes potential attention away from her, so that's not all that crazy. But anyway, no one really got why I liked him, and I couldn't explain it. We just had over a year of experiences built up together that felt like something substantial. And it worked for me. I saw him differently because I knew the things he'd been through and fought against and his insecurities and all that."

I fold the shirt and set it on top of the other one.

"I'm sorry he hurt you. He's a fool."

My heart hurts as I think of Charlie but not in a ravaged, heartbroken kind of way. I never did have that feeling with him. It was more like a betrayal that he lied to me about going on a work trip when, in reality, he was going to see his ex. Deciding while with me if the grass was actually greener on the other side. *Which it was.* Ouch.

"Nah, it's okay," I say. "He was my first serious boyfriend, so I think it meant more to me than it did to him. He had way more experiences with his first love than he did with me. Hence, my theory that first loves are always the most powerful."

I wait for him to give me some indication of what he's thinking. His features remain thoughtful as he presses off the wall and stands tall. But he still doesn't come near me.

"I think you're right in some ways," he says. "I think the deeper your roots go with someone, the harder it is to cut that off. Even if it is sucking poison."

My spirits fall.

His hands go back in his pockets again as the lines resurface on his forehead. "I met Molly right before the start of first grade. Her family moved in next to mine." He wanders around the room. "My dad was a dick back then. He drank a lot and would yell and carry on. It was more emotional manipulation of my mother than anything because Vincent used to take me to the side and tell me how big and powerful we were and how all the garbage he said wasn't true. And I knew that. I mean, we spent so much time with Nana and Pops that I knew nothing was wrong with Vin and me. It was that something wasn't right with Dad."

My chest pulls with the pain of imagining a little Peck scared or worried. I take another shirt, mostly to busy my hands.

"So, one night, Dad pulled his shit. Vincent and I had climbed out of my bedroom window and climbed the big oak tree on the border of our yard and Molly's. We stayed until we figured Dad had passed out before coming back home and climbing through the window." He frowns. "We weren't in there that long before a little rapping sound knocked on my window. I turned to see this little girl with pigtails."

I fold the fabric slowly, watching him choose his next words.

"She'd seen Vincent and I crawl through the window. She was scared." He gulps. "I thought my dad was an asshole, but hers ..." He snorts angrily. "Mine was nothing compared to hers."

He turns and looks at me, a fire in his eyes so hot that I almost flinch.

"She kept coming back. Sometimes with bruises, other times with a swollen lip. Every time scared out of her little fucking mind of this six-foot-three-inch man who had full custody of her and her sister."

"Peck ..." I wad the fabric up in my hands. "I'm sorry."

He smiles sadly. "Vincent and I were her safe place, you know? She'd tell us things he did and beg us not to tell." His fists bunch at his sides. "She'd lay in my bed in her little Barbie pajamas and ask me if she deserved that."

My eyes sting with tears as I imagine children having to deal with the things he's alluding to. It's not fair, and my heart breaks for them.

"I get it," I say, my voice cracking.

"No one knows all that, so I'd appreciate it if you keep those things to yourself."

"Of course."

He nods. "I just ... if people understood what she's been through, maybe they'd have a little empathy for her. Maybe they'd cut her some damn slack. Or maybe not. She is a grown woman and needs to quit using that shit as an excuse."

"That's not really an excuse," I say, unable to believe I'm defending the woman who was just a jerk to me. "That's ... rough."

"Yeah. It is. It's why she can't connect with people. She trusts no one. She sleeps with anyone looking for someone to love her ..." His face falls.

Mine does too. "But you love her," I say cautiously.

He walks around the room. "I do. I love her. For sure. But ..." He glances at me over his shoulder and stills. "Maybe not like I thought I did."

"Oh." My heart beats so hard I can hear it. My mouth dries like it's swabbed in cotton. My brain sings with a mixture of hope and caution because this doesn't mean anything.

This doesn't mean he likes me.

"I've always cared about her," he says. "Like you said, our roots run too deep not to. But it kind of became this … thing. People jumped to, 'Oh, you love her—look at you defending her all the time,' and I went with it. Because maybe I did. I don't know. But looking back on it, maybe … I don't know." He shakes his head.

"Like you said … complicated."

He leans against the wall again. "She deserves a lot of what she gets. As you witnessed tonight, she's not easy to deal with. But it's hard for me not to look at her and see the wounds that I know are there."

"I get that. I do. And you're a nice guy for being her friend when it's not easy to do that."

Bowing my head, I go back to my little pile of shirts. I fold the one in my hand, add it to the stack, and grab another.

I'm on my fifth shirt when I look up. Peck is standing right in front of me.

His lips are twisted into an unapologetic grin. I drop the shirt I'm holding onto the bed in a messy lump.

"What?" I ask, a nervous laugh woven into the word.

"I've had enough talking about Molly."

"Okay." I grin. "And?"

"I didn't think you'd get up there with me tonight."

"On the bar?" I raise my brows. "I'm not going to back down from a challenge."

He laughs. "Good to know."

My breathing matches his as he takes my hands and pulls me up. I stand in front of him, chin up so I can look into his eyes. There's no sign of a thought of anything but me.

I gulp, energy surging through my veins so fast I think I might pass out.

He reaches out. A finger settles in beneath my chin, and he lifts it higher. I look into his eyes as he peers into mine.

I swallow carefully, not wanting to jostle his finger. The simple touch is like a match to a pile of embers deep inside me. My blood is hot as I wait for him to do something.

To kiss me.

"Thank you," he says softly.

"For what?"

"For caring." He smiles shyly, his finger falling from my face. "Don't forget that I'm making you dinner tomorrow."

"Okay," I breathe.

"Good night, Hawkeye."

With a final, lingering gaze, he turns toward my door.

"Night, Wesley," I whisper.

He pauses for a moment in the doorway but doesn't turn to look at me. He taps the wall with his palm, then makes a fist, then disappears down the hallway.

I sit on the bed again, my knees threatening to melt out from under me.

My fingers go to the spot where he touched me as I look at the doorway.

"Damn you, Peck."

I grin, falling back into the pile of shirts stacked beside me.

SEVENTEEN

Peck

"WHAT THE FUCK are you doing here?" Vincent calls out.

I look across the parking lot of the grocery store to see my brother climbing out of his pickup truck. He slides his sunglasses off his face and tucks them into the front of his shirt.

He heads across the asphalt with a rip in the knee of his jeans that's too straight to have been done by accident.

"You didn't buy your jeans with a rip, did you?" I goad him.

He grins.

"Come on, Vin. You're pussying out on me."

He laughs, running a hand through his short hair. "They were a gift. From a very … happy woman."

I slide my cart in the return slot and trek back to my truck.

"I just leave happy women in my wake," he jokes. "So, really, what's up?" He leans against the bed, his forearms resting on the rail. He toys with the handle of one of the bags. "What's all this?"

"Nothing. Just doing a little cooking tonight."

"This have anything to do with that hot little thing Machlan was telling me about last night?"

I unlock the driver's side door and toss my keys in the cup holder. "When did this family turn into a bunch of gossiping assholes?"

"I dunno, but it's better than everyone having a stick up their ass." He laughs. "So does it?"

"Fuck you," I say, shaking my head.

"That's a yes. Good for you."

A car pulls up beside Vincent. A woman who works at Carlson's sometimes gets out. She waves at me before giving my brother a long, leisurely once-over. He nods at her in the subtlest way, as if to say, "I see you but haven't decided if it's worth a full nod yet."

I sigh. "How did you even see Machlan last night? I left the bar around eleven or so, and he was still there."

"He sent me a text after they closed, and I met him in the apartment over Crave. We just shot the shit for a while." He fiddles with the bag again. "It's kind of nice being back home."

I kick at a pebble on the ground, thinking the same thing. It's nice having him home. Sure, I have my cousins, and they're great, but there's a different bond between brothers.

"Where's Sawyer?" I ask.

"Happy as a pig in shit with Nana," he says with a laugh. "She let him have cherry pie for breakfast. Now he's out back fixing up that treehouse in the woods. Kid won't want to go home." He gazes into the distance. "He's happy here."

"Yeah, well, what's not to be happy about?"

He shrugs. "I don't know. I get sick of everyone every once in a while."

"I can see that."

"It doesn't take long to get your fill of Lance," he jokes. "What's that fucker doing now, anyway? I haven't seen him yet."

"Still teaching. Engaged to Mariah. Adopting a kid. Living the life," I say. "I'm sure he'll be at Nana's for dinner after church tomorrow."

He nods. Pressing off the truck, he runs his hands through his hair again. "I forgot about church. Shit. I don't think I brought anything decent for me or Sawyer to wear."

"Nana won't care. She'll just be glad to have you there."

"That's true. She's made it very, very clear over the past twenty-four hours that she's happy to have us here."

"I'm sure she is. She doesn't get to see you or Blaire enough. Speaking of Blaire, she's coming home for a visit too I heard."

"I haven't seen her in forever." He kicks at the ground, his smile faltering. "How's Nana? Really?"

"What do you mean?"

His shoulders rise and fall as a storm brews inside his eyes. "I mean, she looks good. She is good, right?"

Concern is stretched over his face as he awaits my response. Guilt too—the regret of a grandson who hasn't been around a lot.

"She's okay," I say. "We take good care of her. Have a system. I do her medicines, and Machlan takes her for her hair appointment and shopping. Walker fixes shit. Lance pays her bills. Sienna, Mariah, and Hadley help with housework as much as she'll let them. You know how she is." I shrug. "But … she's getting old. You know that."

Just saying that out loud pummels me. I never thought about a life without Nana. And then she had a heart attack and seeing her in that hospital bed struck a chord inside me that I haven't been able to shake.

She was so pale. So … lifeless. I watched her lay there with those monitors beeping, the only thing that let me know she was alive and prayed. I told God I'd do whatever he asked of me if he just let Nana be all right.

"I worry about her," Vincent says. "I mean, she was more like a mother to us than our own mom."

"It wasn't Mom's fault. Dad kept her on the edge all the time."

Vincent's eyes flash with a shot of anger that has me taking a step back. "No. She doesn't get that excuse. Once you're a parent, your loyalties lie with your kids. Period. She *let* Dad run all over her. That was a choice."

I want to argue that because I don't quite agree. But it would be hard considering we haven't seen or heard from our parents in a couple of years. Who knows where they are?

"Anyway, I've been thinking about moving back," Vincent says. "Might be good for Sawyer."

"Yeah, well, it might be good for you too."

We exchange a smile.

"It's a lot to think about," he says. "Sawyer has a great school and a lot of friends. We have a nice little neighborhood with all the fucking fences and flags and shit. I even have a home owner's association."

I burst out laughing. "So that's why you're thinking about moving? They're kicking you out."

"Not yet," he jokes. "But they probably would've if I hadn't fucked the president a couple of times. That got me out of a few fines."

"Only a couple?" I tease.

"She was kind of married," he says, cringing. "But I didn't know that until later. I told her that despite my reputation, I do have some standards. Or one," he corrects. "I won't bang married chicks."

"How benevolent of you."

"I try."

He leans on the tailgate, one foot across the other. It's odd to look into someone's face and see something so close to what you see in the mirror.

Same blue eyes. Same face shape. Same straight hairline with a tendency for hair to fall to the left.

"You know anybody hiring around here?" he asks. "I'm working for a company out of Logansport, but they don't work this far north."

"I'll keep an eye out."

"You do that." He scratches the top of his head. "I gotta get back down here before the whole family loses their balls."

"What's that supposed to mean?"

"Hell, all of you are settling down. Ran into Walker and Sienna—where'd he find her?"

I laugh at the memory of how we met Sienna. "Long story. Funny story, but long story."

He shrugs. "And then Lance is adopting a kid. And Machlan is still

Machlan for the most part, but just as the whiskey was settling in last night, he had to go home because Hadley sent him a text. Probably a nude by how fast he got out of there." He grins. "And then there's you."

I stretch my arms over head and feel the sun on my face. I'm way too relaxed about this conversation to have it mean anything good.

Usually, when people start talking about significant others and projecting their ideas on me, I just go with the flow. There's never been a real plan over here. I take things one day at a time and figure I'm happy, and if this is as good as it gets, I'm still pretty damn lucky.

But today I know he's hinting at Dylan. And I kind of like it. I like the idea of my name and her name being roped together like Machlan and Hadley's. I like the idea of having her be around in discussions like this.

And that can't be a good thing.

This thing with Dylan is a microcosm of my life. It will never last. There will come a day when she leaves, and I'd be stupid not to remember that.

"You think you'll settle down like the rest of them?" Vincent asks.

"Nah."

"Why not?"

"Why don't you?"

He gives me a half-grin. "I totally would if I could find the perfect woman. But usually, I don't get one that can pass the first two levels."

I sigh. "Which are?"

"Level one: get Sawyer's approval. Level two: handle the dick."

I shake my head and walk toward the driver's side door. "You're probably better off alone."

He laughs as I climb in my truck. I shove the key in the ignition and start the engine before looking at my brother through the open door.

His features are void of the humor from a few moments ago. There's a severity there that causes a shiver to ripple down my skin.

"We're both fucked up," he says. I can barely hear him over my diesel engine. "It's taken me a long time to accept that. But we are, and it's not our fault. Our parents were absolute shit. Hell, we were their parents more often than not. And then we had Molly ..." His lips press together. "What's she up to these days?"

"Being Molly."

He blows out a breath. "I should probably go say hi to her today."

"You do that." I pop the door closed and roll down the window. "She's probably pissed at me today, so be warned."

"What happened?"

"Let's say everything you heard about Dylan from last night happened in front of Molly. And then she came up to me and did her usual Molly shit to Dylan, and I had to tell her to back it down a little."

"*Oh.*"

"Yeah."

Vincent blows out a breath. "You've always been her blankie."

I slouch in my seat and let my wrists hang off the steering wheel. The truth of his words sinks into my brain as I stare at the green suburban parked in front of me. It's bright with a glossy finish and reminds me of Dylan's eyes.

"You gotta stop living your life with consideration of Molly," he says.

"I don't do that."

"You do. You always have. Hell, we both did for a while, but your time is done."

I want to argue, which is my standard response, but Vincent was there. He knows. He saw. He held her too.

But he left. And I stayed.

He grabs my shoulder and shakes it. "Remember when you were a junior in high school, and you didn't go to the big field trip to Kings Island because you'd be gone on a Friday night during the first of the month, and that's the weekend Molly's dad was more of a dick than usual?"

My heart sputters as the memories of that night come back. "Yeah."

"You've always worked around her. And that's great, Peck. You're a great fucking guy. But you're almost thirty now, and you're holding yourself back in a lot of things because of a woman who's perfectly capable of living without you."

I don't look at him. I just keep watching the sun glimmer off the paint in front of me.

"I know she appreciates you," he says. "But you've done your job. Hell, it wasn't even your job, and you've done it. You've protected her and been her friend. And you still can. But you don't have to sacrifice your life for her. She sure as shit isn't returning the sentiment."

He's right. That's why it hurts.

Pops always said the truth hurts. He told it to me the first time when he told me not to swing a hammer like I was or I'd hit myself in the forehead. Which I did. *"Truth hurts,"* he'd said as he took the hammer away from me.

I've never forgotten that.

"I like Dylan," I say carefully, testing it out. "But she's …"

"She's what?"

"I don't know. She's … wild." I laugh softly. "She doesn't really want a family. She moved here on what seems like a spur of the moment. Her shit is stacked in my barn, and she doesn't even know what she's going to do with it." I look at my brother as if that explains everything. "What would be the point?"

Vincent taps the side of the truck, a big smile on his face. "The point would be that you thought enough of yourself to give it a try. Now, I gotta go get eggs so Nana can make Sawyer noodles for lunch."

"See you tomorrow," I say.

He gives me a little salute and jogs into the store.

I put the truck into reverse but don't take my foot off the brake. Instead, I look at that green paint again. The sun hits it, causing the golden speckles in the finish to shine.

Just like Dylan's eyes.

I grin. She'd wanted me to lean in and kiss her, and fuck how I wanted to.

But then I recall her eyes after telling her about Molly. There had been real compassion and sadness, something no one else in Linton has every shown Molly. Maybe because they've never known the truth.

Yet Dylan had asked for the truth. Forced me to open up about a subject I'd simply shelved as part of life.

"You're almost thirty now, and you're holding yourself back in a lot of things because of a woman who's perfectly capable of living without you."

Pops is right—the truth hurts. But maybe learning to use a hammer the right way taught me something else too. Doing something properly takes more time to learn but gives better results.

I grip the steering wheel, my palms sweaty.

What would happen if I did things the right way?

With Dylan?

Is something like that possible?

I back out and take off for home.

EIGHTEEN

Dylan

"I'M SORRY I'M LATE." Navie pushes through a rack of clothes and stops on a dime. "It's been a hell of a day."

There's an iced coffee in one of her hands, complete with a pink straw, and a purse dangling over her other arm. Her hair is a mess in some half updo thing. She's still so pretty that it makes me laugh.

"I can believe that." I point at the side of her face. "Lipstick is a little outside the lines on that side."

"Shit."

She runs over to a mirror on the wall and rubs her face until the red is only where it's supposed to be. Pop music plays on the overhead speakers as Navie fixes her hair.

I go back to the rack of clothes in front of me. An eggplant-colored shirt hangs on the end, and I hold it up to my body.

"Not your color," Navie says, coming my way. "I like the cut, though."

"Really? I kind of like the purple."

"I mean, you're the one that's going to wear it, but ..." She plucks a shirt off the rack and dangles it in front of me. "Try this one. Same cut but in blue."

"Ooh. I like that."

"I know. That's why I'm here."

She takes the shirt in my hand, puts it up, and then hands me the blue one.

"What's been going on with you today?" I ask. I spy a cute little dandelion print top and pluck it off the hanger. "You were supposed to be here twenty minutes ago."

"I know. I was watching this video online last night about how to cut up a shirt and make it all edgy and cool."

"That's a good use of your time."

"I know. It was one of those two a.m. rabbit hole things. Anyway, I woke up this morning and wanted to try it out."

"How'd it go?" I inspect a charcoal-gray suit that would look awesome with a crisp white shirt, but it's overkill for the bank, so I put it back. "Not good, I'm guessing, since you look like you've been wrestling a whale this morning."

She sighs. "Very funny. But you're right. It wasn't nearly as easy as the cute little chipper blonde made it look. Hers looked chic and retro. Mine looked like a five-year-old got a hold of her mommy's scissors and hacked up her shirt." She scrunches up her face. "Why are things always harder than they look online?"

"That's not something you hear a lot," I say with a snort.

"What?"

"That things are *harder* in real life than you see online." I wink. "Bad joke. I apologize. But you're right, and that's why I don't attempt that sort of thing."

We walk through the store, holding up various garments for consideration. I've already looked at most of the things in the little shop—the only thing that resembles a department store in Merom. Linton had nothing. Not even a store where everything is a dollar.

Navie slurps the rest of her coffee. The straw sucks air, sending an obnoxious sound through the store that gets her a side-eye from the cashier.

ADRIANA LOCKE

"Can you stop it?" I ask her. "You're going to get us thrown out of here, and I'm not done shopping yet."

She tosses it in a trash can. "Are we just looking at clothes for the bank, or we looking for … other things." She stops in the middle of the walkway and grins.

"Just work," I say carefully. "I don't like that look on your face."

"Ha." She spins around and grabs a light pink negligee. It hangs from her finger like it's made of spun gold.

The garment is beautiful. The fabric begs you to touch it while the lace lining the top and bottom teases you to touch what would be underneath.

My eyes flick to hers. "Navie …" I warn.

"What? You'd look awesome in this."

"Don't *what* me. I know what you're implying."

And that implication has my body humming. Dim lights, candles flickering, Peck's eyes filled with unbridled passion …. I shiver.

"Um, I'm not the one who started this," she says. "You were implying a whole hell of a lot when you were dry humping him on the bar."

"I was not." My face burns. "We were dancing."

"It's a choice of words."

"The correct choice," I say. I take the item away from her and put it back. "Don't start this."

When I turn around, Navie is watching me with a hand on her hip.

"Don't regret that," she says.

I walk away from her toward the perfume counter because it's the farthest thing from her at the moment. My mind ponders her request.

Don't regret that.

Do I?

The back of my brain says I do. It says things are going to get weird between Peck and me. And being that the more I see of him, the more I like him means that I'll probably be packing myself up and out of there. Maybe even with a broken heart.

But my heart has things to say of its own. It doesn't take being shattered into consideration. It's contemplating lazy Sunday afternoons watching football and arguments over who is making dinner—things that I've never really wanted before, and things I have no business wanting now. Not with him, anyway.

The push and pull ripped at me all night after Peck left my room. It was present through my shower this morning, all during breakfast, and accompanied me here.

I'm a mess.

"Does that frown mean nothing happened when you got home last night?" Navie asks. "If you say yes, I'm going to be so disappointed."

I frown deeper.

Her face falls in a dramatic fashion. "No, Dylan."

"We ... talked," I say. "It was fine."

I turn my attention to the sample perfume bottles. Suddenly, I'm very interested in the smell of sunflowers.

Navie leans her back against the glass counter. "You *talked*. After that?"

"Yes. Because we're adults, and adults talk. I don't get why you're making such a big deal out of it."

"I'm not. I just expected ..." She wiggles her brows. "You know. A little more of what I saw at the bar with a lot fewer clothes." She waits for me to respond. When I don't, she sighs. "Talk to me."

"I thought talking disappointed you."

I walk over to a settee next to an ad for handbags and take a seat. Navie wastes no time plopping down next to me.

Setting my potential purchases next to me, I ignore my friend for a moment. This conversation is not going where she thinks it is, and a part of me is a little embarrassed by that. She thinks I'm going to tell her that Peck and I talked about dancing together or ... anything to do with us.

"We talked about Molly," I say without looking at her.

"You've got to be kidding me."

"Nope." I twist my lips together and peer at her. "It's just as well. I mean, she's the elephant in the room with him, right?"

Navie rolls her eyes. "So what did he say? And if you tell me he said he loves her and all that shit, I'll go kill him right now."

"Not exactly."

"Not good enough." She starts to stand. "He's dead."

"Navie, stop," I say, laughing.

"Why would he talk about Molly McCarter when he's got you with him? Alone. In his house?" She shakes her head. "I don't get it."

"It's my fault. I brought her up."

Navie blinks. "Why?"

"She came up to us before I left the bar, and … it was a painful interaction. She's … a lot."

"She's a whore."

I focus on the lines in the tile on the floor.

She might be right. I don't know Molly well enough to know if that's true. But when I open my mouth to say something negative about her, I hear Peck's voice telling me Molly's history in the soft sensitivity he used last night. And I can't do it.

Maybe I can't do it because it feels like a betrayal to Peck and his opening up to me. And maybe I can't because I kind of feel bad for her. Either way, I can't.

"I don't know what she is," I say. "But Peck likes her, and that's that."

"I've never been fully convinced he actually does like her. For the record."

"Well, I'm pretty sure he does." I look up at Navie. "At least in certain ways. I don't know. I just know I don't need that negligee tonight. Or ever."

My spirits sink as I speak the truth. Because it's the truth.

"You don't know that," Navie insists. "Maybe seeing you in that would break the Molly spell."

I lift the shirts I'm going to buy and lay them on my lap.

As Navie said, I was alone with Peck in his house with *no other distractions*. Except that's not true. Because even though he clarified why Molly means so much to him, it didn't mean her presence disappeared.

It's so much a part of him. *She's* so much a part of him. He could've kissed me. I wanted that kiss. But it's not mine and probably never will be. And I can't fault Peck for that. In fact, that loyalty, that ... *honor*, it makes me like him even more.

"I wish there wasn't a Molly spell," I admit. "If there wasn't, I'd be all over that. He's ... like sunshine. He makes you feel good."

She snorts. "I bet he'd make you feel real damn good."

I hit her with my shoulder.

"You need to take a chance," she says.

"You're right. I do. I deserve to be happy and in love. Or just to screw around if that's what I decide to do. But ... I owe it to myself to do that with someone who's safe to do it with."

She cocks a brow. "Define safe."

"Do you know why Charlie left me?"

"Yup. Because he's a narcissistic asshole."

"Maybe, but he's also a decent guy. And while I'm angry that he betrayed me to do it, he really just did what he thought was right for him. And I give him kudos, quietly," I joke, "for doing it when he did and not dragging it out."

She scoffs. "Your logic is irritating."

I grin. "So the answer to my original question about why Charlie left me is that he went back to his first love." My smile falters. "How do you really argue that?"

A flash of understanding billows through Navie's eyes. She nods, her lips parting.

I stand. Tossing the clothes I want to purchase for my new job over my arm, I look down at my best friend.

"If I start a new relationship, I want to do it with a man who's free and clear. One who doesn't have some deep connection with someone else that I have to worry they'll rekindle. I just want it to be easy. I don't want to have to fight for a position."

She nods again. Getting to her feet, she sighs. "I get that. I really can't argue it."

"Right? There's nothing to argue. And with Peck ... he's a great guy," I admit sadly. "If all we can be is friends, then I'll take it. I'd much rather have that then try to embark on some journey that's doomed before it even starts."

Navie throws her arm over my shoulder as we head to the cash register.

"If there's one thing I know for sure about Peck, it's that he's not disappointing."

"Not yet. But everyone will disappoint you at some point."

"Hey," she says, shoving me gently. "I take offense to that."

"I didn't mean you."

"You better not have."

I place my items on the counter and return the attendant's smile. She rings me up, and I hand her my credit card.

"There is an alternative," Navie says.

"What's that?"

"I could hire an assassin."

I laugh. "She's kidding," I tell the woman working the register. "Thank you."

I take my credit card and receipt. Navie grabs my bags. Together, we head into the early afternoon sun.

The air is not too warm and not too cool. The sun is bright as if luring me into happy thoughts.

"You need to stop overthinking everything," Navie says. "You just think and think and think, and before you know it, you're worrying about situations that you'll never even encounter."

"Overthinking prepares me."

"No, overthinking ruins you." She steps away from my trunk as it pops open. "You're so used to being the adult. You've parented your mother and your siblings your whole damn life. Just … be a twentysomething for a while. Cut yourself some slack."

She tosses my bags in, and I close the lid.

"I don't know how to do that," I admit. "It seems … irresponsible."

"You know how to take chances. You moved here on a whim, basically. You danced on a bar last night. You moved in with a man you just met."

"True …"

"So why don't you take chances when the result could make you *really* happy?"

"Living here does make me happy."

She glares at me. "Not what I meant, and you know it."

"Do I?"

"Don't write people off just because you had a bad similar experience. So Charlie didn't pick you. Seriously—good for you. But that doesn't mean it'll always be that same situation with every guy you meet."

"So I'm not the proverbial rebound girl?" I grin. "I'm not the time-killer?"

"Just … shut up." She laughs. "What's wrong in that head of yours?"

"A lot. And on that note, I gotta go. I have a bunch of errands to run today."

"Like what?"

I think back through the list of things I need to do. "Well, I need to run to the post office and drop off some envelopes. I need to do some non-foods and non-clothing shopping."

"What do you need?"

"Bathroom stuff. Notepads. Dish soap."

She nods. "There's a place on the other side of Merom. Follow this street to the right, and you'll see it in a couple of miles."

"Perfect."

"I work tonight," she says. "Come see me if you get bored."

I climb in my car. "Thanks for coming by today."

"I was no help, but you're welcome." She heads across the parking lot. "See ya."

"Bye, Navie."

She walks away like she has no care in the world, but that's not true. She has more cares and problems in her life than I do.

No one knows that, though. She hides things so well. In some ways, we are so similar.

I came to Linton to support Navie, not just because of the Logan business, but because I knew she needed me. But now I think we simply needed each other.

Daily phone conversations, watching movies and then calling each other to rant or rave at the best parts, and planning trips together we'll never take helped us stay close when she moved here. And while I'll never be grateful Logan hurt her or that my family and Charlie about broke me, those things did get me here. Thankfully.

I close the door and turn on the engine. Instead of pulling out, I turn up the radio. An old country song that I remember my nonna playing, about a man loving a woman forever and ever, flows through the cab.

Relaxing back in my seat, I listen to the words.

Is that possible anymore? Or is it always the survival of the fittest?

My phone dings beside me. I pick it up and smile.

PECK: Dinner at seven. Be hungry. ;)

ME: I'll bring dessert.

I LAUGH.

Almost typed *I'll be dessert.*

I toss my phone in the cup holder and head across town.

NINETEEN

Peck

"ALL RIGHT. Let's not fuck this up," I whisper.

The items I bought at the grocery this morning are spread on the table. Packets of steak, giant potatoes that I'll smash with butter and bacon and cheese and chives, and the requisite salad fixings are all displayed in a neat little line for my dinner with Dylan.

I run my hands down the sides of my pants. Sweat from my palms skid down the denim.

"Ugh," I groan. Heading to the sink, I wash my hands.

My stomach has been clenched since I came in from the barn and heard Dylan in the shower. I stood in the kitchen and listened to the water trickle through the pipes in the wall and imagined her standing under the spout.

Wet. And naked.

She's been out for a while now—probably upward of an hour. I told her dinner wasn't until seven, but the longer it takes her to come out, the harder it is to fight my nerves.

"There's no reason to be nervous," I lie to myself. "You're just being polite."

I'd like to politely stick my—

"Hey, Peck."

I wheel around to see her standing in the doorway. A long, brick red dress hangs lazily off her frame, showcasing the delicate curve of her shoulders and dipping sweetly at her waist. Her hair is down, brushing against the middle of her back, and if she has a stitch of makeup on, I'd be shocked.

She's never looked prettier.

"Hey," I say, running my hands down my jeans. Again. "You, um, you look really pretty."

Her cheeks flush. "Thanks. I went shopping with Navie today to grab a few things for my new job and had to have this. It's just so comfortable."

She enters the kitchen, the fabric flowing around her. The room fills with the scent of oranges from her perfume.

Standing next to me, she takes in the ingredients. "What are you making?"

"Steak. Potatoes. Salad."

"I love steak," she says. "And I've never met a carb I wasn't friends with."

I laugh. "Awesome."

"What can I do to help?"

"You totally don't have to help."

She tucks a strand of hair behind her ear and grins. "I know. But I want to. I mean, if you don't mind."

"Yeah. Having you in the kitchen with me sounds like a terrible time," I tease.

"Oh, does it?"

"Just awful."

She grins. "Well, I'll put some music on to help fill all the weird moments of silence that are sure to plague us, considering it's going to be such an awful experience and all."

"Does this mean you're going to dance again?"

150

Her face turns the same shade as her dress. The flush steals my breath as I imagine what she would look like on her back, legs spread, coming all over my tongue. Or on her knees as I take her from behind—

Fuck. Stop. You're cooking dinner, Ward.

"I'm always on the verge of breaking out into song and dance," she says, recovering quickly. "You never know."

I turn back to the table so she doesn't see *my* reddened face. Or my hard-as-nails cock. Because I'm imagining her dancing against me again, feeling every beat, every pulse of her skin against mine.

Holy shit. Stop.

Tonight is about dinner. Not seduction. Because after I left her with nothing but a smile last night, she probably has no idea that I've been fantasizing about her every minute since. And I'm still not sure what I'm doing. *Is this a risk I should be taking?*

"Can you get a gallon storage bag for me? And the foil? They're below the sink," I ask.

"Sure."

When she walks by me, barely brushing against my arm, it sends a shot of energy through my body. Picking up the three kiwifruits on the table, I try to ignore the goose bumps on my skin.

I grab a little cutting board and a knife. When I arrive back at the table, Dylan is there with the bag.

"What are you doing with kiwifruit?" she asks.

"Patience." I peel and slice the fruit and plop it in the bottom of the bag. After giving it a quick mash, I add some olive oil and apple cider vinegar. The steaks go in at the end.

I zip the top.

"I'm so, so confused," she says.

"The kiwifruit will tenderize the steaks. It's so much better than the alternatives of tough meat or overly salty meat."

She snorts. "True. I don't like my meat salty."

I laugh out loud. "Good to know. Good to know."

The oven beeps, alerting us that it's finished pre-heating. I hit each potato with a knife, creating little holes in the skin, and then set them on pieces of foil. I have Dylan add a spoonful of butter on top and then wrap them up.

"You have very odd cooking skills," she says, watching me put the potatoes in a baking dish. "Who taught you to cook?"

"No one, really," I say. "I just kind of … I don't know. I thought about it."

I put the dish in the oven and close the door.

"What about your mom?" she asks. "Does she cook?"

Leaning against the counter, I look at Dylan. "I don't know if she does now. I'd have to know where she is to know if she cooks. But she never did."

Her face wobbles. "Oh. I'm sorry. I didn't realize …"

"It's fine."

"I just saw you with Nana and assumed that your family was picture-perfect."

I take in the concern embedded in her eyes. There's distress in those gorgeous greens because she's worried about *me*.

No one worries about me. It's not something I think a lot about, but I am aware of it. I'm Peck—the guy who will figure it all out. That guy who'll be okay. The guy who's just a goofball at the end of the day, so nothing really gets to him, right?

Wrong. Shit does bother me. I just don't go telling the world about it.

Because the world thinks it already knows. It assumes. Dylan assumes too. But the difference is that she cares when she gets it wrong. It bothers her.

Huh.

"My family is great," I say. "It's just that my parents weren't … that great."

The vacancy inside a piece of my heart that's never quite been filled—the one that I become hyper aware of around my birthday or Mother's Day or the few days a year when I'm basically snowed in. My mother used to love those days. She'd make Vincent and me hot chocolate and snow ice cream, and we would light a big fire in the fire-place. The house always felt like a home on those days.

On other days, it didn't. It was very much my father's house, and we were allowed to stay there. A constant reminder was hauled our way that as soon as we were of legal age, they were getting the hell out of there and living their life.

They didn't even wait that long.

"My dad always resented Vin and me," I say. "I think he had these big ideas for his life, and then Mom got pregnant, and he felt stuck here. With us." I shove off the cabinets, a lump in my throat.

"I'm sorry."

"Don't be. Not your fault. Not mine either."

Dylan bites her bottom lip. "No, it's not. But I can be sorry for you. I know what it's like to not really have the greatest parents in the world. It sucks. My mom is … a handful. And my dad doesn't give a shit."

"My mom cared. I think she knew Dad had a lot of mental issues and got sucked into that." I shrug. "It's her choice. Maybe he needs her more than we do. That's what I tell myself, anyway."

Her laugh is soft and light. "How are you even a real person?"

"What kind of question is that?"

I pull the steaks from the bag and pat them dry. They probably needed another ten minutes or so, but I need to keep moving.

She leans against the end of the table and watches me get them situated on a tray.

"You just told me that you don't even know where they are, and you're like, 'Oh, that's okay.' How are you not bitter about it?" she asks.

Because I've had too many years of disappointment. My expectations have been adjusted back to zero.

"Bitter?" I shrug. "A part of me is, I guess. Vincent definitely is. But I figure everyone does what they have to do. I can't make their choices for them. I can only make mine."

"You're way more of an adult than I am. I'm bitter. And angry. And frustrated."

I look at her. *And beautiful.*

"At least you're honest with yourself," I say.

"But how did you learn to let that go?"

I grin. "The truth?"

"The truth."

"Little League."

"What?" she asks with a laugh.

"It's true. When I started, I was terrible. I mean, awful. Vincent and Machlan were on my team, and both of those bastards were awesome. And then here I come. I couldn't hit the broad side of a barn."

She giggles.

"I had a coach my second year pull me to the side and tell me something that just stuck with me."

She waits for me to continue. When I don't immediately, she motions for me to hurry up. "Come on. Share this golden information."

"He said that every time I let a strike go by, I was fixating on it. That I didn't have a shot in the dark at the next pitch because I was worrying about missing that first one. And he was right. I went to the plate knowing I sucked and expecting the worst. As soon as that first pitch came, I was already so amped up and scared shitless that I swung. Missed. And then I stood there and berated myself over it as the next two strikes went by."

"So you just extrapolated that over your life? Or what?"

"Well, I was twelve." I laugh. "So not immediately. But eventually, I did. And it worked. Helped me not to hold on to a lot of shit."

"See? I didn't play softball. I was a cheerleader."

I nod in appreciation. "I bet you gleaned a few valuable lessons from that too."

"Oh, totally," she says, nodding empathically. "Like how I don't look great in white and olive green. And not to trust the girl who likes your boyfriend to be your back spotter."

"I don't even know what that means."

"The short version: concussions."

"Ouch," I say, flinching.

"Yeah."

I pick up the tray and head for the door onto the patio. "Be right back."

The charcoal is nice and hot. I empty the chimney full of coals and add a few new briquettes. Once the grill is ready, I place the steaks on the grill.

The hair on the back of my neck prickles. Dylan's watching me. I know it. And instead of it making me nervous … I like the feeling of it. I like *the idea* of it. Of her beside me in the kitchen as we prepare dinner while listening to music and talking about our lives. *When have I ever had this?*

Maybe I'd cook more if this was the case.

I grin and shut the lid.

She has a bowl out and is making the salad when I step back into the house.

"I thought I'd go ahead and get this ready," she says. "How many tomatoes do you want me to put in it?"

"However many you'd like," I say from the sink. I rinse my hands and then grab a towel. "Doesn't matter to me."

"Well, do you like a lot of them or not so many?"

"I don't really even like tomatoes," I admit.

She sets the knife down. "Then why did you buy them?"

"I don't know. Don't they go in a salad?"

She cocks her head to the side. Lifting a cucumber, she holds it in the air. "What about these?"

I shrug.

"Do you like them?" she asks.

I shrug again.

"I don't understand," she says.

"The lady at the store said that's what goes in a salad. I don't know that stuff. So if she's wrong, blame it on her. Not on me." I laugh. "I also got sunflower seeds, but I do like those. Never had them in a salad, but I like them for sure."

She laughs, her voice blending with mine. "If you basically don't like anything that goes in a salad, then why are we having it?"

"Don't you like salad?"

Her shoulders fall as a smile graces her lips. "Yes. I do. And I like tomatoes and cucumbers."

"Good," I say, trying not to show her how proud I am of myself.

She turns away, her hair covering the side of her face. A song plays from her phone, the lyrics about candles dripping on bodies striking a chord deep inside mine.

She flips her head so that her hair falls on her far shoulder, exposing the side of her face to me. She chops the vegetables, her hips moving with the beat of the song. The bass is deep, the beat slow and sensual. Her lashes fall closed as she loses herself in the words.

I walk toward her, unable to look away.

Holding her breath as I get closer, she stills.

I stand behind her and peer over her shoulder.

Kissing her would be so easy. Touching her would take all of a half of a second. But if I do either, I'm not going to stop.

And I have dinner to make.

"Looking good," I say.

She blows out a breath.

I'm lying. *She* looks incredible. *She* smells fucking awesome. *She* has shown me more empathy in a few days than many of my friends had throughout my life. *She* is sexy as hell. But she will get to eat her dinner because I'm starting to realize that she deserves someone looking after her.

I laugh at her frustration—because, fuck, I get it—winking as I head to the refrigerator.

TWENTY

Dylan

THE UNEXPECTED CHARM of this man is on full display as he maneuvers around the kitchen with ease. "For someone who doesn't ever cook, you sure know your way around the kitchen."

"It's never been fun to cook for one."

"But it is for two?"

He lifts from checking on the potatoes, gazing through the oven window as if he's admiring newborns in the nursery. When his blue eyes land back on me, my hands press a little harder onto the counter to steady myself.

That level of sexy should be outlawed.

The corners of his lips shoot up. "It is for you."

The kitchen suddenly feels like a hot August day with him standing so close. I look away, directing my attention back to the salad. The blade of the knife slices through the tomato, cracking down on the cutting board.

"Careful," he says, coming around me. "I just sharpened the knives."

He sets a cutting board next to mine and starts chopping the onions. I think it's the first true glimpse of how comfortable we've become in our living situation. I don't know if I should be worried or appreciate it by living in the moment. The latter is feeling like a favorite T-shirt right about now, so I go with what feels good.

Peck Ward feels good. Every brush of his arm against mine, the way his laughter tickles my ear, and the heat that exudes between us is heightened. I finish dicing the tomato and take a step back, leaning against the opposite counter to get a better look at him. From that ass to those biceps and broad shoulders, he knows how to get attention without even trying.

"What are you doing, Dylan?"

My eyes shoot up to find his on me. "Just … thinking."

"What are you thinking about?"

Your body.

"I … um …" I laugh. "Thinking about how that kiwifruit makes things soft."

"Really?" He pretends to consider that. "I don't know that I'd go with soft."

"That's true. Nobody likes soft meat."

His smirk digs deeper as he sets the knife down. "How do you like your meat, Dylan?"

I have no idea if we're still talking about actual meat or not, but I'm willing to play this game. If for no other reason than to see his face when he wears the look like he wants to eat me.

I gulp. "Hearty."

He chuckles.

"Or aged to perfection," I offer.

"Interesting choice of words."

"What word do you prefer?" I ask. "To describe meat, of course."

He sticks his tongue in the side of his cheek. He's such an insane mix of playful and sexy that I don't know which to focus on. My cheeks ache from smiling, but my thighs burn from desire.

"I'd say … hand-rubbed," he says.

"Well done."

"What? My comeback or that's how you like your meat too?"

We laugh together, the sound filling the room.

He plants both palms on the counter behind him and gives it a shove. The momentum sends him across the kitchen toward me.

I can't look away as he gets closer. My heart thumps in my chest, sending a flow of blood over my ears that makes me dizzy.

He stops in front of me and peers down. The playfulness is still there, but it's overshadowed by the heat in his eyes.

I want him even though it goes against everything I know is right for me. He's in love with someone else, and I'm likely just a rebound of sorts who's being used as a tool to the nth degree. And when it doesn't work, he can eject me out of here like yesterday's trash.

But right now, looking up into those gorgeous eyes of his, I just. Don't. Care. I'll deal with it later.

"You standing this close to me isn't fair," I tell him.

"Why?"

His voice is a dead giveaway to the fact that he wants to see if there's any fire under all this smoke billowing between us.

"Because I want to touch you, and you know that."

It takes a few seconds for that to register. When it does, I know.

He adjusts his weight, widening his stance to encapsulate both of my feet. He surrounds me with his wide frame as a grin touches his lips.

"Since when do you not do what you want?" he teases.

"I can touch?" I wink, making that smirk of his grow.

"You most definitely can touch."

Letting my hands land on his abs, I rub around and then dip under his shirt. It wasn't the kitchen that's been bringing the heat. His warm skins heats mine, and my breathing quickens.

"Why are you so irresistible?" I breathe the words out because I'm a hot mess of a turned-on and insatiable.

It's been a long, long time since I've felt like this.

His arms wrap around me. He holds me tight against him, his chest rising and falling as wildly as mine.

His body is hard and steady, and I could stay all day with my cheek pressed against his chest. He leans down, his lips fluttering against my ear.

"I could ask you the same the question," he says. "But why bother with small talk when I can show you."

The moment his lips land on my neck, I close my eyes and tilt my head to the side, never wanting a man more than I do him. I was flirting—both with him and the line between us—but now *I want him*. I need him.

I glance at the oven timer. "We have time. Just saying."

A chuckle vibrates from his chest. "How much?"

My breathing goes in and out at a ragged pace. I lean back to see his face. "Twenty-five minutes."

"I only need ten."

I start to laugh as his face wrinkles in disgust.

"Calling it like it is," he says. "You know what I mean. I'm not going to last long with you."

I slide my hands in his hair. My body angles toward his. "As long as it's a good ten minutes." I can't stop myself from laughing.

He rolls his eyes, but then his arms tighten around me, and he lifts me on top of the counter. "Damn straight, it will be."

"Time's a ticking, Wesley."

He nuzzles his face in the crook of my neck. "I love a challenge, but I'm not sure if I want to win this one or not."

I pull away and take his face in my hands. It's smooth, freshly shaven, as I hold his jaw in my palms. If I continue, this will be a go. There will be no way out. But as I watch him lick his lips, his eyes as constant and unshakable as I know him to be, I realize a truth: I'm already all in.

"How about we race to the finish together instead?" I breathe.

He leans forward and presses his lips softly against mine. His body moves closer until he's up against me. I hook my ankles around the small of his back as he deepens the kiss.

I moan into his mouth; the contact glorious but not quite fulfilling. I need more.

His tongue swipes past my lips. He wraps his arms around me again and draws me even closer.

I'm surrounded by Peck Ward.

He tastes of warmth and wishes, of heat and happiness. There's no rush, no urgency to his sweet kisses. It's as if he has all the time in the world to commit this to memory.

The song changes. Peck slowly breaks the kiss.

I sag as his lips separate from mine. Air is pulled into my lungs, and I search his face, desperate for more.

"That wasn't ten minutes," I tell him.

"Change of plans."

My dress is lifted, and on a gasp, my panties are removed. Sinking to his knees, he presses his silky lips against my inner thighs. I lean back on the counter, propping myself up on my elbows, and watch him watch me enjoy his touch.

"Ah," I eke out as his hands run up and down my legs.

I've missed this feeling of being so desired, so wanted, that my partner just can't wait to have me. I don't even think I had this with Charlie. Not even once.

He bunches my dress at my waist and licks up and down the inside of my legs. Just when I'm about to lose my mind in the feel of his tongue stroking closer and closer to the apex of my thighs, he stands.

"What are you doing?" I ask.

He calmly opens a drawer next to me. "I need to flip the steaks so they don't burn."

"I'm burning over here. With desire." I half-laugh because it's only half-funny. "You're just going to leave me here?"

"Don't worry," he says, clapping the tongs together. "I plan to get back here with plenty of time to take the checkered flag."

"I don't even know what we're talking about anymore, but that better mean what I think it does."

He opens the back door. "It does. Relax." The door closes, and I sigh in frustration. There's no way to actually relax like this—not with my body staging a riot for some kind of relief.

The door opens again, and he tosses the tongs on the counter. He stands between my legs, and I sit up.

"Now, where were we?" he asks.

"If you don't know, I'm not telling you."

"That'd be the first time you don't try to tell me what to do."

I smack at him, but he captures my hand. I'm quickly scooped into his arms and kissed as he carries me to my bedroom.

"Is this okay?" he asks.

"If it makes you remember where we were, then it's perfect."

He grins.

I turn around. Lifting my hair above my neck, I ask, "Do you mind unzipping me?"

He kisses the nape of my neck and plants a few random pecks down the side. My skin tingles with anticipation as the zipper slides down my spine. The right side is taken down my shoulder and then the left before the dress puddles at my feet. I step out of the dress, turning around to face him.

His shirt comes over his head, and all the fun, the teasing, and the games we were playing have been left in the other room. Gentle touches and soft kisses replace the laughter as his hands cover my bare back for the first time.

The reserve that usually constrains my physical interactions with him doesn't exist between us now. Everything he's done is to show me how he cares and that I'm safe with him. So I begin to unbuckle his belt while he reaches around to unfasten my bra.

When his jeans come down and my bra comes off, we don't hide from the sunlight streaming in through the window. We take our time to appreciate each other.

I've never felt more beautiful than I do under his gaze, a smile that's genuine and kind, and hands that touch to explore, not rushing to the next step.

I watch with rapt attention as his Adam's apple bobs with a heavy swallow. His eyes cast down, and when he looks up, I see a struggle in his eyes. "I did this wrong, Dylan."

"What are you talking about?"

"I should have taken the time to kiss you more."

"We kissed in the kitchen, Peck. Checked that box," I say, bringing a finger down and then back up in a check mark motion in the air.

He grins. "But not like I wanted to."

"Then kiss me now."

Strong hands take hold of my face with such care that I cover his hands with mine, feeling weak in the knees. I close my eyes just as our lips press together for the first time in a caress. Our tongues meet, and I wrap my arms around his shoulders, never wanting this moment to end.

When it does, I'm left breathless and sit on the edge of the bed before lying down. "Are you going to leave me waiting? Again?"

"No ma'am, I'm not." His pulls his boxers down, and every thought I ever had about him below the waist were wrong. He's better.

He catches me staring.

"Sorry," I say.

"You know how to build a guy's ego."

"Judging by what I see, you have every right to be downright arrogant."

When he laughs, I smile with him. Whatever this is between us is nice. Hovering over me, he leans down and kisses me again. "So do you. You're gorgeous and *so* fucking sexy."

Since my panties were left on the kitchen floor, there's nothing between us.

He shifts his weight so the head of his cock presses against my opening. I gasp at the contact despite expecting it. Despite *wanting it.*

His Adam's apple bobs in his throat. I reach up and place my palm on the side of his neck. His heartbeat pounds against my hand, and I feel mine amp up to match.

"Peck ..." I whisper.

Our gazes lock, the heat between us sizzling. I try to look away but can't. He holds me in place with nothing but a look as he moves his hips.

Inch by inch, he fills me.

"Oh, my gosh," I pant.

"Open for me, baby." It's a command, there's no doubt about it, but it's said with such a sweetness that I think I might fall apart already.

My knees fall farther to the sides. He slides inside me, fulling seating himself inside my body.

"Damn it," I whimper.

He closes his eyes and doesn't move. The vein in his neck throbs in a look so sexy that I shudder.

His head dips, his mouth covering mine. I press my hands to his chest and then run them up to his shoulders. The muscles flex as he moves, rocking himself into me.

The blanket is soft against my back, his arms hard on either side of me. It's an overwhelming contrast of sensations. I gasp for air but am cut off by his kisses.

Closing my eyes, I let my head fall back into the mattress. He doesn't relent, covering me with kisses, licks, and nibbles across my mouth, jaw, and neck.

I've never felt this treasured, this desired, by anyone in my entire life.

"Peck," I pant, holding his face in my hands.

"Yes, beautiful?"

I grin, bringing his lips back to mine.

"You feel so good," he whispers, dragging his hands up my arms when I raise them above my head and loop my fingers around the rails of the headboard.

"You feel amazing," I say.

He pulls out, taunting my clit, before dipping inside me again.

"Do that a couple more times," I groan, pleasure ripping through my body, "and I'll come."

"I'm having to think about fishing so I don't lose it right now," he says with a chuckle.

I clench my muscles. He feels it because his eyes widen.

"You do that a couple more times, and this is over," he warns.

I lock my legs around him. Digging my heels into the small of his back, I look him right in the eyes and clench again.

"Dylan ..."

He slides in and out, hitting the spot that brings me closer and closer to an orgasm.

"Right … *there*," I say.

It feels so good it almost hurts.

"Look at me," he says. "I want to watch you come."

I do. And when I do, that's it. It's all it takes.

I clench again, a mass of colors tangling through my vision as I melt around him.

His name screams from my lips as a rush of fire floods my veins. He presses harder, faster, driving me into the mattress as he finds his end.

"Fuck," he groans. He stills inside me.

I watch him fall apart. His eyes squeezed closed, his jaw tightened, his biceps strained as he gloriously hits his climax.

The ringing of a bell accompanies our victory lap.

Wait …

He pushes up and looks me in the eyes. "Do you smell smoke?"

I sit up.

"The steaks!" He runs out of the room, and I hear the back door slam against the stopper. "Fuck," echoes from outside.

I hurry into the kitchen. The smoke from the grill has filled the house. I rush over to shut the door but stop when Peck comes inside with the steaks stiff between the tongs … naked.

"Oh, my gosh," I say, wiping back tears from my laughter. "Now that's a sight to see."

He drops the charred meat on the cutting board. "So much for impressing you with a nice meal."

His disappointment isn't just seen in his expression, but defeat drops his shoulders. I stop laughing but continue to smile.

"Everything is fine." I lean against his back, resting my cheek to him. "You wanted to impress me?"

"Yeah, but I screwed it up."

"You sure did." I slip around him, coming between him and the steaks. "In the best of ways." With wide eyes and a big sassy grin, I ask, "Want to go screw up again?" I reach up and rub his shoulders. "I was thinking we could try your bed this time."

When his hands grab my hips, I know I've got him just where I want him. "How do you feel about the shower?"

I tug him toward his room. "Better get me dirty first."

"We'll be getting dirty all right." Lifting me, he puts me over his shoulder and smacks my ass. "I wasn't hungry for food anyway."

"What are you hungry for then?"

"I'm famished. For you."

TWENTY-ONE

Peck

"PECK WARD, you have some explaining to do." Nana brandishes a wooden spoon my way. "Why wasn't your butt in a church pew this morning, young man?"

"Let me get in the house first. Geez," I say, closing the door behind me.

Machlan and Lance stand at the island, clearly enjoying their position as the good grandsons. That doesn't happen often with either of them.

"Oh, leave him alone," Lance says, popping a cashew in his mouth. "I think he was getting a little last night."

"Hey, Lance. Shut the fuck up," I say.

"Really with that language on the Sabbath?" Nana asks.

"Sorry."

Lance laughs. "Getting laid brings out the feistiness in ya. I like it."

"She'd make you feisty too," Machlan teases. "Peck's got himself a hottie."

"And it's not Molly. Hey, that rhymed," Lance says.

I have a half a notion to turn around and walk out. I've got enough shit on my mind besides listening to these two idiots tease me all day.

Was I getting a little, as Lance so eloquently put it? Yes. Does Molly need to be included in this conversation? No. And is any of this their business? Absolutely not.

But they're ... them, so they'll make it their business.

Assholes.

Nana turns back to the stove. "Well, if Peck was entertaining a lady last night"—she pauses and looks at Lance as if to make a point—"and that lady was Dylan, then he gets a pass."

"I never got a pass," Lance points out.

"Because you would've needed a pass every other week," Nana tells him. "Peck is a good boy. He shows up for Jesus every week without fail." She sets the spoon down and looks at me. "So were you with Dylan last night?"

Machlan and Lance burst into laughter as my jaw drops. I stare at my little grandma as she waits patiently for me to tell her who I was sleeping with.

"Nana ... no," I say. My response only makes my cousins laugh louder. "We really don't need to discuss this."

"I don't want to discuss it. I know the mechanics of having sex, Peck," she says.

I think Machlan is going to piss himself.

"All I'm asking is if you were having sex with Dylan," she says calmly.

My hands go in the air as I walk in a circle. "I have no idea what happened to this family. It's like y'all went off and lost your damn minds."

"Couple of 'em in here didn't have any minds to start with," Walker says, shutting the door behind him. He looks around the room. "What are we laughing about?"

Lance points at Nana. "She just told Peck she wants to know who he was fucki—screwing last night."

Nana's hands go on her hips. "I did no such thing. Not with those words, anyway."

"I can tell you that," Walker says, knocking me off-balance with his shoulder as he walks by. "He's been worthless since she got to town."

"Fucker," I say, ignoring Nana's gasp. "I have not."

He picks up a handful of cashews and pops them in his mouth. He's completely nonplussed.

"I hate you all," I tell them. "Except you, Nana. I love you."

She raises a brow and goes back to the stove. The oven door is opened, and the smell of cornbread fills the kitchen.

I take a seat next to Lance. He and Machlan argue about lottery odds while Walker kisses Nana on the cheek.

"I was going to fry some potatoes too, but I'm just too tired," she says. "Cooking takes a toll on me these days."

"We keep telling you to stop it," Machlan says. "Let the girls cook for you."

"Or for us," Lance says.

Nana shoves that idea away with the back of her hand. "Don't be silly. I just need to go a little slower than before. I'll get my strength back up. I just need some time."

"Sienna would've been here to help, but she had to fly to Los Angeles yesterday over some contract for her company. She got a deal to design for a place that does evening gowns or something."

"Yeah," Lance says. "Mariah would've been here too but volunteered to make a bunch of cakes and stuff for the nursing home in town. They were having some birthday month party thing," he says, unsure. "She got Hadley to help her."

Walker looks at me. "Where's Dylan?"

"You too?" I ask, raising a brow.

He grins.

"Look, you guys. Dylan and I are just …"

My voice trails off because I don't know what we're doing now. I suppose the accurate term would be sleeping together, but that doesn't feel quite right. That feels … careless. Replaceable. Those aren't two words I care to place on whatever last night was.

It was a good night of fucking. I know that. I'll probably go home today, and she'll act like nothing happened. But as I lay there in the early morning hours with her wrapped around me, her hair in my face and arms tucked around me, it felt like something happened beyond a few amazing orgasms.

It felt like … I wanted to do it again. Not just the fucking, but the rest of it too. And that's worrisome.

"You and Dylan are engaging in adult activity." Lance grins. "See, Nana? I said that in a clean, politically correct way."

"Good boy," she says.

"Right," I say, uncomfortable with that description too. "But it's not like you should expect her here on Sunday afternoons or give her hell when you see her. Okay?"

Machlan plucks out a couple of cashews. "We'd never do such a thing."

"Right," I say again as the door behind me opens again.

We all look to see Vincent and Sawyer walk in.

My nephew is a miniature version of his father. He has dark blond hair, crystal-clear blue eyes, and a hefty dose of freckles across the bridge of his nose like Vincent and I used to have when we were younger.

"Hey, Uncle P," he says, leaning against me as I pull him into a one-armed hug.

"Hey, buddy."

I look down at him and smile.

I've never really understood the feeling I get when I'm around Sawyer. I don't get to spend enough time with him to know his favorite foods or colors or what he likes to do besides fish. But I do know that if the kid called me at two in the morning for anything, I'd be there. I know I wouldn't question his bail money if he grows up and does something harebrained like his dad and I did, and if anything ever happened to my brother, I'd take this kid in a heartbeat.

A fuzzy feeling fills my chest as I think for a split second what it might be like to have a Sawyer of my own. To have children and a wife that the rest of my family could ask about and want to see. To have a little blond-headed, maybe green-eyed kid running around, asking me to go fishing too.

I shake my head.

Too fast. Way too fast, Peck.

Nana dabs her eyes with the towel on her shoulder.

"Knock that shit off," Walker says, pulling her into his side.

"I'm just so happy," she says. "There are no words to explain the love you have for your grandchildren. I loved your father," she says, looking up at Walker, "and your mother," she says, looking at Vincent and me. "But you kids are just something special."

"Well, we think you're something special," Sawyer says.

I pat his back. He looks up at me and smiles.

"You wanna tell her?" Vincent looks down at his son.

Sawyer stands tall. "Nana, guess what?"

"I don't know. What?"

"Dad and I were talking today. And we made a decision." He rubs his bottom lip with the side of his finger, a habit of his father's.

Vincent watches Sawyer proudly. I see why. This little dude has the confidence of a kid twice his age, and he's definitely got Vincent's swagger.

Vincent is definitely fucked.

"Well," Machlan prods. "What's happening?"

"We figure maybe we'll stick around." Sawyer looks at his dad and smiles. "We kind of like it here."

Nana's eyes fill with tears again. Her arms spread open. "Come here and give your Great Nana a hug."

Sawyer struts across the kitchen and falls into her arms. She kisses his head, wiping her eyes with her towel.

"Yeah," Vincent says. "I figure I've done a thorough search of the counties down there for a stepmom for Sawyer. I need some new options."

Nana fires him a look. "Don't talk that way in front of him."

"Why?" Sawyer looks up at her. "I need a stepmom. The right stepmom," he insists. "This kid I go to school with—his name is Pete. Well, Pete's dad got remarried in a hurry, and his stepmom is a nightmare. So if Dad needs to take his time in picking one, I'm okay with that."

Nana looks relieved. "That's right, sweetheart. Your dad is just being cautious."

Sawyer walks toward me with a mischievous look on his face. "I'm not dumb," he whispers when he gets to me.

"You little shit," I whisper back.

He laughs. "Can I go outside and check out the treehouse before we eat?"

Walker nods. "Yeah. Go ahead."

"But dinner is ready," Nana says.

Machlan walks around the island. He motions for me to get up. I head that way, rolling up my shirtsleeves.

"Peck and I will help you fry some potatoes," Machlan says.

"You boys don't have to do that."

"Nah, we do," I say.

"You boys are too good to me." She reaches up and kisses my cheek. "But I do wish you had brought Dylan."

"Nana ..."

She swipes her towel at me. "She's a nice girl. And it's clear she's smitten with you."

"Oh, she is not."

My stomach clenches. I open the refrigerator and pretend to look for something just so my cousins don't see my face.

Dylan isn't smitten with me. Is she? What does smitten even mean, anyway?

Her face pops up in my memories—her head thrown back, mouth forming a sexy little 'o' as she dropped all her reservations and gave herself to me.

As if she can read my mind, my phone buzzes in my pocket. I take it out and look at the screen.

DYLAN: I'm heading out with Navie for a while today. I made some lunch. Leftovers in fridge if you want some although I'm sure you won't want any given you're at Nana's. Say hi from me.

I CLOSE the door and look up at my family. They're laughing as Machlan peels a bag of potatoes and Vincent tells Lance about some encounter he had with a woman on a boat. Walker sips a glass of tea, leaning against the cabinets, taking it all in. The only thing missing from this scene is Dylan.

I wish she were here.

He catches my eye. The joking from earlier has subsided and in its place is a knowing look. It wasn't that long ago that Walker was in my place and trying to decide how to deal with things with Sienna. I wasn't sure he'd figure it out. But he did.

Maybe there's hope for me.

For us.

TWENTY-TWO

Dylan

NAVIE GASPS.

I knew she would. She has some kind of Spidey sense about things like this … things that have to do with sex or things that include me being embarrassed.

This one is a double or nothing.

"Dylan," she squeals as I come through the door.

"I'm not even fully in your house yet, and you're already squealing."

"You're glowing," she says.

"I'm not pregnant, Navie."

"No. Maybe not. But if I'm guessing, I'm going to say that you've been partaking in activities that could result in a little baby Ward."

I don't mean to laugh, but I do. "That's not funny," I say, despite the chuckle.

She plops down on her sofa. She's downright smug.

I sit in the chair and try to maneuver the conversation to other things … before we come back to my glow. There's no doubt we'll discuss it. And I kind of want to. I need a sounding board.

"That new movie I was telling you about—the one with the strippers—it's playing in Merom. I saw it on the sign yesterday," I say.

"Mhmm."

Redirection might be harder than I thought.

I just need a minute to get my bearings. My plan was to figure things out in my head before seeing Navie, but that proved to be difficult—if not impossible.

"Want to get some dessert?" I ask. "I've been wanting to check out Carlson's Bakery."

"Mhmm."

"Navie …"

She laughs. "What I want is for you to tell me what put that look on your face. You want to do that in a movie theater? Cool. At Carlson's over a Reuben sandwich? Awesome. I don't care. Pick whatever venue you want, but we're discussing this."

Plucking my favorite blue pillow from beside Navie, I tuck it next to me on the chair. Might as well get comfortable. This may take a while.

"Okay. Where do I start?" I ask.

"Just answer this first, and then you can go wherever you want with it: is he as amazing in bed as I imagine?"

My skin heats as I recall Peck's firm yet gentle touches. My lips part as memories of him taking control with his mouth flood me. My thighs squeeze as I remember what it's like to have his head, his hands, his cock between them.

Dear lord. I might never be okay again.

"That's a yes," she chirps. "I knew it. I can tell."

"Well, it's not like it was hard to guess correctly. You've seen the man move."

"And you've felt it." She scoots around in her seat. "So give me the details. Are you guys a thing now?"

I force a smile to hide my uncertainty. Truth be told, I know we aren't *a thing*. I'm not messed up about that. But I don't know what we are.

Friends? Friends with benefits? Lovers? Two people who made a mistake?

When we curled up together and fell asleep moments before dawn, I had one opinion. And when I woke up alone this morning with a note that he went to Nana's, I had another.

It wasn't as if I expected anything to change because we'd been intimate. But it does make me feel a little off-balance that he left me in his bed when I'd met Nana before.

"I'm overthinking everything," I tell Navie.

"Of course you are. I'm here to help break all that down."

I bite a fingernail, mulling everything over.

"Dylan. Stop it."

"I just …" I drop my hand. "I don't know what to do. I can't wrap my head around it."

She wiggles her eyebrows. "But could you wrap *your hand* around it?"

I throw the pillow at her.

Laughing, she hands it back to me. "What's the problem? Honestly. What are you all hung up about?"

"It's like … now what? He's great. We've slept together. I freaking live there. There's no way, *no way, Navie*, this can end well."

"And why the hell not?"

I spring to my feet and walk around the little room. Days ago, my stuff was stacked in the corner of this space. Days ago, I was waiting to strike out on my own. Days ago, I had a clear picture of what the next phase of my life would look like, but now I don't freaking know.

"Look," I say, stopping next to the television. "Peck was gone when I got up."

She thinks. "He goes to church every week. I bet he didn't want to wake you up."

"Maybe. But the point is, I haven't had time to talk to him, to even see him, since about five minutes after he pulled his cock out of me. And by that, I mean I don't know what he's thinking."

"Probably that you looked like an angel in his bed and he wanted to leave with that imagery," she offers, speaking slowly. "Like you said, you're overthinking. Breathe. Relax. Go make yourself some tea."

I shake my head. "If I go back and things are weird, do you know how awkward that will be?"

"Pretty damn awkward." She gets to her feet. "But I highly doubt that's what's going to happen."

"Fine. What if I go back and he's like, 'You are the love of my life'?"

She laughs. "Also highly doubt that's what's gonna happen."

"Gee, thanks." I bury my head in my hands. "I just feel like this happened so naturally and so fast that I've lost all perspective." I look up at her. "A few days ago, he was professing his love for Molly, according to you."

"He was lying," she scoffs. "You've given him a taste of the real thing. He probably doesn't even remember who she is."

I roll my eyes but give her a smile.

This is why Navie is my best friend. She knows what to say and always has the utmost confidence in me. I love her.

I sit back down again. My feet curl up beneath me as I try to settle my thoughts into a more manageable stream.

"Okay. Here's the thing," I say slowly. "I did what I always do—I jumped in too fast. I threw caution to the wind and—"

"And there's nothing wrong with that."

"No, there's not. Except for the fact that now I have to deal with the consequences." I frown. "Peck seems like a really good idea. A damn good one. But … am I prepared to deal with a man right now? One who may or may not have an unrequited love for a very specific woman?"

Navie holds up a finger, heading toward the kitchen. It gives me a small moment to consider things about Molly.

Unrequited love isn't really true, I guess. Peck told me he'd love Molly forever, but after our talk the other night, I know he's reassessing *how* he loves her and what that love means. But it doesn't necessarily mean he's emotionally available for me. I mean,

Peck's a virile man, and I'm sure he's slept with many women over the years.

And they've never amounted to anything.

Gah! Brain, stop thinking.

Navie comes back with a glass of tea, handing it to me and then sitting on the couch.

"If it's what he wanted—to try to see what was between us, if anything, and it could stay so easy breezy, I could go for it. But if it's going to get all complicated and I have to jockey for a position with Molly, I … I don't wanna do that, Navie."

"I get it."

"But I also don't want to sleep with a guy who I could be good friends with otherwise and screw it all up because of the actual screwing." I blow out a breath. "I shouldn't have done that."

Navie leans forward, putting her hands on my knees. She looks me right in the eye. "Yes, you should've. Because you have to learn to trust yourself. Something in your brain told you it was okay to let your guard down, and you have to trust that voice."

"But that voice has led me astray before."

She grins. "Even inner voices have bad days." She sits back again. "You need to calm down and stop thinking about all the bad things that might happen and focus on all the good that's possible."

"Like …?"

"Lots of orgasms, from the sound of it."

I laugh. "Girl …"

She laughs too. "See? And what if this whole thing turns out to be something good. Then what? Then you'll kick yourself for doubting it in the first place."

I take a sip of the tea and try to do as instructed. I try to relax.

My body is still buzzing from last night. My muscles ache, and some feel stretched. It's a lovely feeling and would be even better if I could kick this mental silliness.

"Let's think proactively," Navie suggests. "What can you do to make yourself feel better about this? Besides talking to him, which I'm assuming you'll do when you go home."

"That's the plan."

"Okay. Good. Now let's develop the rest of the plan."

I rest my head on the chair and ponder my situation. If I boil it all down, the part that bothers me the most is being stuck there in a situation I don't want to be in. If I didn't live with him, I'd be more open into seeing where things could possibly go between us.

"I need to have another housing option in my pocket," I say. "Speaking of which ..." I set my tea down on the end table and slip my phone from my pocket.

"What are you doing?" Navie asks.

"Hang on."

I open my text app and then scroll through my contacts until I find Joanie's name.

ME: Hi, Joanie. It's Dylan Snow. I was wondering if you found the information for the house we were discussing. I'm still very interested in it.

I LOOK up to see Navie's watching me.

"What?" I ask.

"What are you doing?" she repeats.

"Just seeing if Joanie, my boss at the bank, found any information on the house she knew about for rent."

Navie's lips twist. "I can't argue your logic there. Maybe it would be better if you weren't staying with him. I can see how that would muck stuff up."

My stomach settles, and a calmness sweeps over me. It's from the tea or the text or from discussing things with Navie. I don't know which, but I do know I'm grateful to feel it.

"Okay. Now lunch?" I ask. "I really want to try the coffee cake at Carlson's."

"It's the best. You should just buy the whole cake and eat the rest for breakfast. That's what I do," she says with a shrug. She glances at her watch. "Or we could grab something real quick and still make the movie."

I nod.

Even though our decision is made, neither of us moves. I just sit and revel in the knowledge that I have Navie so close to me again. It feels so good to have someone in your corner.

The moment is broken when my phone buzzes in my head. I look down.

MOM: I called you a couple of days ago. Koty needs to borrow some money for Gia's birthday party. She'll be eight, if you didn't remember. Could you send a check? A couple of hundred should be enough, I'd say. I told her you would.

I ROLL my eyes and turn my phone off. "Are you ready?"

"Yup. Let's go."

TWENTY-THREE

Dylan

THE TELEVISION IS ON. A sitcom I've never seen before plays out in front of me. It's not really that interesting, and I don't get the humor, but it's enough of a distraction to warrant leaving on.

The movie Navie and I saw was great. The buttery, salty popcorn was even better. But now I'm home again. Alone.

I glance at my phone, but there's no text from Peck. No missed call. No anything. I don't know what to make of that. And even though Navie had my nerves mostly chilled out by the time I dropped her off at her apartment with a tub of leftover popcorn and a loaf of coffee cake, I've lost the chill. Now, I'm anxious.

What does his non-reply mean? Does he regret being with me? Does he regret the fact that I'm here?

I have no idea, and I wish I did.

Picking my phone off the coffee table, I re-read Joanie's text. The information about the rental is in front of me. The name of the landlord, the fair asking price, the fact that it's available now—all of it is right there, waiting on my move.

But I don't know what move to make.

I want to stay here, but I know I should go. It's a tough call to make when I have no help in making it.

The door opens and shuts. Peck's footsteps scoff against the floor. I hold my breath as I watch his shadow stretch across the doorway. Then, finally, after what feels like an eternity, his handsome face comes around the corner.

He stutter-steps as he walks by. His hand grabs the doorframe, and he stops.

A mix of emotions crosses his face as he looks at me sitting on the couch. I fidget, unsure of what to say.

"Heya, Dylan," he says. Slowly, his face breaks into a smile.

Relief courses through my veins as he enters the room.

"How was your day?" I ask. Glancing at the clock, I see that it's nearly dinner time.

He walks straight over to me with a dose of hesitation in his eyes. Leaning down, he holds my face in his hands and presses a kiss to my lips.

It takes me by surprise.

"Oh," I say when he pulls back. "I wasn't expecting that."

His posture relaxes as he settles himself into an oversized leather chair.

In dark jeans and a blue button-up with the sleeves rolled to his elbows, he looks delicious. But his eyes still don't quite share the same casual vibe as his dress.

"I'm sorry about today." He clears his throat. "I missed church, which pissed Nana off. But I got up and got to her house before lunch."

"That's good."

He nods. His chest rises as he sucks in a deep breath. "I'll be honest here—I didn't know whether to wake you up today or not. I just … my whole family was there, and they're a lot to deal with and—"

"Peck. It's fine."

He lights up. "Really? Because I really thought I'd probably fucked up. And the longer I went and didn't call you or text you, the worse I figured it was. But I just … I didn't know what to do."

I rearrange myself on the couch so my feet are on the floor. I tug a pillow onto my lap for a flimsy guard to my ego and heart.

"Nana asked about you," he says. "She was kind of pissed you didn't come."

Well, I wasn't asked.

"That's nice," I say. "I'm glad she likes me."

"That's for sure."

He holds my gaze. I think he's as unsure of what to say as I am. So I jump right in. Might as well.

"I get what last night was," I say.

"You do?"

I nod. "And I don't expect you to want to drag me in front of your family because we slept together. I'm a big girl, Peck. I didn't read into it." *Ish.*

"No. No, no, no," he says. He moves to the edge of the chair. His elbows rest on his knees. "You're wrong. That's not it at all."

My body still as I take in the seriousness in his face. I'm afraid to reply—to say anything at all—in case I just misinterpreted that.

He blows out a breath and smiles. But it's a gesture that's not made to ease my mind, but a sign that he's trying to get himself together.

"Let me ask you this," he says. "Do you think yesterday changed anything between us?"

I consider his question. "Well, I know now that you can deliver an a-plus orgasm."

He grins.

I grin too.

"I'm glad that we still have this," he says, looking relieved. "I was afraid we'd messed this up somehow."

"Me too." I set the pillow to the side. "I've worried all day about it. And then you didn't call and stuff and I—"

"That was my mistake. I'm sorry. I should've." He clears his throat. "I just want you to know, without a doubt, that last night … well, it meant something to me. I don't know what, exactly. I'm still a little confused, to be honest. But I … there's … you know."

I do know. I think. And it's how I feel too. But hearing him admit that out loud, his voice so earnest, does something to me—something deep and powerful.

I smile and try not to blush.

"Thank you for saying that," I say. "But you don't owe me an explanation. You don't owe me anything."

He sits back in his chair again. "I believe that. I actually think you owe me at this point."

"What?" I laugh.

"Well, I bought an expensive set of pots and pans because of you. I'm renting you a room in my house—and a bathroom. And you got off … four? Five times yesterday? You clearly are in debt to me."

My shoulders fall as the tension that's built all day melts away. "I don't pay my debts. Just so you know."

"Oh, thanks for telling me now." He winks. "But seriously, I'm sorry if I made things weird today. It was just … a weird day."

I nod, mulling that over. My gaze goes back to the television, and I act like I know what's going on. Really, I just want a minute to decipher what he said.

It was just a weird day.

What does that mean?

"My brother announced today that he and Sawyer are moving home," Peck says.

"That's great. Are you happy?"

"Yeah. Sawyer is a cute little shit. I'm excited to get to show him the ropes."

"You mean make him ornery?"

Peck laughs. "Oh, he's already ornery. I had no part in that."

I watch his face light up. He seems completely energized and over the moon about Vincent's news. It makes my heart happy.

It's not hard to imagine Peck running around with a little kid as a sidekick. The idea makes me grin.

"I bet you're a great uncle," I say.

"I hope I am. I didn't really have that level of family growing up. I had Walker's dad, but he was always working at the shop, so I didn't see him much. And he was pretty standoffish when it came to things like life lessons. You just kind of knew what he expected … and also knew he'd stick a boot in your ass if you didn't follow along."

I laugh.

He rests his elbows on his knees again. His head is free from a hat, which doesn't seem to happen often. His hair looks like he's run his hands through it a hundred times today, and I wish I could reach out and take a turn.

"How was Nana today?" I ask.

"She was good. Great, actually, since Vincent told he they're staying in town." He sighs happily. "Being there and watching her with us boys was pretty special. It's … what matters in life, I think."

He turns slowly, lifting his eyes to mine. Our gazes connect like two superheroes colliding above a battlefield.

I sit back, absorbing the impact of his stare. He leans forward as if it will help him dig deeper into my thoughts. All I can see is how he cared for Nana. How he'd do anything for her, and I'm guessing that would extend to all his family.

All those he loves.

"You'll be a great dad," I tell him.

"What about you?"

"What about me?" I ask.

"Do you want to be a mother?"

My breathing quickens. I fiddle with the edge of a pillow.

"I don't know," I admit. "Sometimes I do, and sometimes I don't."

"Can I ask why?"

I stand and walk over to the little fireplace beneath the television. There are pictures on the mantle. I gaze at them, taking in Peck's smiling face as a little boy and pictures of him and his cousins.

"Things like this," I say, pointing at the images. "This makes me think that having a family would be amazing. But then I remember my own familial experience, which was nothing like this at all, and I'm not sure." I furrow my brow. "Does that make me a bad person?"

He shakes his head. "Not at all."

"I've never known a love like you should have for your kids," I admit. "I've never felt anything like that coming from me, and I've never felt anyone else love me like that. So what if I can't ... do it? What if it doesn't come naturally to me?"

"I think that's probably something a lot of people worry about."

I shrug. "I don't want to mess someone up because a gene is omitted in my genome that gives me a mother's unconditional love. Besides," I say, "I'd have to find someone who wants to build that kind of life together. And I'd have to trust them explicitly to get to that point. And, well, I'm not even sure if that's practical. Or realistic."

"I have the same worries sometimes."

"Really?"

He stands too. "Yeah. I mean, I want a family someday. I want the life my nana and pops had. But my luck, I'll fall in love with someone who doesn't want those things too."

My heart hurts for him. He deserves every good thing in the world, and the idea of him not getting it seems ... tragic.

But does that mean he's not in love with Molly?

He walks my way, reaching for me.

My heart leaps in my chest as I place my palm in his. He rubs his thumb over the top of my hand and grins.

"You are blissfully unaware, aren't you?" he asks.

"Of what?"

He laughs. "So let's get the elephant in the room out in the open."

I gulp. The elephant isn't just too big to be ignored, but it's sweaty and stinky and right in front of our faces.

I don't know how this is going to go. My first instinct is to protect my heart, to build a wall as tall as I can so it doesn't hurt when he tells me he wants to cool things off. But as I look into his eyes and feel his smile settling over me, I'm not afraid.

"I know you're wondering what's happening between us the same as I am. And if you aren't, well, I guess I look like a pussy now."

I grin. "I guess if that's the case, you'll just have to prove your manhood."

He shakes his head, trying to hide his smile.

"But, yes, I have wondered a time or sixteen thousand today," I admit. "Last night was kind of amazing ..."

He pulls me close, our hands locked together between us.

"Tell you what," he says. "Let's take things a day at a time. If we want to hate each other one day, then fine. If we wanna fuck each other's brains out another day, awesome."

"No, that's better than awesome."

He chuckles. "And if we want space and room to sort of do our own thing, then that's perfectly fine. But I like having you around, Hawkeye."

My heart flutters in my chest at his simple, sweet words. *I like having you around.* That might be the nicest thing anyone has ever said to me. Period. Because it's not a comparison or challenge of some sort. It's a statement. One that warms me from the inside out.

"And I kind of like having you around, Wes."

His brows shoot to the ceiling. "So it's Wes now, huh?"

"Wesley is a mouthful."

"Is that one of your innuendos?" he teases.

"Well," I say, batting my lashes. "I don't actually know that to be true or not. But we could remedy that."

"Name the place and time, sweetheart."

I unwind my hand from his and take a step back. His eyes grow wide as I grin lasciviously.

"How about right here, right now?" I ask.

"I like it."

"You will. I promise," I say, working at his belt. "You will."

His hands capture mine. He brings them to the small of my back as he tugs me close to him again. He kisses the tip of my nose.

"I'm going to hold you to that little promise," he whispers. "But can I just kiss you first?"

I stand on my tiptoes and bring my lips to his. God, I love kissing this man. And I'm in awe that he didn't want me on my knees first, pleasuring him, but wanted to kiss me before. First. Like it was more important.

What sort of a man does that?

This one. The one with a massive heart and a beguiling soul. And it's at this moment that I know, without a doubt, there aren't walls big enough to save me from him. If he wants to break my heart, I can't do anything to stop him.

TWENTY-FOUR

Dylan

I KNOCK on the front door.

As soon as my knuckles touch the wood, I second-guess this decision. All of it. Not just the knocking on the front door as opposed to the back—the one that Peck and I used when we were here together, but also the fact that I'm even standing on Nana's porch in the first place.

The materials I found at the hardware store in Merom today are piled at my feet. There are trays, rails, screws, and a battery-operated drill that I found in Peck's garage. I also found some prepackaged hooks for kitchen cabinets to hang small saucepans or towels or bottles of cleaning liquids.

"I shouldn't be here," I singsong through clenched teeth. I bend to scoop up the stuff and scramble out of here when the door swings open.

Nana's face lights up when she sees me. "Dylan! Oh, honey. I'm so glad to see you." She scoots back so I can walk by. She spies the boxes at my feet. "What's all that?"

"Well, I realize now that this might've been presumptuous of me, but I was bored today. I don't start my job for a few more days. So I ventured over to Merom and spotted the hardware store, and before I knew it, I was leaving with the stuff to fix your cabinets." I shrug meekly. "I hope that's okay. If not, I can come back or even leave the stuff—"

"Stop," she gushes. "This is the nicest thing. Please, come in."

I hold the boxes in my arms and carry them inside. Nana shuts the door behind me.

She leads me through a formal living room that's really not formal. Pictures dot the walls—tons of them. Baby pictures, others that I recognize as Peck and Machlan. The one closest to the doorway has to be a young Nana and Pops.

I pause, taking in the image. They're standing in front of this house. Her arm is wrapped around his waist. She has the biggest smile on her face as she looks up at Pops. He's tall, way taller than Peck, with shoulders that span a mile. He has a head of dark hair and a smirk that makes it impossible for him to deny Peck. It's exact.

"What I wouldn't give for those days," Nana says. She's standing beside me, looking longingly at the picture. "We had just had Eddie and Jessica."

I furrow my brow.

"Eddie is Walker and the boys' dad. Jessica is Vincent and Peck's mom." She smiles sadly. "He probably hasn't told you much about her, has he?"

I shake my head. "Just that he isn't really that close to her." I leave out the bit that he doesn't even know where she is to spare Nana any pain. I'm not sure what the deal is or what she knows, but I don't want to make waves. It's not my place.

Nana nods. "Well, my daughter hasn't been that kind to her children. It breaks my heart." Her voice quivers. She places a hand on her throat as she looks at the picture of her and her husband. "Jessie was a good girl. Absolutely beautiful. Smart as a whip. I just knew she was going to be a veterinarian as much as she loved animals. She'd spend every waking hour at the farm down the road if I let her."

She looks lost in a memory I'm not privy to. I just stay quiet and let her work through whatever is going through her mind.

"Something happened to her. Drugs, I think," she says. "She got with Mel—that's Peck's dad—and she was never the same. Still funny and could tell a story like nobody's business." She grins. "But she just … disconnected. It's like she was afraid to get too close to anyone."

"That must've been hard for you," I say, balancing the boxes in my arms.

Nana's hand drops to her side. "Listen to me jabber while you just stand there holding those boxes. Just tell me to hush next time." She scoots down the hallway toward the kitchen.

I place the boxes on the island.

"Can I ask you a question?" I force a swallow as Nana nods. "How long has Jessica been gone?"

"She left for good when Peck was fifteen. Vincent was a senior. That was a hard year. Poor Vinnie acted out, causing mayhem, and Peck sort of internalized it. It was rough."

I press my hands against the island and think of the weight Peck must've been carrying around. The loss of his parents. Taking responsibility for Molly and her problems. The poor kid must've been ready to break.

"He seems to have turned out all right," I say.

She grins. "That he did. He's a very good boy. If I need something, he's there. He's there before I need things." She laughs. "I guess, in some ways, I'm all he has. It's why family is so important to him, I think. He's already lost so much of it."

My throat tightens as I take in her words.

"All my boys are good, family-centric kids," she says. "But Peck … it's different with him. I don't care what Machlan does to him or how many of my cheeseballs Lance takes or how much he and Walker bicker at work, Peck doesn't hold grudges. He lives and loves and lets go. The other boys can be mad for a while."

"I know he's happy Vincent and Sawyer are moving back."

"Me too." She ambles over to her rocker and gets settled. "The boys think I want them all together because it makes me happy. And it does. It thrills this old heart to death. But you know why I really want Vincent back here?"

"Why?"

"Because once you get to be my age, you realize family is absolutely all you have."

I sit on a barstool. The weight of her words falls on my shoulders, pressing me down into the hard wooden seat.

"That's unfortunate for people like me," I say.

"Why is that, honey?"

"My family … isn't like your family. We just aren't close."

I look at the ceiling, concerned that I feel so comfortable with this woman to be opening up like this. But now that the sieve is open, I can't close it. I don't want to. With every word, I can feel my load lightening.

"What are they like?" she asks.

"Well, my dad is gone. My mom …" Tears well up in my eyes. "She doesn't really even like me." I blink back the water that threatens to spill over my cheeks. I can feel my nose turn red as I try to rein in my emotions. "I don't know what I ever did to her, but … I have to earn her love, and that's hard …"

She rocks gently back and forth in her rocker. The sound is soothing in a very strange way.

"Dylan, sweetheart, I'm going to tell you something. And this is a fact with my hand up." She waits for me to look at her. "That's not love."

I try to speak, but my mouth is too dry.

"You don't have to earn someone's love. Their respect? Yes. Their loyalty? Absolutely. But true love comes freely. You can't stop it or start it. You have no control over it."

Her words hit me in the chest, digging right into my heart. I think they should hurt. They should cut me deep with the truth that my mother doesn't love me. But it doesn't. It doesn't hurt. Because I accepted it as truth a long time ago. But clearly, from these tears, I haven't fully grieved the loss of love from my mother.

"But here's another thing for you," she says. "Parents always, always love their children."

"But …"

She sighs. "Parents are people too. Take my Jessie. I know she loves her sons. But someone looking from the outside may think, 'How could she? She left them. She wasn't a great mother.' Those people have never considered that maybe the best thing she could've done for Vincent and Peck was to leave them."

I think about that. If she was strung out or into bad things, maybe Nana's right. But I wouldn't have thought of that.

"Parents make mistakes," she says in that steady way of hers. "Sometimes, they don't know what to do or say. Sometimes they don't even realize how badly they've treated you. They're just dealing with things the best way they can. Does that make sense?"

I nod. It does. I'm going to need to really think about that to absorb all of it, I think, but it makes sense.

It also hurts my heart.

"Will you promise me something, Dylan?"

"Um, sure," I stammer.

"Always remember what I just said."

"What part?"

She smiles. "All of it. One of these days, I'm not going to be around. I haven't told the boys yet because they'll just worry themselves crazy, but I had some tests come back not too good. I meet with a specialist next week."

"Nana," I say, mouth agape. "You have to tell them."

"I will. I promise. But I've been sitting on this information for a month, just waiting on the right time to tell them." She looks at me intently. "I'm fine with whatever happens. I've had a great life. I'm ready to go if the good lord calls me home. All I have left are Peck and Vincent, and Vin has Sawyer. Peck has no one. And I've sat here praying for God to send him someone …"

I swallow. *Hard.* "Oh, Nana. I'm not sure that …" I laugh nervously. "I mean, Peck and I aren't … together. We aren't serious."

"You'll see."

As though that says it all, she stands up. A satisfied look is on her face, but I don't feel like this can be over. I can't have that thrown on me. Is she nuts?

"Nana, with all respect, I promise you that I'll always … be there for Peck if he needs me, but …"

How do you tell a woman that you can't promise your everlasting love to her grandson?

I stand in her kitchen, mid-shrug, when she laughs.

"You've failed me already," she says.

"How's that?"

"You forgot what I said."

My brain clouds with what feels like a thousand things she just said. "What part, exactly?"

She stands in front of me, taking both of my hands in hers. They're cool to the touch. The veins sit at the top of her skin as she squeezes me with the grip of a baby.

"You can't start or stop love, honey," she says. "It's just there, or it's not, and it's present between you and Peck. Everyone can see it. Maybe not you yet because it's a scary thing to finally see. It took Walker forever." She laughs. "But you will. You can't deny it forever."

"Okay …"

"Just … love him. Like you, he's never really had someone love him unconditionally but me, and I don't count." She smiles like she's won a prize. "I promise you that he'll be patient with you. He'll be kind. He'll drive you crazy with his incessant need to make sure you're all right." She laughs. "Please just be the same to him. For me."

I stand, bewildered, as she squeezes my hands again. Before I have to figure out how to respond to that, the back door opens.

And there he is as bewildered as me.

"Um, what are y'all doing?" Peck asks.

Nana winks and drops my hands. "We were saying a prayer before Dylan starts remodeling my cabinets. Never hurt to ask the lord to be in the midst of a kitchen."

I bite my bottom lip to quell the laughter that shakes my chest.

Peck walks my way. "Okay …" He makes a face like he's as

confused as I am.

I hold my breath as he reaches me. He smells of sweat and diesel fuel, and there's something entirely hot about that.

My fingers itch to touch him, but I'm still not sure where we stand with all that. *It depends on the day*, he said. But every day would be a touching day if it were up to me.

He leans forward, his lips hovering over the shell of my ear. "You look so damn good that it's hard not to put you on that island and bury myself inside you."

"Stop it," I whisper.

He plants a kiss behind my ear. "I think today is a fun today."

"What's that mean?" I bend away from him so I can see his face.

"That means when you're done doing whatever it is here, we have plans."

"Doing what?"

"It's a surprise."

I'm not sure how I feel about a surprise, but I know how I feel about that look on his face. And that second, much longer kiss behind my ear? Almost has me salivating.

"So what are we doing here, ladies?" he asks, walking around me. "Did I hear cabinet reconstruction?"

"I got these things at the hardware store. I thought I could put them in the bottom of her cabinets so she can just slide them out when she needs something. That way she doesn't have to bend over," I say.

Peck gives me the sweetest smile. "I like that." He looks at Nana. "You good with that?"

"I'm great with it," she says.

I pick up his drill. His eyes go wide.

"Is that my drill?" he asks.

I hit the trigger, making it spin. "Yup."

"We need some boundaries, woman," he says. "You never take a man's drill."

I turn my back so Nana can't see my face. "I'll make it up to you later."

He grins, and all is right in my world.

TWENTY-FIVE

Peck

"WHAT ARE YOU DOING?" Dylan squeals as I take the corner a little sharp. "Peck!"

Her laughter fills the truck. It even drowns out the roar of my diesel. While I love few things more than hearing an engine roar, the sound of her laughter would be one.

My lips twist into an amused smile as I hammer the gas.

"Oh, my gosh." She reaches up and grabs the *oh shit* handle. "I never should've agreed to this."

"You love it, and you know it."

She looks at me and beams. "Okay. I kind of *doooo* ... Ah! What are you doing?"

I laugh as I pilot the truck up the hill toward Bluebird Hill.

The sun sets behind us, casting pinks and purple rays through the sky. We hit the top of the hill, and I ease up on the gas.

The vision of Dylan and Nana together comes back to me as the truck slows. To say I was blown away today by this woman sitting beside me would be an understatement.

What kind of girl spends her afternoon helping out an old lady rearrange her cabinets? Out of the kindness of her heart?

I look over my shoulder to see that woman gazing out the window.

My heart tugs in my chest.

"Oh, wow." Dylan gasps as she takes in the view. She unbuckles her seat belt and looks over both shoulders to get a panoramic view. "This is beautiful."

I look at her and grin. "Yes, it is."

She smacks my knee, leaving her hand to rest on my thigh. Her fingers press against my jeans as she scoots closer to me.

Her hand is heavy on my leg. I try to ignore it so I don't get distracted as I whip the truck around to face the valley. I park it right next to the edge and cut the engine.

Pine trees cover the hills and valleys surrounding Bluebird Hill. It's my favorite spot in the world.

"Peck," she says. "Wow. *Just wow.*"

"Right?"

"How did you even know this was here?"

"Well, there's a sign ..."

She jabs me in the side with her elbow.

I laugh. "Everyone knows about Bluebird Hill. It's not a hill, really. Just a change in elevation. There's a little wooded area over there," I say, pointing to the right, "where everyone goes to park in high school."

"Oooh," she says.

"And back there is where everyone fights." I gesture toward a spot behind a giant rock. "But my favorite spot, besides this one, is the one I'm going to show you next."

"Is it better than this?"

I stick my tongue in my cheek. I can't wait to see her face when we get back there.

"Maybe," I say. "We'll see what you think."

I start the engine again and stick it in reverse. Gravel and dirt go flying as my tires dig into the ground. Dylan is all smiles.

My spirits are high. Things are just … good. Damn good. Better than I ever imagined things could be.

A part of me doesn't want to think about it too much. Acknowledging how great things are going will undoubtedly jinx it, and I just want this to last as long as it can.

"Okay, Hawkeye," I say. "You ready?"

"I mean, I don't know. Am I?"

Excitement flickers in her eyes as she takes in our surroundings. I veer off onto a path that only locals would ever see. It meanders through a patch of woods, the limbs scraping the paint on my truck, before opening into a field.

A field of mud.

"Oh, shit," Dylan says. "Can you back out of here?"

"Nope." The last syllable pops.

"Um, then what are we going to do?" She looks around. "I mean, there are trees on three sides of us and a giant field of gunk in front of us. I don't think you really have any other options."

I roll my eyes. "Of course we do."

"And what's that?"

"Buckle up, baby. And hold on." I grin, my heart beating hard in my chest.

She looks at me warily. "Peck …"

"Five … four …"

"But you aren't buckled up," she says, grasping for the seat belt.

"Because I'm an expert. Three … two …"

"Wait!" she exclaims with a nervous laugh. "Is this even legal?"

"One. No. Here we go."

I wait until I hear the click of her seat belt before I stomp the gas. She clutches the handle above her head, her eyes as wide as saucers.

The engine roars to life as our speed increases. I move the truck a few feet to the left of center. From experience, I know that the mud pit isn't quite as deep there, and we can rip through it a little easier.

"Peck … Ah!" She screams as we hit the mud.

Thick, brown gunk flies over the truck and coats the windows. I flip on the windshield wipers even though it won't do any good. It'll only smear it. Still, it's good for the experience.

We're midway through and blind from the mud. I keep the engine roaring as we plow through the wet muck. Dylan giggles beside me, her hand on the ceiling as she tries to keep herself pressed in the seat. I take every chance I can get to take a quick peek at her. The excitement in her eyes is worth every bit of time it'll take tomorrow to clean this fucker.

"This … is … awesome," she says, her voice vibrating with the movements of the truck.

"Yeah?"

"Yes!"

I maneuver the truck through the last bit of mud and coast up the other side.

Adrenaline races through my veins. I'm not sure if it's from the mudding or because Dylan is beside me. … In the mud.

She unlatches her belt and spins to face me. "That was so much fun," she says. "What is that called?"

"Um, mudding," I say. "That was mudding."

"Mudding. Right. Can we do it again?"

"It's not as fun going back from this side," I tell her.

"But wouldn't it be the same thing?"

I flash her a look. "No, you wannabe country girl. The ruts ride differently. Take it from this side and get stuck out there. Sound fun?"

"Maybe?" She winces. "Yeah. Kind of."

I laugh. "Okay. How does calling Machlan and Walker to come get us out sound?"

She makes a face like she sucked on a lemon.

"Exactly," I say. "So grab the paper towels under your seat and lets clean off the glass."

"Um, what?"

"How else are we gonna see to get home?"

She gives me a strangled laugh. "Um, I don't know, but that's a lot of mud."

"Yup." I hold out my hand. "Towels, please."

She digs under her seat and finds a roll of paper towels. They land in my palm. I crack open my door to see her still sitting in her seat.

"Hey. You gotta help," I tease.

"But ..."

I raise a brow.

"Fine," she huffs playfully.

We climb out of the truck. Soft dirt that's not quite mud squishes under my boots. On the other side, Dylan groans.

I head to the front when a set of bright red and blue flashing lights ripple across the field. Kip, the county sheriff and a distant cousin, gets out of his car.

Dylan races as fast as she can around the front of the truck. She grabs my hand and stands beside me.

Her breath comes out in quick rushes as she watches Kip walk closer.

"What are you two kids doing out here tonight?" he asks.

He damn well knows the answer. Hell, he probably saw me pass by Goodman's Gas Station on the way here and followed me. *Fucker.*

"Oh, I don't know, Officer," I say. "Just looking for a picnic spot."

"Peck," Dylan hisses. She takes a deep breath. "We're sorry, Officer. We didn't know we weren't supposed to be out here."

Kip eyes me curiously. He's amused, and that only means this is going to get interesting. Except for the fact that I know he won't haul us in. Not for this. He would've over those gas cans from Tad—if he could catch me—but he won't from hauling my truck through the mud. He's been through that hole as many times as I have over the years.

"I didn't say you weren't supposed to be out here," he says.

"Oh." She looks at me. "Well, we didn't do anything wrong. I swear."

Kip lowers his chin. "The first indication of someone doing something wrong is them telling you they aren't. Now, do you want to tell me what's going on out here, or do you want me to give you a ride to the pokey?"

The pokey? I start to laugh, but a warning shot is sent my way from Kip, so I choke it back.

"Sir, Officer, I can't go to jail. Not over this." Dylan looks up at me. "You said this was safe."

I shrug, still not one hundred percent sure what Kip is up to. But I'm willing to play along.

"Damn it, Peck," she says.

"What? I didn't do anything wrong," I insist.

"Clearly, something is wrong, or this nice officer wouldn't be out here messing with us." She bats her eyelashes at Kip. "Right?"

"Is that true, you little nice officer?" I ask.

She rams her elbow into my ribs, making me yelp. Kip tries to hold a steady face but loses control.

"I had you going, didn't I?" he says with a laugh.

Dylan's jaw drops.

"I couldn't figure out what the hell you were doing," I say. "What's up, Kip?"

"Not much. I had a report of vandalism on the cabin on the East side. I saw the headlights back here, and thought I'd see what was happening."

"Wait?" Dylan says. "You two know each other?"

"Cousins," we say at the same time.

"That figures." She grits her teeth, but her eyes shine. "You both are assholes."

"Did ya think I was taking you in?" Kip asks.

"To the pokey?" I tease.

She turns away. I look back at Kip when a handful of mud slams into the side of my face.

"You're on your own now," Kip says and runs back to his car.

I head to the driver's side of the truck and load my palm with mud.

Blood soars past my ears as I anticipate Dylan's next move. The mud squishes as she tries to sneak up on me from behind. I crouch next to the tire and wait for her pretty little head to pop around the tailgate.

Splat!

My handful of mud finds its target and sticks to the front of her chest. She screams, the sound embedded with a laugh, as she launches her own ball haphazardly. It misses.

"Maybe I should give you a new nickname," I say, scooping up another handful of gunk. "Something like—hey!"

A glob of mud smashes me in the side of the face. Dylan cheers, jumping up and down. She's filthy and downright, absolutely gorgeous.

I lunge forward and am in front of her before she knows what's happening.

Pinning her to the filthy tailgate, I take in the wildness in her eyes. I haven't seen them this lively before. It's amazing to witness.

Her breathing is ragged, matching mine, as I hover my lips over hers.

"Kiss me," she demands.

"Eh, maybe."

She palms the back of my head and tries to lower my mouth to hers, but I resist. It takes everything I have, but I manage it.

"Kiss me," she says again. "Please?"

"On one condition."

"What's that?"

She has mud stuck to her hair, the side of her face, and the corner of her lip. Her clothes are filthy, and her shoes might be ruined. But, I don't think she cares.

"When we get home," I say, letting my finger trace the side of her face. A dark brown streak is left in its wake. "You have to take a bath with me. Not a shower," I say, thwarting her interjection, "but a bubble bath."

"Let's think about that for a second. Do you want to sit in a mud bath?"

"I'd sit anywhere with you."

She grins.

"But," I say, "fair point. Shower first to get the mud off. Then a bubble bath."

She acts as though she's considering it.

"Think fast," I prod.

"Fine," she gushes. "I guess—"

I stop her words with the kiss she wanted. I halt all the over-thinking we're both about to do with my tongue. I pause all thoughts of anything besides her and me right here, right now, with my body up against hers and kiss her until the sun sets behind the tree line.

Then, and only then, do I take her home.

TWENTY-SIX

Peck

"WHAT ARE we going to snack on?" I ask.

Dylan's legs swing back and forth off the countertop as she watches me take inventory of the pantry.

"What are my choices?" she asks.

"It looks like you can have popcorn, raisins, or barbecue potato chips that might be stale." I look at her. "Actually, they are stale. I bought them for New Year's Eve like two years ago."

"Nice."

I shrug.

She pretends to give this every ounce of consideration that choosing your last meal would require. Not so much just a snack for a movie night, but whatever.

I watch her little nose scrunch up as she sorts through her choices. There's still a piece of mud stuck in her hairline. I almost tell her but don't. I like thinking of the fun we had tonight every time I see it.

I've never seen Dylan this carefree. This happy. Granted, I haven't really known her all that long, but even in the moments we've shared, I haven't seen her like *this*.

It's as if she's at peace. Settled. Maybe even content. It's my most favorite look on her—even better than the flush of an orgasm or the mischief of a smartass remark. Those are both memorable but not my favorite. This little grin plastered across her cheeks tonight is the best one.

"I'm going to say popcorn since we're watching a comedy," she says.

"A comedy? I thought we were watching that action flick."

"You thought wrong. Besides, action flicks require ice cream, and we don't have any. And I can't get ice cream delivered here in less than four days, which is stupid. The brambleberry one is my favorite, but it'll take two weeks to get it or something." She frowns. "That's what happens when you live in the middle of nowhere, I guess."

"Breathe, Dylan," I tease.

She smiles, and I forget all about the popcorn.

I mosey my way across the room. She's wrapped up in a giant blue towel. Her hair hangs straight and is damp from our hour-long bath. My hands go on either side of her, locking her in place. She scoots to the end of the counter and presses her lips to my forehead before resting the top of her head against mine.

My stomach pulls. It starts somewhere deep inside me, somewhere that's never been accessed before. All I know is that I'm in serious fucking trouble with this girl.

In a short time, she's rearranged my entire life. And not just my kitchen cabinets, which she has plans to do tomorrow, apparently. The nights I'd spend alone at Crave, listening to Machlan or Navie jabber on about their lives, are now spent doing things like having a mud fight on Bluebird Hill or playing tic-tac-toe on the shower wall with bathroom chalk—something I'm not sure how or why I even own. But I do. Or she does. Either way, I love it.

"What are you thinking?" she asks.

"Just thinking that you're a giant pain in my ass."

She laughs, pulling away. She brushes a stray lock of hair off my face. "I don't believe that's true."

"You don't, huh?" I grin.

"Nope. I think—Ah!"

I grip her sides, right below the bend of her hip, and tickle her. She squirms in my hands, her hair flying everywhere as she bends and contorts in the sexiest of ways. I have to stop before I'm thinking with my cock and not my head. Again.

Stepping away, I watch her straighten her towel.

"I'll get the popcorn," I say. "You get the movie on. Deal?"

"Deal."

She hops off the counter and swipes a hand against my ass. I turn to grab her again when the doorbell rings.

"Why don't you get that?" I ask. "I'll get the popcorn on."

"Um, I'm in a towel."

"My robe is on the chair. Slip that on," I offer.

She grins and drops the towel right where she stands. Her body is round and full, and seeing her breasts hang—full and vuluptous—makes me hard.

"Dylan ..."

She laughs, pulling my robe around her and tying the belt. "I'll be back. Stay focused, Wes."

I shake my head at the nickname as she disappears around the corner. Retrieving the box of popcorn, I take out a packet. The plastic is removed and in the trash when I hear her feet come pitter-pattering down the hallway.

Glancing over my shoulder, I expect to see her prepping a story about the kids from the house down the road pranking us. Instead, her jaw is set.

I stop in my tracks. "What's going on?"

"You have a visitor."

Her words are short. Crisp. Cold.

"Who is it?" I open the microwave and shove the bag of popcorn inside.

"Molly."

Oh, fuck.

I hit two minutes on the microwave and then start. And then, with *a lot* of trepidation, I turn around to deal with the latest development in my life.

"What does she want?" I ask.

"I didn't ask."

"Okay." I think as quickly as I can. "Do you want to go out there with me?"

That might be the worst idea I've ever had—or close to it, anyway—but I don't know how else to manage this. If Molly is here, maybe something is wrong. She never shows up here just for the fuck of it. But under these circumstances, with Dylan living here and ... being with me, it feels wrong. To me. I can't imagine what Dylan is thinking.

I run a hand down my face because I haven't thought this far ahead. I should've, though. I should've had a game plan.

"I think I'm going to stay here," she says.

"Dylan, I ... I didn't invite her here."

"I know." She forces a swallow. "I guess, really, there's nothing wrong with it. I mean, she's your friend. Right?"

Her attempt at being reasonable knocks the wind out of me. I pull her into me and kiss the top of her head.

Something washes over me. It's a feeling I've never had before. It's the best, warmest, quietest feeling that's also the most powerful thing I've ever felt. I feel ... calm. Which is completely at odds with this circumstance.

The doorbell rings again, and Dylan sags into me.

"I'll go handle that, and then we'll have a movie night, okay?" I look her in the eye. "I just ..." I gulp. "I'll be right back."

She nods, tucking a strand of hair behind her ear.

My insides twist as the words I was about to say so nonchalantly are still sitting on my tongue. *Are they true? Do I really feel that way?*

Before I can think about them too much, I have the door handle in my hand. When I swing it open, Molly is standing on the porch. I'd hoped she'd changed her mind and left.

"Hey," I say, shutting the door behind me. "What's up?"

"I need to talk to you."

"Well, here I am. Shoot."

She looks over my shoulder, presumably to see if Dylan is anywhere in sight. "I, um, I just … I don't want to talk about it here. It's private."

Irritation claws at my brain as I try to stay calm. I just want to get back in there with Hawkeye and watch our stupid romantic comedy and eat popcorn that will make my stomach hurt all night.

"Fine. What do you want to do?" I ask.

She starts down the sidewalk. I follow. When she hits the gravel of the driveway, I start to wonder if something really is wrong.

This is unlike Molly. She's usually so self-centered that she plays a very forward card.

"Where are we going?" I ask.

The night is dark, but the sky is clear. The moon gives off plenty of light to see. Stars sparkle overhead. Molly sits on a wicker bench by a patch of sunflowers that have seen better days.

I sit next to her. "Look, I'm happy to help you, Molly. But I have plans tonight, so if you could spit it out, that'd be great."

"Peck, I'm scared."

"What are you scared of?"

She shrugs.

"Like, is someone messing with you? Are you afraid of the dark? Did you sleep with someone's boyfriend? Again?"

She shoots a dirty look my way, but I'm not sorry. The question is reasonable, considering she's come to me for advice about this very thing three times before.

She sighs. "Do you remember when you, me, and Vincent camped out behind your house? And there was that serial killer on the loose in Iowa, and Vincent had us scared that he was going to find us?"

"Yeah. I'd forgotten about that."

"Vin came to see me today." She smiles sadly. "After he left, I just … Things were so much easier back then."

I nod. "They were in some ways. In others, they're easier now."

"How do you figure?"

"Well, we control our own destiny now. Back then, we were at the mercy of our parents. Now, we could be the parents." I grin at the thought. "We decide who is in our life and who isn't. Where we sleep. What cell phone company we want to pay the bulk of our paychecks to."

That gets a smile out of her.

"I'm just figuring things out," I say. "There's a lot I don't know yet. But one thing I'm realizing is that life is never easy, and when you do find something, or someone, who does seem effortless, you better lock that shit down."

My body pulls toward the house. The popcorn is probably done by now, and Dylan's probably watching the previews.

I glance over my shoulder.

The lights are all on, and the girl I can't get enough of is inside. She's waiting on me, knowing I'm out here with another woman.

But the longer I sit with Molly, the more definitively I know that I don't have real feelings for her. I never did. In the twenty-five or so years that I've known her, I've never come close to feeling what I feel for Dylan.

"You like her a lot, don't you?" she asks.

"I do. I like Dylan a lot."

"Do you love her?"

I stretch my legs out in front of me. The question somehow tightens every muscle in my body. But, for whatever reason, it doesn't get an automatic no from me. I almost lean toward yes.

"You do, huh?" she asks.

"I don't know," I say carefully.

Her eyes fill with tears. "Do you love me, Peck?"

It's a loaded question, maybe the loaded-est question I've ever been asked. As I watch her struggle with reality and the tears fall down her cheeks, I know the answer.

I don't love her. Not like she's asking me. The way I feel about Molly is similiar to the way I feel about Sienna or Hadley—a friend that I'd take a beating for, but not one that I'd go to war for. Not like I feel about Dylan.

"That's my answer," she whispers.

"I've always cared about you."

"But you've always said you love me too. Now you don't."

I sigh. "I do ... love you, just not like I ..."

I can't bring myself to say the words to her—not before I find the courage to say them to Dylan first.

"So what happens to me now?" she asks, wiping the tears with her hands. "You're the only person in the world who likes me."

"Well, that's not true. But you could attempt at being a little more likable. That wouldn't hurt."

"Everybody already has their mind made up about me." She sniffles. "I don't even think it matters what I do anymore."

"Stop mean-mugging everyone," I say, bumping her with my shoulder. "And taunting people. And ..." I wait until she looks at me. "And show people who you are. Let your guard down a bit. Give people a chance."

"They already hate me."

"They don't hate you because they don't know you, and instead of showing them who you really are, you just feed into their assumptions."

I look back at the house. Desperation to get to Dylan eats at me, but I know I need to have this conversation.

"I'm not like her," Molly says. "I'm not all cheerleader-y sweet."

"She's not always sweet," I joke. "But honestly, listen to me. You are better than what you show the world. Deep down inside that little black heart of yours is a girl who's funny. And fun. And thoughtful."

She rolls her eyes.

"Remember the time you brought me that friendship bracelet?" I tease.

"I was eight."

"And you told me if I told anyone that you'd kill me. But," I say as we both laugh, "it proves you got it in ya."

"Maybe."

"You do. I know it."

We sit quietly, the crickets chirping around us as Molly digests my advice. I have no idea where all that came from, but I'm glad it did. I'm even more glad that she seems to be listening.

I stand, and she follows suit. We trudge our way back up the driveway. Some of the lights inside have been switched off.

We reach Molly's car and stop. She looks up at me with mascara streaks painted down her cheeks.

"Are we still friends?" she asks.

"I told you a long time ago that I'll always have your back. And I will. But I'm not the same person I was a month ago."

"Do you think she's changed you that much?"

"No. I don't think she's changed me. I think she's shown me things about me and about life. She's given me hope, you know?"

"I need someone to give me hope."

"You work on you. Stop worrying about everyone else and looking for someone else to validate you, Mol. Use that power you have for good instead of evil."

We exchange a smile.

"Thanks, Peck."

"Anytime." I start toward the house but stop. "No. Wait. Not anytime." I face her. "Real quick—I'll always be your friend, but we gotta have some boundaries."

"I don't do well with those." The corner of her lip turns toward the sky. "I'm kidding."

"Just ... no coming by here unless you're running from zombies. And probably shouldn't text or call, you know? And Dylan is a great girl."

"I'm good with all this, but can we leave off that last part?" she jokes.

I think.

"It would serve you well to make friends with her," I say.

She opens her car door and climbs in. "I'm sure your girlfriend wants to be my friend." She rolls her eyes.

"You never know."

"Yeah. See ya later."

"Bye."

I head back toward the house. I hear her car door shut and the engine start, followed by the tell-tale sound of gravel crunching as she backs out.

I don't look back.

The front door is partially open, and I step inside. "Dylan?" I walk through the house until I find her standing in her bedroom. Not mine. "What's going on? What about the movie?"

"I got tired."

"Oh." I look around. She's pulled her blankets down like she's preparing to climb inside. "You sleeping in here tonight?"

"I didn't want to go to your room without you."

That makes sense, but I don't like it.

"We could bring some blankets into the living room and turn the movie on," I say. "Wanna?"

"I'm not really in the mood." She blows out a breath. "I guess seeing you walk outside to talk to another woman kind of fucked up my energy flow or something."

I reach for her. She lets me take her hand and pull her against me. I wrap my arms around her as tightly as I can and nuzzle my face into her hair.

"You could've come out there with me," I say.

"I know. I'm just ... jealous."

The thought makes me smile. *I'm a total dick.* "Well, so you know, because it's important to me that you do know—I told her not to come by. Or call. Or text. Or be a jerk to you or anyone else, actually."

I feel her smile against my chest. "Really?"

"Yes, really."

I lean back and brush the hair out of her face so I can see into her eyes. I feel it again, stronger than ever. It's that rush of comfort, of being perfectly content with your life. With your partner.

With the woman you love.

"What?" she asks. "Why are you smiling at me like that?"

"Come on. Let's go to bed."

"But ..."

I tug her hand and guide her to my room.

To our room.

I just have to figure out how to make that happen.

We climb in bed. She snuggles up against me, her hand flat against my heart.

"Peck?"

"Yeah, Hawkeye?"

"I didn't like it when you left with her just now."

"I know, and I told you that she won't—"

"I meant, that it was different. When Charlie left me for his ex, I was angry and felt betrayed. But I don't think I ever actually felt jealous. Is that weird?"

I think about it. "Probably. Maybe. I don't know." I pull her closer.

"But tonight, with you … I don't know. It just didn't feel good."

I truly am a dick because that makes me feel pretty darn good. But I won't leave her hanging. Even I have limits on dickiness.

"I know," I say. "And every moment I was outside with Molly, I wanted to be inside with you. She saw that. She knew. She commented on it, actually."

"She must hate me, huh?"

"Not sure, to be honest." I kiss the top of her head. "But I did tell her that things have changed. For the better. For you." *And me.*

I feel her smile against my shoulder, and nothing feels better than this moment. Dylan in my arms. In my bed. In our bed.

I gulp.

"Okay," she whispers. "Night, Wes."

"Night."

It doesn't take long before she's sleeping peacefully.

I grab my phone and dim the light and type in, 'How to tell someone you love them.'

Because what the hell do I know about this? Not a damn thing. I'm not even sure if this is the right thing to do.

I look down at her and smile.

Even if it's not the right thing, I'm going to try anyway.

TWENTY-SEVEN

Dylan

"WHAT ARE YOU DOING TODAY?"

Navie's voice is chipper, especially for nine in the morning. As a bartender, she doesn't keep early morning hours.

"I'm screwing off today," I say. "I start work next week, so this is my last hurrah."

Navie laughs.

"Really I'm just trying to get my life in order over here. I made a list of a bunch of things I need to do before my life get hectic again." I tap the steering wheel as I wait at a stop sign. "Why couldn't I have been born a rich princess and just paid someone to do my life's paperwork for me?"

"Girl, don't even start with that. That's my dream right there. I'll still work for a living. I just want to find someone to come over and handle my life. Like ... a wife. I need a wife."

"Same," I say with a laugh.

I pass a sign for Bluebird Hill. My face lights up as I remember our night up there. I'm still picking mud out of my hair, which is slightly annoying, but I wouldn't change those memories for anything.

That's the epitome of why I fell for Peck. His silliness and fun-loving side are balanced with a part of him that's so effortlessly sexy. He's the perfect package.

I was so happy last night when we got home. On top of the world, even. But then Molly McCarter showed up and put enough of a wobble in my universe that I'm not quite perched on the top of Mount Happiness anymore.

"Why are you up so early?" I ask Navie.

"The neighbor's dog, actually. It started barking at six thirty. I'm not thrilled that I got virtually no sleep, but damn, I feel accomplished already today. Is this what the rest of the world feels like when they get up at the crack ass of dawn?"

"Not usually," I say, laughing. "We're usually more bitter about it."

"Well, I don't think I'd want to do it every day."

My phone buzzes in my cupholder. I look down to see Joanie's name on the screen. Goodman's Gas Station is up ahead, and I pull my car into the back entrance. I park next to the side of the building and put it in park.

"Hang on, Navie," I say.

I look down at the screen again.

JOANIE: Hi, Dylan. Did you decide anything on the house? He has someone else interested but wanted to give you first dibs. Please let me know.

I STARE AT THE PHONE. In the back of my brain, I've known I needed to respond to this. It's sat there and prickled me over and over again. I don't know why I haven't sent her an answer. But I have to now. Time's up.

My thumb runs over the screen as I consider my response. Even though I already know what I have to do, I think about each option.

If this text had come through yesterday, I probably would've told her I pass out of some orgasm-fueled optimism. But today is not last night, and my optimism game is waning. It's not dead, but it's not killing the world either.

"Are you there?" Navie asks.

"Yeah. Hang on."

A pang of anxiety sits in the middle of my abdomen, wearing a hole in my stomach since I opened the door and saw Molly on Peck's porch. The most frustrating thing about it all is that I trust Peck. I do. I know he would never hurt me intentionally. But the fact remains that Charlie didn't necessarily set out to hurt me either.

ME: Hi, Joanie. Thanks for the text, and I'm sorry for not responding more promptly. I thought I had a solution to my housing issue, but it turns out, I don't. I'd love to rent the house. I know I haven't seen it, but as long as it's not full of cats, we'll be fine.

JOANIE: Oh, great! I think you'll love it. I'll get with Peter and have him get ahold of you. It's okay to give him your number, right?

ME: Yes, please.

JOANIE: Great. He'll be in touch soon.

ME: Thanks again.

I STARE AT THE SCREEN. The deed has been done.

"Dylannn ...." Navie sings. "Just call me back, fool."

"I'm here. I'm here," I say, bringing the phone to my ear. "I just, um … Well, Joanie texted me about the house she found, and I had to make a decision."

My throat burns as I swallow.

It's the right choice. I know that. But it doesn't mean I like the idea of leaving Peck.

Last night, sleeping in his arms, still felt right. Right but just … unsettled. He told Molly that things were different now, but she's had unlimited access to him for over twenty years. Will she really give up and bow out? She may not have loved him, but she's owned him, more or less, I think. And me? I've only known him for five minutes.

The original plan was for me to move out. Just because things took a turn with us romantically doesn't mean he's ready for me to live with him. I'm not sure I'm ready for that either.

That doesn't mean it'll feel good to go.

"You told her no, right?" she asks.

"I told her yes. I'll take it."

"Um, why? Am I missing something?"

"Well," I say, "Molly came by last night and—"

"What?" she squawks.

I sigh. "It's … fine. I think. I guess. I don't know. I think he did the right thing."

"Then why are you moving?"

"Because time never hurt anyone. I rushed in to my relationship with Charlie and—"

"He's not Charlie."

"Clearly. I just get in over my head all the damn time, and I don't want to do that with Peck. If things can work out between us, I want it to happen organically. Slowly. Without the pressure of having me already moved in."

She considers this. "Makes sense."

I open my mouth to respond, but the words fail to come. Instead, my eyes are glued to a man and a woman who look incredibly familiar. He has a blue hat on his head.

No.

They turn ever so slightly, and I get a better look.

I almost drop the phone.

Molly and Peck. It's them. Without a doubt. They're walking across the parking lot next to each other.

Maybe he's just here getting gas. Maybe Walker needed fuel for something at work. Coincidences happen.

My stomach sloshes, threatening to expel the coffee I drank this morning. I grip the steering wheel so hard that my knuckles turn white.

"Navie? I'm gonna have to call you back."

The words come out wonky. Even I can hear the emotion in my tone.

What the hell is going on?

"What are you doing?" Navie demands. "Are you okay?"

Molly climbs in a little black car, and Peck walks to the other bank of pumps. His truck is partially hidden by the fueling equipment and other trucks in front of it.

The black car speeds out of the parking lot and takes a left. I watch, holding my breath, as Peck comes to the mouth of the parking lot.

Turn right. Turn right towards Crank. Come on, Peck.

"I'll call you later, Navie."

I still don't hang up. I'm too scared to move. If he turns left …

A small gasp squeaks out of my mouth as Peck's truck turns left. Toward the direction Molly went. Away from Crank.

There's nothing down that road but a few houses. I ventured that way yesterday morning on a boredom adventure.

"What's happening?" Navie demands.

I wish I knew.

"Dylan! Damn it."

"Sorry," I say. My voice sounds weak. I hate it. "I just, um, well, I just saw Peck follow Molly away from town from Goodman's."

"No, you fucking didn't."

"Yes, I fucking did."

"Dyl …"

I put my car in drive. "This doesn't mean anything," I tell her. "Maybe it's a coincidence. And even if it's not, they're friends. They're allowed to be friends."

"Fuck that."

"Navie ..."

She rambles, her emotions about this situation as all over the place as mine. It makes no sense, and I refuse to believe he's up to no good. That's just not Peck. I feel it in my stomach.

But I also feel that this is something I'm going to have to figure out how to deal with because she's not leaving. And I can't ask him not to be friends with her. I'm not that insecure girl, and I refuse to be.

My spirit feels deflated as I pull out onto the road. And head right. Toward Peck's.

He's serious about me. I believe that. But I also believe that this thing with Molly is going to have to be navigated, and I don't know how to do that. I didn't give myself a whole lot of time to think about it. I did what I do—I jumped in and didn't consider all the consequences.

Damn it.

I squeeze my temples as I pull into Peck's driveway.

"Can I stay with you tonight?" I ask Navie.

"I didn't know if you remembered I was here or not," she says. "But, yes, of course."

"Thanks." I turn off the car. "The guy who owns the house is supposed to get ahold of me today, so I'll know more then. But even if I can have the keys right away, I don't think I can sleep there tonight. I won't have a bed or anything."

Tears flicker in my eyes. They're hot, almost scalding, as they topple onto my face.

"Don't cry," she whispers. "This will all be fine."

"I know. It will." I swallow hard. "I'm just, um, I'm going to get my personal things in a box and figure out what to tell Peck. I'm too emotional to really put things in a great way right now."

"Want me to tell him?"

I laugh, wiping my face. "No. Thanks. I'd rather not have him hate both of us forever and ever."

She laughs too. It's a sad sound, one that's filled with pity. And I hate that, but I am pretty pitiful at the moment.

"Come by anytime. I work at four, but I'll be here until then," she says.

"Okay." I climb out of the car and face Peck's house. "I'll talk to you in a bit."

"Bye."

I shove my phone in my pocket and take in the cute little house with the rose bushes.

"Fuck."

I head inside to pack up my life.

Again.

TWENTY-EIGHT

Peck

"WHAT A FUCKING DAY."

I park my truck next to Dylan's. It's a simple thing, an action that becomes routine. A habit. But every time I pull in my driveway and see her car setting there, something happens inside me. The thought alone makes things feel different. And good. And that the possibilities of life going forward might be endless.

I hop out of the truck and jog to the front door. It occurred to me today that she hasn't eaten at Peaches yet, and while I would like to spend a lazy evening with her in the kitchen, I know I won't be able to keep my hands off her. Plus, I'd like to take her out and make her feel special.

The door swings open. With a furrowed brow, I step inside. A banging sound followed by a thud comes from Dylan's room.

"What the hell?"

I walk down the hallway with my senses on high alert. Peeking in her bedroom, I spot a large box from the barn on her bed … and her standing at the foot.

She looks up. Her eyes are vulnerable yet guarded. It's not the Dylan I know.

"Hey," I say.

She smiles. Sort of.

"What are you doing?" I nod toward the box. "Did you carry that inside all by yourself? You could've waited on me to help you, you know?"

"No. I, um, well, I did. But it was empty."

"Empty?"

I pause and look around. The suitcase in the corner is zipped up instead of propped against the wall with its contents spilling every-where. The cup of water that's sat by the bed since the first night she was here is gone. Her deodorant and girlie stuff have disappeared from the dresser, and the books and papers that she's been sorting through off and on are gone.

Oh, fuck.

My throat feels too tight to pass a swallow.

"What's going on?" I ask.

She fiddles with the lid. Her eyes avert from mine. She switches her weight from one foot to the other as she tries to avoid my question.

"Dylan?"

"Oh, well, do you remember the house I was telling you about? The one that Joanie, my new boss, told me about. I think I mentioned it to you."

What the hell is she talking about? A house? For what? What's it matter?

And then it hits me. Like Walker slugging me in the stomach for a joke I made at his expense, I feel like the wind is knocked out of me.

"What does that have to do with you?" I ask carefully.

She forces a swallow. "Well, Joanie messaged me today about it because I hadn't responded to her earlier text. And she said I basically had to jump on the rental or lose it because someone else was interested."

"What did you say?"

She looks into the box. Her face is flushed, her lips swollen, and I wonder if she's been biting them.

Why?

"I told her I'd take it," she says.

I grab the doorframe to keep myself steady.

She'll take it? What the actual fuck?

My first instinct is to grab her and hold her against me and not let her go. Not let her ruin this thing between us because it's the greatest thing I've ever had. But she looks at me, and a fire burns through my veins like wildfire, and I can't move.

"Why did you tell her that?" I ask. "Do you not like it here?"

She smiles, but it's not for me. "It was never the plan for me to stay here long term."

"Well, it was never in the plan to have you sleeping in my bed either, but I'm not arguing that."

"Maybe I shouldn't have been doing that either. Thank you for pointing that out."

I raise a brow. "What happened today? I feel like I went to work with one life and came home to another."

"I don't know, Peck. What did happen today?"

"Nothing that I know of."

She nods. "Well, I think it's best that we have some space for a while. As you mentioned, I ended up in your bed awfully fast, and I think it makes a lot of sense to let things simmer for a while and see how we feel."

"I know how I feel." I take a step toward her. "Don't you?"

"I do. That's why I'm doing this."

She makes no sense. She's lost her damn mind. Leaving me because she wants to be with me ... *She never said that.*

"Dylan, do you want to be with me?"

The pause is too long. The silence too deafening. The hesitation lingers in the air until I release a frustrated chuckle.

"I do," she says. "I do. You're ... great, Peck. But I have some things I need to sort out before we go any further."

"Like what?"

Her eyes fill with an uneasiness.

My brain trolls through every minute we've spent together. From the day she stormed up to the truck at Old Man Dave's house to last night when she fell asleep in my arms, I go over it. Nothing is there that would be a straight line to this.

Except Molly.

My shoulders tighten.

"Is this about Molly?" I ask.

"Not really."

"Molly McCarter has no bearing on us, Dylan. None."

She stands up, her gaze fiery. "You're right. It shouldn't. It absolutely shouldn't, but it does, Peck. It does. *She does.*" Her jaw sets. "I saw you with her today and watched you follow her out of town, and I *hate* the way I feel about that. It's not me. I don't want it to be me."

She storms past me. Her jaw is set as she grabs one of her T-shirts off the back of a chair.

"So what? Yeah, I saw her today," I say. "I helped her sister, Megan. Her battery died."

"And they couldn't have called a tow service?"

"Yeah. They could've. But I happened to be getting a coffee at the gas station and offered to go down there and help them. Because that's my job. I did my job, and I came home. *To you.*"

She spins on her heel. "You're right. It is your job. And they're your friends, and you would have been a dick if you didn't help them."

"Yeah. I would. But if it drives you this fucking crazy, I won't anymore. Ever again."

Her throat bobs as she swallows. She wads the shirt up and tosses it in the box.

She sits down again. It's as if all her energy has vanished. I want to sit beside her or pick her up and put her on my lap. I want to help her, to make her better, but I'm the one she's mad at.

I think.

A tear threatens to spill over her eyes. I reach for her, but she pulls away.

"I don't want to be this person," she says.

"What person?"

"This one. The girl who feels so insecure when a girl shows up that I know you don't love. I just … it makes me feel all kinds of ways, and I hate that, Peck. It's not good for me or you or even Molly although I can't say she's high on my list of priorities." She looks up at me with tear-filled eyes. "I want to be good enough to be the love of someone's life. The kind of love you have with the first person you fall for—that unconditional, inexplicable kind of love."

"Dylan …"

My head spins at her admission. I don't know what she's saying. Does she not like the person she is when she's with me? Does she think she's worse for wear now that we've been together? Does she not believe I'm capable of love?

Am I capable of love?

"This isn't about you," she says softly. "Or Molly."

"Then what's happening right now?"

I kneel in front of her. She turns her head and looks at the wall. The sight of her so sad, so upset breaks my heart.

"Relationships are hard for me," she says.

"I think they're hard for me too … because you're making it that way."

She almost smiles. "I've always felt second or third or, hell, even fourth sometimes in every relationship I've been in. From the one with my mother to the one with my Nonna to the one with Charlie."

"You're first with me. You're the only one in the game, sweetheart."

I look at her with every bit of sincerity I can. I love her. I know it. There's not a doubt about it. But if I tell her now, maybe she'll just feel sorry for me. Maybe she'll stay for the wrong reasons. Even though I'm desperate to stop this madness, I know you can't make someone stay if they don't want to.

I stand. This feels horribly familiar.

Closing my eyes, I'm bombarded with the words on the note Mom wrote. All I can visualize is the way her handwriting slanted to the left and got thicker in the loops. The paper. The confusion …

. . .

VIN AND PECK,

Dad and I are taking a little trip. I'll call you as soon as we get settled. I love you boys. I love you with everything in me. If you need anything, see Nana, okay? And just remember your mom loves you.

Love,
Mom

THAT'S. Not. What. Love. Does.

The sting hits me in the heart like it did the day I found it after school. It's like a scorpion stung me over and over. She loves me with *everything in her*, yet it wasn't enough for her to stay with us. With me.

Why did I think I was?

Nothing hurts as bad as someone you love choosing to leave you. Not a damn thing.

My eyes open to see Dylan watching me.

The last time someone told me they were leaving and would be back, I never saw them again. If Dylan walks out of here, will the same thing happen? I would've scaled the moon for my mother, but it didn't matter. Maybe it won't matter if I promise the world to Dylan.

My heart breaks as a tear falls, trickling down her cheek. I catch it with the pad of my thumb. My eyes get watery, too, as I feel the invisible clock ticking down.

"I'm not saying that's not true, Peck. That I'm not first with you. But I have to get to a place where I believe this thing between us is going to work."

She's going to leave. I see it in her eyes. The decision is over.

And I can't stop her.

I shouldn't.

It's her choice to make.

"I wish you wouldn't go," I say. My voice threatens to break. I cover my mouth with my hand and face the wall.

"I'm not saying we'll never see each other again. I just think we need some space."

I'll call you as soon as we get settled.

I nod. "Okay."

The room seems to grow smaller by the second. I think I'm going to pass out as the walls seem to crush in on me.

I spin around and grab her box. "Is this ready?" I ask.

Her eyes go wide. She nods subtly.

"I'll carry it out for you." I head to the door. I stop but don't turn around. I don't want her to see the single tear flowing down my cheek. "Let me know if you need anything, Hawkeye. I'll, um, I'll give you some space to get your stuff."

"Peck …" she calls out.

But I'm already gone.

TWENTY-NINE

Dylan

I SIT ON THE COUCH. Navie's blue pillow, my favorite, sits beside me. It reminds me of Peck's stupid beautiful eyes, so I pick it up and chuck it into the kitchen.

And.

I.

Cry.

I hate crying. It makes me feel weak. It pisses me off, and that just makes me cry more.

I'm not even sure why I'm crying. My brain tries to make sense of it, putting ideas and memories into little boxes while my heart orchestrates the rest of my body.

"Ooh …" Navie appears out of nowhere. I look up through my tears and see her standing a few feet in front of me. She places a Carlson's box on the coffee table. "This isn't good."

"No," I say, sucking up the snot that's gathered on my top lip.

"You sounded so much better on the phone." She makes a face. "Can we go back and get that Dylan? I like her better."

"Fuck off."

She sits beside me and wraps an arm over my shoulder. No words are spoken. No questions are asked. The only thing put forth between us is Navie's presence.

I miss him already. It hasn't even been thirty minutes.

I'm not strong enough for this bullshit.

"Okay," Navie says. She slips her arm off me. "That's enough."

"Enough what?"

"Enough crying. And wallowing. You're dripping snot on your shirt." She makes a face. "I mean, really."

I sniffle. "I'm sorry I'm not reacting in a way that's good for you."

"Girl, let me tell you something. This isn't good for you either."

"Well, I'm about ready to add to the HAS Line. That'll be damn good for me."

She rolls her eyes.

She stands and walks around the apartment. The pillow is launched from the kitchen, landing beside me. My purse is picked up off the floor and set on the table. She finds my keys in the sink and holds them in the air.

"Don't ask," I warn.

"Noted."

She sets them by my purse.

"If you wanted a friend to coddle you and tell you that everything you're doing is right, you picked the wrong friend." She crosses her arms over her chest. "In case you've forgotten, I'm not kissing your ass just because your feelings are hurt or whatever."

I settle back on the sofa. "Of course you're not."

"I'm giving you the first point—Peck and Molly are beyond irritating, and he needs to cut her off."

"He did. I think. Or so he said. But he jumped to help her again today so …."

"Part of that is that it's Peck. It's in his cellular DNA to help people. He's like a … service dog or something."

I laugh even though I don't feel much like laughing.

"But this is where things change." She busies herself in the kitchen,

229

making two glasses of tea. "You have to make some tough choices here, girlfriend."

"I moved out. That's a tough choice."

She looks over her shoulder. "Okay. Noted." She messes with a box of tea bags.

Navie's antics aren't what I want or need right now. Sleep is. Or whiskey. Or brambleberry ice cream.

My phone buzzes in front of me. It's a text from my mom. I roll my eyes and silence it without even reading it.

"Who was that?" Navie asks.

"Mom."

She makes a face. "Have you talked to her lately?"

"Not since I got here."

"You've never texted her back?"

"Why? She just wants money."

Navie carries two teacups to the couch. She hands me my favorite, the one with hot air balloons, and then sits in the chair beside me.

"Does she?" she asks.

"What?"

"Just want money?"

"It's all she ever wants. She's not even nice about it."

She sets her teacup on the coffee table. It clinks as it settles.

"Have you ever wondered if maybe she's also checking on you? Making sure you're okay?" she asks.

"No."

She shrugs.

"She doesn't care, Navie. You know that. She just worries about Koty and Reese."

"Wouldn't it be funny if Koty and Reese were sitting around right now saying, 'Mom totally favors Dylan. When something goes wrong, it's Dylan to the rescue.'"

"I doubt it," I scoff.

"Well, maybe not, but that's how I would feel. I mean, I was talking to my sister this morning, and we got into this argument about our parents. I think they think more highly of Armie because she's in college, wearing pleated skirts, and dating a soon-to-be doctor. She apparently thinks they think I'm a badass who doesn't need our trust funds and isn't afraid of hard work. That I'm going to rule the world someday with my work ethic." She grins. "Talk about a change in perspective, right?"

I grin. "You are pretty badass."

"Obviously."

I think about what she's saying, but I still can't imagine my siblings thinking that.

"I thought of something else," she says. "Can you imagine what Molly must've thought when Peck told her to scram? I mean, she must've thought you were the alpha woman."

"But he helped her again today."

"And went home to you."

Her words remind me of what Peck said. My heart squeezes. I wish he was here to give me one of his famous hugs.

But he's not. Because I left.

"I just don't want to be the jealous girlfriend, Navie. And I don't even know if I can do a relationship. He wants to have a family and a dog, probably. I'm not there. What if I don't get there?"

Navie smiles. "Look at me."

I do.

"Peck picked you. He chose you to share his bed. He came home and climbed onto a set of sheets with who? You."

"Because I was already there."

"And if he didn't want you to be, he would've asked you to leave." She sighs. "You need to look at things from other perspectives. I think we, as human beings, have a darker version of our reality than the people around us. I see it all the time at the bar. One guy thinks the guy to the right is slaying it because he has a fancy watch. And that guy thinks the other guy has it made because his wife doesn't call him every ten minutes. But the guy with no wife would kill to have a woman bother him like that. Does that make sense?"

"Kind of."

She leans back in her chair and watches me.

I attempt to use her theory as I think about Peck. What would he be thinking right now? That I don't want him? Because I do. That I think I'm too good for him? Because I don't. That he's not worth the effort? Because he is.

This probably looks like an entirely different situation from Peck's perspective, and I hate that. I hate that he might be hurting because of me.

"Do you think I'm selfish?" I ask her.

"No. Not at all. I just think you've been hurt a lot and are afraid of being hurt again."

"One of the main reasons I left is because I think he needs the space the same as me. His life is going through a lot of big changes too. A new girl who's moved in and sleeping in his bed and acting all crazy jealous when he's acting like a decent guy. He doesn't need that."

"Then don't be crazy jealous." She scoots to the end of the chair. "Trust him."

"I do."

She calls me out with a single glance.

"I do," I insist again. "I just ..."

I think about the feeling in my stomach when I think of him with Molly. Whether it's innocuous or not, it terrifies me.

"Molly is not your competition," Navie says. "You are your own competition. And you might kick your own ass." She shrugs as she stands. "Now, I have to get to work. You're welcome to stay, obviously. Just think about what I've said, okay?"

I nod.

She blows me a kiss and walks out the door.

I grab my phone and stand. Walking around the room, I think about what she said. It's not much different from what Peck said about Molly, actually, and how people assume they already know everything there is to know about her.

And about him.

He is happy-go-lucky, will-do-anything-for-you Peck, but he's also devastated, untrusting Wesley, who lost his mom because she picked her husband over her boys.

How did I not think of that before?

But will he ever trust me? He said that he let others believe what they wanted about his feelings toward Molly because it was easier that way. Easier for his heart in some ways. He never feared that Molly would leave him ... *because he never really gave her his heart.*

Shit.

My heart falls to the floor.

I'm an idiot.

I should call him and am about to when I pause.

He doesn't need me to check in on him and apologize. He needs me to make the choice to stay. To validate *us.*

Maybe I need to work out things with my mom first. Navie's right. I have no clue what my mother or my siblings think about me. I'd already decided. I just didn't realize it until now. Just as I assume I know what Peck thinks and wants and what my mother thinks. And maybe I'm right. But maybe I'm wrong.

I flip my phone over and hit the button to call the last number in my call log. It rings twice before I hear her voice.

"Hello? Dylan?"

"Hi, Mom."

"I was wondering when you'd call," she says. "Did you get my texts?"

"About Koty needing money? Yeah."

She groans. "I told her you'd send it. Have you?"

"No."

"Well, we need it, Dylan. Can you send a check or wire it or whatever this week?"

My spirits fall. "I'll do my best." It's probably not worth mentioning that I haven't had a job for the past two weeks.

"These siblings of yours will be the death of me. I told them the next time they need money, they're calling you themselves and trying to talk you into it. I'm tired of begging you."

I start to fire back my standard response—a groan and an excuse to get off the phone. But Navie's words niggle at my brain, and I take a deep breath instead.

Imagining Mom not seeing me as the fixer of her problems, but being grateful to have me as a resource, I try a different approach.

"How are things with you?" I ask. "Do you need anything?"

She doesn't answer me for a long moment. So long, in fact, that I pull the phone away to see if she's still there.

"Do you know how long it's been since anyone's asked me that?" she asks.

"Yeah, well, I'm trying a new approach to life tonight. Just testing it out."

"I … I don't need anything, Dylan. But thanks for asking."

The sound of her voice—relief, maybe? Appreciation, possibly?—makes me feel warm. I grin.

"You're welcome. I need to go though, okay?"

"Sure," she says. "Just don't forget that money."

"Okay. I won't." I pause. "Love you, Mom."

"Yeah. I love you, kiddo."

The line goes dead.

I sit back down and tuck my phone under the blue pillow. I rest my head against it.

Navie's words float back through my mind as the stillness of the apartment takes hold. *Molly isn't your competition. You are your competition.*

I mull that over, tossing it around and around. Even when I close my eyes, I can't stop her words from bouncing inside my skull.

If she's right, I'm not only my own competition, but I'm also my own worst enemy.

I sigh. My entire body hurts. I curl up in a ball on the sofa and try to go to sleep.

THIRTY

Peck

"TAKE IT EASY," Walker shouts across the bay. "For fuck's sake, Peck. You're gonna tear everything we got up if you don't stop your bullshit."

It's funny that he thinks I care.

I was up all night. I didn't even go to bed. My linens still smell like oranges, and I just couldn't handle it. Not without Dylan in bed with me.

It took four hours to decide if I wanted to call her or not. I mean, I wanted to call her. Hell, I wanted to go find her and bring her home with me. But she left. She wanted to. I begged her to stay, and she didn't. But I called her because I'm a fucking idiot, and her phone went straight to voicemail. I didn't leave a message because I didn't know what to say, and I didn't want to be a stuttering fool—more of a fool than I already am.

"You're lucky I'm even here today," I bark.

I take a hammer and whack the rim in front of me.

"I'm lucky?" Walker yells over my second strike of the hammer.

"Yeah."

His laugh is more of a rumble than anything. It means one thing—he's pissed. *Well, good, motherfucker, because I'm pissed too.*

Walker throws down the cutting torch in his hand and stalks across the shop. I consider that maybe this is the universe's way of taking care of my problems.

Death by Walker Gibson.

I hit the rim for the third time.

There are worse ways to go. At least that would let me go out with a little dignity.

I miss her. Fucking hell, I miss her. I'm so helpless to fix this, and the knowledge of that binds me up. I feel like I can't move. I can't go. I can't think or process or figure a way out of this maze.

"Seriously, Peck. What the fuck?"

"What the fuck, what?"

He snatches the hammer right out of my hand. "I watched you do this all morning, and I've had it. Either talk or walk."

"Oh, look. You're trying to be funny," I say.

He scowls. "I'm not trying to be funny. I'm trying to save your life."

"You should be sure someone wants saving before you go playing hero."

His eyes narrow and his jaw tenses as he tries to bend me to his will. Usually, I'd cut a joke right here and end up annoying him, and he'd go back to whatever he was doing and leave me alone. Today, though, I'm not in the mood for cutting jokes.

I just lost my girl.

Sure, she said we were just getting space. But this space feels like a fucking universe. I don't like it. *I hate it.* And I can feel the depths of the divide between us, and I know it's not going to close.

The door to the office opens and in walks Vincent and Sienna. They exchange a grin as they see Walker and me ready to square off.

"Take it easy, boys," she says. "What's happening in here?"

"I'd love to know," Walker says, staring me down.

I don't answer either of them.

CRAZY

Vincent leans against a work table and slides his sunglasses off his face. He hooks them in the front of his shirt.

"If I were a betting man, and I do love me some gambling," Vincent says, "I'd bet my brother here is having girl problems."

I consider testing my brother's mettle these days and throwing a solid right hand. But if I do, Walker will get involved, and we'll all die.

Sienna puts a hand on Walker's bicep. Instantly, he relaxes.

"Peck, what's going on?" she asks. "Can I help with anything?"

"Nope."

"Okay, cut the shit. What did lover girl do?" Vincent shrugs when I send him a death glare. "What? I didn't fuck her. I don't care what you heard."

My right hand isn't fast enough. Walker's hand clasps around my forearm, and he jerks me around in a circle to face him.

"Wanna fight?" Walker asks. "Let's fight."

"Walker ..." Sienna sighs.

"I don't want to fight you, Walk. I wanna fight him."

"You sure about that?" Vincent raises a brow. "You wouldn't stand a chance. And I was kidding about fucking her. You know that. Chill out."

I give him my most befuddled look. "Really? Pretty sure I can take a guy who wears a button-up shirt with fucking flamingos on it."

"This shirt is cool." He lifts a piece of the fabric and lets it billow back to his body.

Sienna waves her hands in the air. "Okay. Enough of the pissing match. What is happening? Are you having lady problems, Peck?"

"Yeah. He's on his period," Vincent jokes.

"Shut. The. Fuck. Up."

He just laughs.

"Okay," I say, turning to Sienna. "I need advice. Wanna give me some?"

"Sure. What's going on?"

I walk around the shop bay, circling wide so as not to get into Walker's or Vincent's spheres. While I don't think either one would try to shoot a double-leg on me, I'm not *that* sure—not sure enough to get in their line of fire.

"So I have this girl. Dylan. She moved in with me as friends, and I don't know. She just … stole my fucking heart, Sienna. Yes, we slept together, but it was more than just fucking. And you know … I like her a lot."

More than a lot. I love her.

"That's great," Sienna says.

"Yeah, except she thinks … I don't even know what she thinks. She moved out yesterday and said she thinks we need some space and that she couldn't compete with Molly, which is stupid …" I sigh. "What the fuck do I do, Sienna?"

Walker steps between us. His hands are out to the sides. "Let me take this one."

"I don't have time for your bullshit," I say.

He faces me, and the annoyance at my antics from moments ago is completely gone. All I see is a sincere desire to offer advice—advice that'll likely suck ass, but at least he cares enough to offer it.

"Okay, Walker," Sienna says. "Go for it."

"This I gotta hear," Vincent chimes in.

Walker smiles. "First of all, tell me in the quick notes version how Molly is involved."

"She's not. I mean, she came by the house, and I told her not to. That she needed to stand on her own two feet." I look over my shoulder at my brother.

He grins. "Great advice, bro. Sounds like a genius gave you that."

I laugh.

"Okay. Got it," Walker says. "Listen to this, Slugger," he says to Sienna, then returns his focus to me. "So Molly knows that you like Dylan. You told her basically that you chose Dylan over her. Right?"

I nod.

"But Dylan doesn't know that."

"No, she does. I told her that. I told her she was my number one."

Walker chuckles. "Man, you gotta make shit crystal clear. Like crystal fucking clear." He doesn't flinch when Sienna sticks her elbow in his side. "You have to spell this out for Dylan. Tell her you're an open book. That you want her—be explicit about it—that you want her to live with ya, if that's what you want. That you love her. Just like that. I love you. Three words. Look her in the eye."

"Aw," Sienna says. "That's great advice, baby."

"I know." He grabs my shoulder and shakes it. "You probably think, 'Man, Walker. I did that shit.' But I guarantee you that if you had done it just like I said, she'd be back. If, you know, she likes you."

"So I haven't been clear enough?" I ask.

Vincent shoves off the table and walks our way. "Nah, I think he's right. I'm not really one for females who need a lot of coddling. I don't coddle. But I do see what he's saying because women do need that confirmation that they're wanted. I mean, I don't get it, but it's true."

Sienna wraps an arm around Walker's waist and leans her head on his side.

"Women need to feel like they have a purpose in the relationship," Sienna says. "We need to be needed. We also want to be seen, and last but not least, we want to feel safe in the confines of that situation." She looks at me and smiles. "I bet if you think about it long enough, you'll figure out what you need to do."

I scuff my shoes against the floor. "I just panicked. Flat-out panicked. I saw she was leaving, and I just felt like …"

Vincent looks at me. "Like everyone ends up leaving."

I nod.

"Well, I get it. But I still think you need to do something. Don't let this one go," Vincent says. "If not, I'll go find her—umph."

I tackle him low and hard, smashing his back against the wall. If I were really trying to wrestle him, I wouldn't gotten him a few inches lower and planted his head into the asphalt. But because I'm just fucking around, I grabbed him high.

"Stop it, you fuckheads," Walker bellows.

Vincent reaches around and grabs my hand. I tap his back, and we call a truce.

Breaking apart, we're panting and laughing.

"Damn, you're quick," he says.

"And you're stronger than I remember."

"Okay, enough fucking off. Back to work, Peck." Walker kisses Sienna's cheek. She follows him back to the spot where he dropped the cutoff saw earlier.

Vincent joins me by the truck that I've been working on all morning.

"You really like this chick, huh?" he asks.

"Yeah."

"So how are you gonna get her back?"

I shrug because I don't know. I'm not sure if she's still mine or not. She's not mine like she used to be—the way I want her. And I want to fix it. I just can't figure out what to do.

Vincent rifles through a coffee can of screws. "You need a grand gesture. That's what you need."

"How do you know?"

"The last girl I was fucking was big into those female-centric networks." He shrugs. "I'll learn if someone wants to teach."

I work on the lug nuts on the tire as Vincent fucks around.

A grand gesture. *What the hell is that?*

Walker whistles through the bay. He holds open the door to the office, and Sienna goes inside. He motions for Vincent to come too.

"See ya later," he says.

"Yeah."

The garage quiets down and allows me to think. A grand gesture. Would that work? Is that something I can do to drive home my point to Dylan? Because I need one good solid try to win her back. If it doesn't work, then I'll have to let her go.

But it'll work. It has to.

THIRTY-ONE

Dylan

LAST NIGHT SUCKED.

Come to think of it, so did yesterday and this morning and this afternoon too.

I've always been one of those people who doesn't mind being alone, and I can entertain myself like nobody's business. But Navie worked all last night and slept all day today until an hour ago when she got up and is prepping to go back to work. I've been alone too much. It's taught me that Navie was kind of right: I am my own worst enemy.

The dialogue running through my head isn't exactly kind. It's not cheerful or positive. But ... it's real. It's the truth.

And the truth is that I'm not a whole lot different than Molly. That's a hard, jagged little pill to swallow.

It hit me around three a.m., the witching hour. The hour in which songs have been written about its loneliness. The hour that's not quite today and not quite yesterday, an hour of time that exists to haunt you.

And haunt me, it did.

I might not sleep around, as I've heard Molly might do. I don't stop at men's houses that might have had a thing for me when someone else has moved in and try to play a card to get them back in my graces, as I'm pretty sure she did. I haven't ever gone up to a woman at a bar and picked a fight or tried to intimidate someone to stay away from a guy I didn't even like so he'd just like me.

That being said, I'm desperate for love. I have acted foolishly because I'm scared that someone isn't going to love me back. And my behaviors probably stem from the way people have treated me growing up, and I haven't been able to break that mental connection. Just like Molly.

I laugh out loud. It's not a sound full of levity or humor. It's a motion packed with disbelief and sadness and a little disgust.

I'm not better, no different, than Molly McCarter.

I take the blue pillow and press it against my eyes.

Neither one of us deserve Peck. When I think about the things Nana told me, and how his mother left him and how awful it must have been for him growing up, I realize how strong he is. None of that bullshit has stopped him from opening his heart. But when she implored me to love him …

"You can't start or stop love, honey. It's just there or it's not, and it's present between you and Peck."

The look in her eyes. It was clear how much she adores here beautiful grandson.

"Just … love him. Like you, he's never really had someone love him unconditionally … He'll be kind. He'll drive you crazy with his incessant need to make sure you're all right. Please just be the same to him. For me."

I've already let Nana down. I didn't trust him to keep my heart safe. I didn't love him unconditionally.

Is that what this is? It's that I love Peck?

"Hey," Navie says.

She runs a brush through her hair. She's irritated with me, and I know it. But I'm irritated with myself, so there's that.

"I'm sorry," I tell her. My voice is muffled under the pillow, but she gets the gist of the sentiment.

"Yeah, well, apologize to yourself." She puts the brush on the table and works to pull her hair on top of her head. "Are you coming to Crave tonight?"

"Nah."

She rolls her eyes. "Look, you can stay here all you want. My house is ... not yours, but you're welcome here. But, and this is a big but, if you think you're going to stay here and mope around because you are, in fact, a fucking idiot, then you aren't so welcome."

Her words are harsh, but the look on her face is not. A smile touches her lips.

"Gee, thanks," I kid.

"It's for your own good. I can't let you sit around here and add to that HAS Line."

"Um, what?"

"Oh, nothing. I just woke up to six shipping notifications expected to arrive at my house in the next three days."

I cringe. "Yeah. But two of those are ice cream. There's a new Banana's Foster flavor that really screamed my name."

"Oh, so it screamed Hey Fool? Awesome name for an ice cream flavor."

I throw the pillow at her. She laughs when it lands a few feet from her, not even getting remotely close to its target.

She sits in the chair. I sit up too so I don't feel like a therapy patient getting help for my issues. That would only embolden her to give me a lecture, and that's not what I need. Not that I particularly know what I need right now, but that's not the point.

"Look, it's the middle of the day," she says. "You've literally not gotten off the couch today."

"I'm sulking."

"Really?"

"Yeah. I'm avoiding my problems."

She smirks. "Seems like that would be hard to do when you are your problem."

"Navie ..."

"Have you even called about your rental?" she asks. "Or are you just pretending life off my couch isn't happening today?"

"Yes, smartass." I take out my phone and look at the screen. It's blank. "No one has called or texted."

She quirks a brow. "Not even Peck?"

"Once last night." I half-groan, half-whine as I sit back against the cushions. "It was when you forced me to get into the shower and said I looked like the bride of Frankenstein."

"Did you call him back?"

"No."

"Dylan, you ... Ugh."

I throw my hands in the air. "What should I say? I don't know whether to be mad at him or at me or at Molly or at the world or just ... fucking ... I don't know. I. Don't. Know. It's all confusing. I don't even know anymore."

Navie shakes her head. "Honesty coming in five seconds."

I make a point to grab on to the edge of the couch, making her laugh.

"When things get all confused in your head, it's fear," she says. "You are the most logical person I know. Except the HAS Line. But anyway, other than that, you're great at breaking stuff down. At sorting your problems. At making decisions. But when that all gets muddy, it means there's fear packed in there. That's why it's all jumbled."

It actually makes a lot of sense logically. It also makes sense knowing how I feel inside.

I am scared. Scared shitless. I'm scared of falling in love with Peck. I'm terrified not to love him too. I'm scared of spending my whole life and never feeling the way I do when I'm with him.

What if I screw it up? What if I become a jealous monster because surely every person who lays eyes on him wants him? What if I end up disappointing him the way people always disappoint me?

I probably already have.

I rub the corners of my eyes. My heart aches when I think about him. I try to think about things from his perspective, and I think I might puke.

My breathing shallows as what has to be adrenaline shoots through my veins. My hands pat the seats next to me in a steady rhythm as my brain begins to rapid-fire a series of feelings and ideas.

Even though I told him we just needed some space, it doesn't feel like that. I know it can't feel like that to him either. He must feel like I walked out on him and left him.

Because that's what I did. But it's not what I really meant.

I was scared, and like Navie just said, fear makes a mockery out of you.

Maybe that's what happened to Jessica too. Maybe she was scared. I don't know what of, but maybe that's why she could leave her two sweet boys behind.

He deserves better than that for once. He deserves better than that … from me.

The idea of doing that, of being there *for Peck* makes me happy. Being the strong one, the forgiving one, the one he knows he can come home to and be safe—that concept makes tears well in my eyes. Maybe, just maybe, he's like my mom too. Maybe no one has asked him if *he* needs anything. He's always given. Been kind. *Forgiving.* Maybe no one's asked him *what* he wants. *Who* he wants. And maybe, just maybe, that could be me.

It feels absolutely, positively right. Because not only does he deserve that, but so do I.

I ignore Navie's curious look as I stand. Thoughts are coming so quickly that moving seems to help make them easier to process.

I think of Charlie and the few men who came before him. Of my mother and Koty and Reese and even my relationship with Navie. In all those, without knowing it, I waited on someone to save me. I gave them the power to either make me happy and fulfilled and accepted … or to pass.

Maybe I'm the hero of my story.

Or at least, maybe I'm the co-writer of a tale as old as time, of a woman and a man who have all kinds of fears and bruises but come together to work them out.

I know. Suddenly, *I know.* This is what love feels like.

It wasn't the lust and desperation I felt toward Charlie. It wasn't the intense crushes I had on men before him. And it wasn't the way I felt when I met Peck under that stupid truck or the way I felt when we burned the steaks.

This is love. It's the moment when I realize just how bumpy this ride might be. It's when I accept that I'm all kinds of bruised up, and he has scars deeper than I can see ... and I still want to take his hand and navigate the waters with him. Even though his scars and my bruises together might make for some waves. And storms. And asteroid collisions. It's still worth it. It's still preferable even with the fear rolling around my stomach.

"I'm in love," I whisper.

Navie grins. "I know."

"No," I say with a nervous laugh. "This isn't an infatuation or a crush or just not wanting to be alone. Or even just not wanting to sleep on that couch again."

She laughs.

"I love him, Navie. Like I love him like Nana loves Pops."

"Huh?"

"Never mind."

My heart fills with a contentment that I've never experienced. It assuages some of the sharp edges of being scared and lets me know this is the right answer.

"This is what they mean when they say, 'When you know, you know.'"

"Good. Now I wanna know what you're talking about."

I grin.

Navie stands and adjusts an elastic in her hair. "So what do we do with this revelation?"

"I'm not sure ..."

I wonder where he is and what he's doing. I could call him, for sure, and I want to. I need to hear his voice.

But he deserves more than that. And that's what I'm going to give him.

"Can you do me a favor?" I ask carefully.

"Sure."

I grin. "I have an idea …"

THIRTY-TWO

Dylan

"CHANGE OF PLANS," Navie says through the phone.

"What do you mean, 'Change of plans'? We can't change the plan now."

My voice is borderline frantic. Change the plan? No. We can't. Not now.

Oh, shit.

I look ahead at the couple nearing the door to Crave.

She wasn't kidding.

The bar.

Machlan's bar.

At nine o'clock at night.

"Navie, this idea just got seriously out of hand," I groan. "Um, is Machlan there?"

"Yes. That's not the problem. The problem is … well, I can't tell you the problem. But—"

"Okay, I'm cutting you off because this is way more important than whatever you were about to say." I gulp. "Nana is walking into the bar."

"What?" she squeaks.

"Yeah."

"What bar? You mean, like, the prescription counter at the pharmacy, right?"

"Nope." I wince. "I mean like you have Nana *and a date*—"

"*Shut the fuck up.*"

"Sorry."

She gasps. "Oh, my gosh, Dylan. The boys are all here. Machlan will burn this motherfucker down."

I want to cry. I'm not sure if it's because Nana is actually beaming at the little old man who has her by the hand as they amble toward the door or because I know she's right and her grandsons are going to kill her.

Or that they're going to kill me because, unfortunately, this entire thing is kind of my fault.

"Well, go take the matches away while you can and prepare," I say.

"Shit. Okay. I gotta go … do …. What, I don't know. Maybe take cover."

"Gotta go."

"Hey, wait. About that change of plans—"

I end the call. I don't have time for her shenanigans.

Nana is dressed in a bluish-purple dress that hits her mid-calf with giant white and red flowers on it. She also has on pearls. She looks absolutely lovely. And like she's going to church. Not her grandson's bar.

I want to cry.

"Hi," I say as I reach them.

"Hi, honey," Nana says. She pulls me to her and kisses my cheek. "I'm so excited for this." She pats my hand.

She's beaming. The woman is absolutely beaming. And as much as I want to redirect this little date or whatever it is, I can't. I can't take that happy away from her.

I'm here to bring happy. Not kill it.

"Um, so, you know that this place gets a little, you know, wild at night?" I say with a nervous laugh.

"We've been to bars before." The man looks down at her and locks his hand with hers while he beams. "Not together, of course. This is our first time together, right, Michelle?"

She looks up at him and smiles like a high school girl going to prom.

They're going to kill me. Peck is going to kill. Me.

"Let me get the door for you," the man says.

"Dave, you're such a gentleman."

The door pulls open. Sounds of Crave billow out onto the sidewalk and past our ears. I'm pretty sure I hear someone shout something about dick popsicles, but if Nana hears it, she doesn't seem to mind.

"Thank you for inviting us," Nana says. She places her hand on my forearm as she steps inside.

I laugh, my face screwed up like I might cry.

Because I might.

My nerves are so high I need a drink. My plan was to get a couple of shots of tequila before Peck gets here, and I put this harebrained plan into motion.

Nana's eyes go wide as she takes in the fruits of Machlan's labor. And the couple grinding so hard in the middle of the dance floor that they may as well be screwing.

"Ooh," she says.

"Yeah. We can turn around and go back home," I say, trying to steer her to turn around.

Dave laughs. "We're old but not dead, Dylan. We've seen these things before."

"In your grandson's bar?" I ask Nana.

"Well, dear, no," she says, clutching the string of pearls around her neck. "But Machlan can't help if these people ..." She gulps as the woman starts twerking. "Do whatever ... that is." She looks up at me. "Times sure have changed."

I bet.

My eyes find Navie's behind the bar. She looks as nervous as I feel.

I hold out my hands to say, "I'm sorry," but she fake cries, and I know we're dead.

Or I'm dead.

The plan to win Peck's heart is going to end with my heart and possibly other organs, depending on how mad they are, being nailed to the bulletin board and having darts thrown at them.

At me.

Like a witch in Salem.

I start to scan the bar for Peck. It's not necessary, though. Because I have four of the hottest, most handsome, and shocked men barreling toward me.

This time, I clutch Nana's hand. Even though she's kind of the enemy right now. But they won't kill her. They love her.

Which is why they'll kill me.

I drop her hand and give her a small grin before stepping to the side and a few inches closer to the door.

My plans are halted, probably indefinitely, as I focus on preserving my life.

"What in the ever-loving fuck is this?" Machlan asks.

He and Peck stand shoulder to shoulder. Lance and Walker are behind them, whispering. I'm not sure which set of men I'm more worried about at the moment. The two in the front, ready to throw tantrums, or the two in the back who are whispering back and forth.

"Machlan, I don't care that we're in your bar," Nana says. "I still won't listen to that mouth."

"You're about to hear a lot worse than that," he says. "What on earth are you doing here? Please, someone tell me."

Nana's face breaks into a smile. And I know she's going to do it. She's going to out me. She's going to throw me under the bus.

"Well, I can't really say because I think it's a surprise. But when Dylan invited me tonight, I had to come."

And dead.

All four of their heads, six if you count Nana and Dave, whip around to face me. Machlan is seething. Walker isn't amused, but Lance is. I think. And Peck …

I can't tell if he's happy to see me or not. He starts to smile and then realizes his grandmother is two feet from him in a place where we dirty-danced not that long ago.

I wave. "Um, hi." I smile. I shrug. I pray for my soul.

"I have so many questions right now," Peck says.

"Me too," Machlan adds with a glare.

Walker motions for me to follow him. So I do. Because there's really no other choice.

My heart pounds harder than it's ever pounded before, and I think I might pass out. Peck doesn't say anything to me, just kind of watches me in shock as I follow his cousin a few feet away.

I want to attach myself to him, to kiss his face and ask for forgiveness. To tell him I'm here for him, and that I love him, and that … I didn't invite Nana here. But I'm not sure what he would do, and there's a burly man who apparently expects to have a conversation with me.

Now.

Walker spins around. "Gonna need you to explain."

"Um …"

"That's not an explanation."

I blow out a breath. "Yeah. I know. So, um, you see, I kind of acted like an idiot to Peck and—"

"I know. Should I bill you for the day's work Peck didn't get done yesterday? Because he was worthless as fuck, and I'm still gonna have to pay him."

I gulp. I'm not sure what to say. Just as I'm about to volunteer to do just that, Walker tips his hand. The corner of his mouth starts to lift before he twists his lips into a grin.

"I'm kidding," he says. "I mean, I'm not. He was worthless. But it was kind of nice to see him all pissed off over a woman for once."

"That's happened before, I'm sure."

"Never."

"Really?"

"Yeah. He's never really given a fuck about anyone. Molly, but not like yesterday. Not for real."

"Oh."

I glance at Peck over my shoulder. He's positioned himself so he can watch me and listen to Lance and Machlan interrogate Nana and Dave too. I smile. He does too. Kind of. He also kind of looks … worried.

There's nothing I can do about that right now. Maybe ever. So I focus on Walker because maybe I can have one Gibson not hate me.

"So," Walker says. "Why is there a nana? In a bar?"

"Okay, let me explain."

My brain spirals from one topic to the next too fast for me to grab on to one of them and go. Do I start with why I ended up at Nana's this afternoon? Or why I think Nana is here? Or that I forgot Peck's drill battery over there the other day and told myself I needed to retrieve it before he realized it was missing, but really I just wanted the comfort Nana provides?

I don't know. I. Don't. Know.

"Please." He waits. "Anytime now."

"Okay." I hold my hands up, gathering myself. "So I was at Nana's today, and I could tell you why, but I bet you don't care."

"Nope."

"So when I was there, she sort of … plucked my emotions right out of me."

He nods with a level of sympathy only someone can have if they've encountered a lesson-wielding Nana.

I've now experienced it. Twice, really. But both times were about the same situation, so maybe that only counts as one.

"She was telling me …" I stop. The boys don't know about her test results, and I'm not about to add that to the mix tonight. It's not mine to tell anyway. "She was just telling me that you only live once, and that you have to just … go for it. Live the life you want. Forget whether it might be scary or appropriate or if you'll … piss your grandsons off."

He folds his arms across his chest and looks over my shoulder. "Is that why she's here with Old Man Dave?"

"I think your grandmother might be in love."

A series of emotions pass through his eyes. "Well," he says finally, "she's entitled to a little love of her own. Pops has been gone a long damn time now."

"I'm glad to hear you say that."

"But she still doesn't belong in a fucking bar." He looks at me all serious again.

"Well …"

Before I can try to explain that, Machlan comes up beside us. He's bemused.

He points at me. "Talk."

"I … um …"

"Yeah. If she has a heart attack tonight, it's your fault."

"That's not fair, Machlan," I say.

"I don't give a rat's ass if it's fair or not." He glances at Walker. He must find something in him to settle him a bit. "But … it is kind of funny."

My shoulders sag as I watch these two men try not to find amusement in this situation. But the longer they try to hold it in, the harder it is. When Lance walks up, they all start to laugh.

He leans forward, his head dipping into the odd-shaped circle we've formed, and whispers, "I think Nana's getting lucky tonight."

Walker shoves his brother, knocking him off balance.

"So," Machlan says, running his hands through his hair, "I still don't know why you thought it was a good idea to invite her here. I'm never gonna be able to look at this place the same way again."

"No shit." Lance nods toward the actual bar. "Our grandmother just ordered a drink. With her date."

"In pearls," Walker adds.

"I think it's kind of cute," I say.

"No one asked you." Walker grins. "Okay, so I've had enough of this fucking gossip bullshit tonight. I'm going to go find some whiskey and watch this play out. You," he says pointing at me. He pauses as if he was going to say something else. Instead, he shakes his head with a little smirk and walks away.

I scan the bar but don't see Peck. I wonder if he left. Panic begins to set in as I turn a complete circle and come up with nothing.

"Hey," Machlan says.

I turn back around. "Yeah?"

"All joking aside. What's happening?"

"Okay. I needed to do something to show Peck that I love him. I just, um … Well, I want him to trust me. That I won't leave him. That … just …"

I don't know how to explain it. Not really. I don't know how to put into words that I want him to know I love him, and I don't want to say those words until I say them to him. Because I'm not sure anyone's ever really said that to him and meant it like I do.

Lance nods. "We get it. We may act all tough on the outside, but we're really pussies when it comes to our women."

"Fuck you. I'm not," Machlan says.

Lance rolls his eyes.

"I was telling Nana today that I wanted to do something really special for him. To show him that I love him, but I didn't know what to do or how or when." I blow out a nervous breath. "So we decided I'd do it here. In front of his friends. Just put it all out there. And the next thing I know, she's decided she's coming."

Machlan's head cocks to the side.

"Oh, don't look at me like that," I say. "Like I want to profess my love for your cousin in front of your grandmother. In a bar. Come on now."

Lance puts a hand on his brother's shoulder. "I believe you. I think Nana just wanted a night on the town. Look at her."

We turn to see Nana and Old Man Dave dancing some 1930s jig. I'm sure the tempo would've been faster and probably not to today's hip-hop, but it works. Strangely. And it's one of the sweetest things I've ever seen.

"That's what I want out of life," I say.

"It's what everyone wants," Lance agrees. "I mean, mostly. I don't think Mariah is the type to order a Manhattan, and I'm definitely not wearing a tie with … are those koalas?"

"Maybe," I say, unsure.

Machlan sighs. "Well, I'm not thrilled she's in here. But I am happy she's ... I guess she's happy."

We watch as Nana throws her head back and laughs a full-bellied laugh.

"I think that's a safe bet," Lance says.

"Yeah."

My heart warms as I watch her. If Nana can find the balls to show her love in a bar, then so can I.

"Machlan, would it be okay if I borrowed your bar?" I ask.

"I think you already have."

"No," I say. "Like, for real. Can I jump on the bar and—"

"Can I have your attention, please?"

My stomach bottoms out as I turn and see Peck standing in front of Navie.

On the bar.

The music has been stopped.

A few shouts come from the back for Peck to dance, but he runs his hand through the air. "No dancing tonight. Sorry. I know you really just come for that."

Machlan scoffs beside me, making me laugh.

"Tonight, I want to make a little announcement." He looks around until he finds me. His face softens, and a smile that I only see when it's the two of us graces his lips. "I want to say something to the woman I love—"

"No!" I don't mean to shout it through the bar, but I do. "Stop!"

Peck's face falls.

My stomach twists as I dash toward him. I climb on top of a barstool, wobbling as I get my balance, and step onto the bar.

The eyes of everyone inside the establishment are on us, on this little show we're putting on that should really be done in private. But this is not how it was supposed to go down.

"What are you doing?" he asks.

"Don't steal my thunder."

I face him, my chest rising and falling. His cologne hits me and almost knocks me on my ass.

I've missed him so much.

He watches me, unsure as to what I'm doing and what I mean.

"Let me finish. Please," he says.

"No. My turn."

"It's not your turn," he says. "I haven't had mine yet."

"Because I'm going first."

"Will one of you just fucking go?" Machlan shouts.

The people in the bar laugh. I vaguely hear their voices.

I turn toward the bar. "I want you all to know something," I say.

No one says a word. It's absolute silence as I scan the crowd.

Machlan and Walker stand side by side with amused grins on their faces. Lance stands next to Nana. She clutches his arm and watches us … proudly, I think.

Old Man Dave nods slowly, his golf-style hat propped poshly on his head. And then there's my best friend, Navie. She stands at the end, her elbows resting on the counter.

"Get him," she mouths, making me laugh.

"If anyone is curious, even if you're not …" I look at the man beside me. "I'm sorry."

"You wanted to tell us that?" Lance yells. "Come on. Give us something good."

"Lance, you be quiet," Nana says.

The bar laughs, teasing Lance, as Peck reaches for my hand. We step closer as I put my palm in his. Just like that, the world shifts. The ball of pain in my stomach and the crack in my heart begin to heal.

"I'm sorry," I say again. "I got scared."

"I'm sorry," he says, repeating my words. "I should've come to get you, but I just … panicked."

"You shouldn't have had to come. I should've stayed."

We exchange a soft smile.

"I have this … fear," I say, "that I won't be able to handle things as good as you do."

He laughs. "It's cute that you think I know what I'm doing."

"We're a pair, huh?"

"Let's just … agree that neither of us leave. That we talk things out," I say.

"Oh, like I wanted to do yesterday?"

I take our hands and shove him. He uses the motion to tug me even closer.

I look up in his eyes, the pools of blue that have captured my attention from the first time I saw them. When I thought he was Logan and a pots and pans thief.

"The past few hours have been a revelation to me," I say.

Something catches my eye. I glance down and see Molly standing there. She stares at me, and I'm not certain that she's not going to grab my leg and jerk me on my ass.

But she doesn't.

Instead, she gives me a smile that's kind of sad but maybe resolved. I smile back. She tucks her chin with a little nod and disappears into the crowd.

I turn back to Peck. "You were right about a lot of things."

"I'm always right." He winks. "Especially this." He removes his hand from mine.

Sucking in a lungful of air, I watch as he brings his hands to my face. Cupping my cheeks, he plants a kiss against my lips.

The crowd cheers, and I think someone tries to spray us with beer, but I'm not sure. I'm too absorbed by this man and this kiss.

His forehead rests on mine as a shy smile touches his lips. "I love you," he says.

My chest swells as tears prickle my eyes. Because he means it. It's the one thing in life I'm absolutely sure of.

I pull away so I can look into his eyes again. "I love you," I whisper.

The grin he gives me could fix the world.

"That's enough," Machlan shouts. "Get off the bar. Drinks half price for the next ten minutes!"

The crowd goes wild. We don't move. We just stand on the bar as chaos ensues around us. The music starts, and it's the same song that has nothing to do with a pony that we danced to before.

Peck laughs. I think he's going to start dirty dancing with me again, but he doesn't. Instead, he takes one of my hands in his and puts the other on the small of my back. And we dance, just differently this time.

Because this time, *it is* different.

But it's us. And it'll always be a little crazy.

EPILOGUE

Peck

"WHY ARE YOU ALL SO LOUD?" I ask.

I wince as Dylan and I step into Nana's. It's loud as hell, my family going balls to the wall for some weird reason.

And then I see that weird reason.

Old Man Dave is here.

Nana has a date to Sunday dinner.

"Your reaction looks about the same as mine," Vincent says as he walks past me.

Dylan elbows me in the side. "Breathe." Then she snickers. "How's it feel to have your words delivered to you?"

"Baby, as long as it's you bringing it, I'll take it."

She smacks my stomach.

Mariah and Sienna come over and whisk Dylan away. She's never met them before, but you wouldn't know it. They just envelop her like she's family.

Because she is.

I don't care that I haven't really known her that long or that we've already kind of broken up once. Or that I still don't know her mom's name or what she wanted to be when she was a kid. I know what matters.

I know the sound of her feet when she's coming to bed and how off-key she is when she's making dinner. I can tell you how fast it will take her to reach out when she thinks I'm having a shit day and the tenderness in her eyes when she's helping me sort Nana's medicines on Monday evenings.

It's been a great couple of weeks since our little performance at Crave. The me before would've thought I was jinxing it. I would've been waiting for her to get sick of things and pack up and go. But she's already done that. She won't do it again.

I won't let her.

"Look who I found out front," Vincent says, coming through the back door. Behind him is Blaire.

"We saw her last night," Walker says. "Not impressed."

She points a manicured finger her way. "You. Shut it."

Everyone laughs.

"How are you all?" she asks, slipping off her jacket. "Hey, Peck."

"Hey, Blaire."

I watch her move through the room with an air of sophistication. It's easy to see how she's so successful. She commands a room. You can look at her and see how intelligent she is. And beautiful. She reminds me a lot of her mom.

She tosses her jacket on the back of a chair and slides up next to me.

"You forget how boisterous they are." She laughs. "Wait. I'm talking to you. You're usually the loudest one of them all."

My gaze finds Dylan. She's taking a pie out of the oven and chatting away with Sienna. As I watch them, I wonder if I could ever be happier than I am right now.

"Yeah, well, I'm settling down, I think," I admit. "I'm good with being a wallflower."

I watch as Lance comes up behind Dylan and whispers something in her ear. She turns and looks at me and starts laughing.

"Stay away from her," I shout across the room.

Blaire laughs. "Yeah. You're a wallflower, all right."

"I'm working on it." I take a sip of sweet tea. "So what are you up to these days? We haven't seen you around in a while."

"My job has been killing me. I had a trial that went on forever. But I won," she says, smiling proudly.

"So you're taking a little time off for once? Good for you."

She does a very un-Blaire-like thing. She blushes. "I'm actually heading down to Savannah for a few days."

"Oh."

"I ..."

"She's fucking some guy down there," Machlan says.

Blaire casts him a stern look.

"Are you making love? I'm sorry," Machlan teases.

She sets her sights on her brother. "No. We are certainly fucking," she says, enunciating the word.

Machlan curls his nose. "Well, that wasn't as fun as I thought it was going to be."

"You've said that many times over the years," I joke.

"Change the topic," Blaire says sweetly. "Hi, Nana."

She walks up to our group. Grabbing Machlan's arm, she grins so wide I think her face might split in two.

"Can someone please go rescue Dave from Walker?" she asks.

We all glance over at the couch. Walker and Dave sit on each end. Neither are talking. And when Dave starts to stand, Walker fires him a look, and he sits back down.

"I think Walker has it under control," I say.

Nana sighs.

"You know what? I don't want to hear it," Machlan says. "You always want to give us advice, which we take and that probably saves our lives. But this is Walker's way of giving Old Man Dave some advice."

I snort. "His style is very ..."

"Formidable," Blaire chimes in. "But honestly, Nana. He looks like a nice man. Just be sure that you're—"

"We're using protection, thank you," she says. "This isn't our first rodeo."

Blaire's face drops, and Machlan and I ... die.

"Nana. Nana. No," I say, not sure whether to laugh or gag.

"I'm out." Machlan shakes his head and goes out the back door.

I pat Nana on the arm as I walk away. "We'll talk later, Blaire."

Dylan walks toward me. Her hair was down when we got here, but it's on the top of her head now. I spread my arms, and she falls into my chest.

I hold her, kissing the top of her head, and consider just standing like this through dinner. We don't need to eat. Or talk to people. Or do anything but this.

"I love you," I tell her.

"I love you."

Sawyer stops beside us. "Hey, Uncle P."

"Yeah?"

"So Nana has a boyfriend."

"It looks like it."

"Does that mean ..." He gives me a look like only a son of Vincent could. Raised brows. Shit-eating smile. Naughty look in his eyes.

I laugh. "Ask your dad."

He pouts. "He won't give me accurate information. He tells me we'll talk later. When I have hair on my balls."

"Oh, my gosh," I hear Dylan say against my chest.

I try not to laugh and encourage his behavior, but I can't help it. "Tell you what. We'll go fishing next week, and I'll tell you what you need to know."

"Really?"

"Yup."

"Cool." He bumps my knuckle with his. "Thanks."

He struts away like he's the king of the world. I know the feeling. I used to think that too. But now I see the fallacy in it all.

I don't want to be king of the world. I don't even care if I'm king of the county—a title I'm fairly certain I kept in some circles for a while. Now, I just want to be the king of Dylan's heart.

ADRIANA LOCKE

"Dinner is ready," Mariah shouts.

Everyone files into the dining room and takes their seat at the big, fold-out tables Nana gets out for these things when we are all here. Nana sits at the head, per usual. I sit to her left across from Old Dave. Dylan sits on the other side of me.

I look around the table at my family. This wild, crazy bunch of characters who round out my life. I love them all. Even Walker.

He sits at the foot, opposite Nana. He listens intently as Sienna tells Mariah about her trip to California. Lance and Machlan argue about something that shouldn't be discussed at Nana's table, even if they're using substitute terms for the dirty ones.

Hadley and Dylan chat about making homemade noodles and how to make them not stick to the bottom of Nana's kettle. Apparently, there's a mess in the kitchen to be cleaned up after dinner.

Vincent and Sawyer whisper at the other end. I think it's about me and my offer to go fishing because I get a glare shot my way from my brother.

Blaire and Dave listen as Nana tells a story about their night in the bar, a night that Machlan has made her promise never to repeat. I think she told Machlan that every time he misses church, she's coming in for a drink. His ass will be in a pew for the rest of his life.

Dylan takes my hand and gives it a squeeze. "I've been thinking," she says.

"Me too."

She smiles. "How do you feel about starting a family?"

I think my cock just got hard.

"Are you serious?"

She nods. "I mean, we are doing things in the wrong order—"

"Attention, please," I say, scooting my chair back.

Everyone stops talking and looks at me. It's only now that I realize I've done it again: talked without thinking it through. Only, this time, I don't give one fuck.

I look at Sienna. She grins. We discussed this loosely a couple of days ago, and she told me to follow my heart. Well, I'm following that or my cock. Not sure. Except I think they're sort of one and the same at this point. They both belong to Dylan.

"What are you doing?" Dylan mutters.

I move my seat away from me. And, with a gulp, hope, and a prayer, I drop to one knee.

There are gasps. Someone uses profanity to express their shock. Nana yelps.

And Dylan? She covers her mouth with her hand.

Tears fall down her face as her eyes go wide. "Peck …"

"You make me so happy. And I know I want to marry you one day," I tell her, taking her hands in mine.

Her lips tremble as she watches me. In awe, I think.

My heart overflows as she squeezes my hands in hers.

"You were right about something," I say. "You can't compete with first love. And you are mine. The first woman I've ever loved, and you'll be the last."

"You're damn right I will be," she says.

"I don't have a ring because I'm unprepared, which I know shocks you. But Sienna told me to follow my heart and that I'd know when the time is right. It's right." I clear my throat and ignore the way my heart feels like it's going to explode. "Dylan Snow, will you marry me?"

"Of course. Yes."

She launches herself at me, knocking me onto my back. She takes my face in her hands and kisses me.

My cousins go crazy. The girls squeal. The guys chide me and some clap, and Lance yells something lewd that gets him reprimanded by Nana.

It all dissipates into the background as I look in my fiancée's eyes.

"Wanna skip dinner?" I ask her.

She grins. "That would be rude."

"It was rude of you to mention having my children when I couldn't do anything about it."

She laughs, the sound making me smile.

"I'm not kidding," I say. "Let's blow this popsicle stand."

"Okay."

I kiss her again before we stand.

"Nana, we're gonna have to miss this dinner."

"But Blaire is here," she says. "And Dave."

I give Dave a little salute. "Come by and see me at the shop tomorrow, Dave."

"Will do. Good luck to you, boy. And you," he says, nodding at Dylan.

I take my girl's hand and walk around the table. Blaire stands and gives me a hug.

"Be safe," I tell her.

"I will. It was nice to meet you, Dylan." She pulls her into a hug too. "If Peck ever gets into trouble, call me. I don't know if anyone has given you the Gibson Boy protocol yet."

We all laugh.

With a wave over my shoulder, I head to the back door. Dylan is at my heels when I step outside.

The afternoon is warm, and a breeze ripple through the yard. I stop and stand at the rail.

"I knew then," I say.

"What? You knew what when?"

I turn and look at her. "The day we were at Nana's. The day I brought you here for dinner. I knew that day that I loved you."

She grins.

"Promise me something," I say.

"Okay."

"Promise me that you'll always talk to me. If you feel any sort of way, like you're overwhelmed or if you're—"

"Shh." She touches my lips with her finger. "I'll follow through right now. I'm feeling a certain way right now." She taps my lips before pulling her finger back. She leans forward and hovers her lips over mine. "Like I'd really like you to put a baby—ah!"

I pick her up and put her over my shoulder and head to my truck.

"Peck! You're crazy!"

Damn right, I am. Crazy for you.

CRAZY

The End

Where to go next?
If you haven't met Walker, Lance, and Machlan, check out Crank now. Live on Amazon and in Kindle Unlimited.
If you have read the Gibson Boys, check out the Landry Family (Sienna's family!) in Sway. The first chapter of it is up next.

267

SWAY

Chapter One
Alison

"This is a single girl's paradise."

"No," I grimace, blotting the spilled cheese sauce from my shirt. "Paradise would be a tropical island with a hot cabana boy at my beck and call ... and an endless supply of mojitos."

Lola laughs, the sound barely heard over the chaos of the kitchen. Chefs shouting instructions, event planners panicking, plates being dropped—the world of catering is a noisy endeavor.

I step to the side to allow Isaac, a fellow server and Lola's gorgeous friend with benefits, to scamper to the ballroom a few feet away. He's tall with a head full of dark curls and a laugh that makes you involuntarily smile. Lola is crazy for keeping him at arm's length, but that's how she operates. He has little money; she has limited interest.

"Cabana boys may have hot bodies and virility, Alison, but they lack two very important qualities: fame and fortune."

"So, what you're saying is that you'd take a limp dick over a hard one? Interesting," I say, rolling my eyes and tossing the sauce-soaked rag into the linen bin.

"No, that's not what I'm saying, smart ass. I'm saying I'd take a solid bank account over a solid cock. Think about it—with all that money, he could never fuck me at all and I wouldn't care."

"If that's the case," I retort, grabbing another tray of drinks, "there are tons of opportunities out there to *not* get fucked."

I laugh at the dreamy look on her face, partly because it's hilarious and partly because I know she's not kidding.

Lola and I are a lot alike. We both come from meager backgrounds and Luxor Foods is our second job. There's no doubt we both would rather not be here because serving rich bitches can be a very humbling experience. But they are also the best parties to work because they tip. Very well. Of course it's so they can feel above us most times, but we'll take it. It's money in our pockets, and if they get off on it in the process, good for them.

That being said, Lo took this job to afford her manicures, pedicures, and eyelash extensions. I do it to take care of my son, Huxley. Lola's first job is working at a salon and her career goals include marrying up in the world. I, on the other hand, work at Hillary's House restaurant during the day and go to school for journalism in hopes to one day write pieces that might inspire someone.

"Speaking of fucking," she says, her eyes aglow, "did you see Mayor Landry?"

"I love how you segued into that," I laugh.

"It's a linear comparison. Tell me that fucking isn't the first thing that comes to mind when you think of him, and I'll call you a liar."

Of course it's the truth. It's the first thing that comes to mind … and maybe the second and third too.

Thoughts of the recently crowned Most Eligible Bachelor make me a swoony mess. Barrett Landry's thick, sandy brown hair that always looks perfectly coiffed, his broad, friendly smile that makes you feel like you could tell him your darkest secrets without judgment, his tanned skin, tight body, wide shoulders—the list goes on. But it all leads, as Lo so candidly pointed out, to thoughts of him stripped down and wearing only his charismatic grin.

I shiver at the thought.

"See?" she grins, waggling her finger in my face. "Linear comparison."

"I'll give you that. He's *so* seriously fine."

"Have you had a chance to get close to him? To breathe him in?"

"Breathe him in?" My laughter catches the attention of our boss, Mr. Pickner. He twists his burly body our way, letting us know we'd better get to work.

"I haven't," I say, turning back to Lola. "Even though I've been around men like Landry before—well, not quite like him, but as close as a mortal can be—I don't think I could handle it, Lo. He scrambles my brain. I'd probably fall face first into him and dump the drinks in his lap. Then we'd *both* be wet."

She swipes a tray off the table and shoots a wink at Isaac as he walks back in. "It would so be worth it if you played your cards right. You could probably get away with running your hands through his hair and maybe even licking his stubbled jaw. A kiss would probably be over the top, but his Southern roots would keep him from causing a scene and asking for security."

"You've thought this through, haven't you?" I ask in mock horror.

"Of course I have and every other woman in here has too. Hell, half the men probably have," she giggles. "In my fantasy, he gazes at me with those emerald green eyes and leans in and—"

"Ladies! Back to work!"

We sigh as Mr. Pickner barrels by. He's an overweight, balding, temperamental asshole of a man, but he owns the premiere catering company in all of Georgia. So we deal. Barely.

Lola bumps me with her hip. "Seriously. Stop being so goody-two-shoes and go out there and snag you a man and a retirement plan."

I bite my tongue. We've had this conversation a number of times before and she just doesn't get it. I don't fault her though. Most people don't. They see the glitz and glamour, the designer labels and fine wine and get drawn in like a Siren's call. That life looks too good to resist, too good to be true.

The thing is—they're exactly right. It is.

She reads the look on my face and we start towards the door. "I know, I know. You lived like that once. It's a fantasy, smoke and mirrors ..."

"Yup."

"Well, I say I'll play in the smoke as long as the mirrors make me pretty."

I snort, pushing open the door to the ballroom. "You go right ahead and dig that gold all the way down the aisle."

"I've got my shovel right here." She shimmies her backside in my direction. "See that one over there?"

Following her gaze across the room, I see a man I know is one of the Landry brothers. There are four of them and two sisters, twins, if I'm not mistaken. I don't really follow that kind of thing much, but they're basically Georgia royalty, and even avoiding current events as I do, you can't help but pick up on some of their lives. Every newscast, it seems, has something Landry-related even when it's not election season.

"I'm going to check him out," Lola says and takes off, leaving me standing with my tray of ridiculously overpriced champagne.

I roam the outer edges of the elegant ballroom, giving a practiced smile to each person that plucks a drink off the tray. Some smile widely, some try to chit-chat, some completely ignore me like they probably do the paid staff at home. It's fine by me.

A few years ago, I attended events like this. Married to my college sweetheart, a newly minted judge in Albuquerque, we went to balls and galas and swearing-in ceremonies often. It was a magical time in my life, before the magic wore off and everything exploded right in my face.

"Well, aren't you a pretty little thing?"

I spin to my right to see an older gentleman grinning at me like a snake ready to strike.

"Would you like a drink?" I offer, knowing good and well by the color in his cheeks that he's already had more than enough.

"No, no, that's fine. I was actually just admiring you."

Pasting on a smile and tossing my shoulders back, I try to keep my voice even. "Thank you, sir. Now, if you'll excuse me—"

"I was thinking," he says, cutting me off, "how about you and I take a little stroll? Do you get my drift?"

"With all due respect," I say through clenched teeth, glancing at the wedding ring sparkling on his finger, "how about you take a stroll with your wife?"

I swivel on my heels and head off as calmly as possible, blood roaring in my ears. I can hear his cackle behind me and I really want to turn around and slam my fist into his beefy face. It's behavior that's typical of people like this, thinking they can get away with whatever they want with the bourgeoisie. I just so happen to have an overdeveloped sensitivity to it, being that my husband did the same thing to me as soon as he got a little power.

Lola catches my attention as I pause to settle down. She points discreetly to the other end of the room and mouths, "Over there." The gleam in her eye tells me she's spotted the mayor, but I can't see him.

I shuffle through the crowd and finally spy the man of the hour walking out, his arm around the waist of a woman that's been acting crazy all night. Her head is leaned on his shoulder, her hand resting on his backside. Laughing, I catch Lola's eye and nod to the exit.

"Bitch," she mouths as she approaches the same man that approached me earlier. I want to warn her, but don't. For one, I know it won't do any good, and for two, I can't take my eyes off Landry.

People literally part for him to walk through. It's like he's Moses. They're more than willing to be led through the Red Sea, divided by his power and influence, and into the Promised Land.

I'm off in space about what precisely that land might entail, when my shoulder is bumped, rustling me out of my Landry-induced haze.

"Excuse me," I say. When I realize who I've just ignored, my cheeks heat in embarrassment. "I'm so sorry," I stutter, handing Camilla Landry, one of the Landry sisters, a glass of champagne.

She's even more beautiful in person, a textbook example of poise and sophistication. In the media a lot for charity work with her mother, her face is easily identifiable with her high cheekbones and sparkling smile.

"Don't worry about it," she breathes, waving me off. "I can't take my brothers anywhere without women getting all mesmerized. Especially that one," she laughs, nodding to the doorway Barrett just went through. "Although, between me and you, I don't get it."

Her grin is infectious, and I can't help but return it.

"I'm Camilla," she says, extending her long, well-manicured hand like I don't already know.

I balance the tray on one side and take her hand in mine. "I'm Alison. Alison Baker."

"You helped clean up a sauce spill earlier. You put the lady that had the accident at ease when you took the blame and kept the attention off her. I wanted you to know I saw and respected that."

"It really was no big deal."

"In this world, *everything* can be a big deal. Trust me. You probably just saved my brother a couple of votes."

"Just doing my part," I laugh.

She smiles again, her chic sky-blue dress matching her eyes and heels. "Well, on behalf of the mayor, thank you. He seems ... occupied, at the moment."

I wink. "I have no idea what you're talking about. I didn't see a thing."

She nods, looking a touch relieved, and thanks me again before turning away and greeting the older lady from earlier, the one that spilled her dinner all over me. Camilla takes her hand and helps her into a chair.

Her elegance is breathtaking and she has a charm about her, an easiness even though she's clearly blue-blood, that I've never seen before. It's exactly what the kitchen is buzzing about with Barrett—a charisma you can't quite put your finger on.

Read more here.

ACKNOWLEDGMENTS

This book couldn't have been written without the help from my team.

First and foremost, I'd like to thank God. He comes first. Always. Without his love and favor, I would be nothing.

I'd also like to take a moment to thank my family for their patience, love, and support. Saul, Alexander, Aristotle, Achilles, and Ajax—y'all are the best. And my greatest blessing.

My Mom is my biggest cheerleader and I know my daddy is cheering me on just as hard from heaven. I have the best in-laws in the world. I love you all so very much.

Kari March is my partner-in-crime and quite possibly the most talented person I know. Thank you for making my book covers perfect … and for being my friend. I treasure you.

Tiffany Remy and Kim Cermak are the workhorses behind the scenes. You two are more than assistants or friends. You do so much for me with a smile (usually—ha!). Thank you for everything. I mean it.

Carleen Riffle, the other half of Team Mess, amazes me with her brilliance every time we work together. You are so intelligent and so kind, so wonderful in every way. I love you.

Thanks to Marion Archer for always finding room in her schedule and love in her heart for me and my projects, and to Becca Mysoor for being the sunshine in my life.

Jenny Sims with Editing 4 Indies impresses me continuously with her sharp eyes and sweet soul. Thank you for working with me. I'm honored.

My life became infinitely better the day I met Mandi Beck. She's the one I can call with anything in the world and sure she'll answer. I love you, Pres.

S.L. Scott is the steady half our friendship. I'm blessed to know her and call her a friend. Thank you for the strategy sessions and love and kindness … and for the cupcakes in the jars. Really the cupcakes in the jars.

Jen Costa and Susan Rayner have been with me from the very start. Your energy and enthusiasm for my stories keeps me going most days. Thank you for being my friend.

Ebbie Moresco, Kaitie Reister, Dana Sulonen, and Stephanie Gibson are the women who keep my groups running. You are amaze me with your energy. I appreciate your time and dedication to Team Locke.

And to Dave and Michelle. Keep on loving each other and inspiring everyone else.

Sincere gratitude to the bloggers who continue to show excitement for my stories.You amaze me. Thank you for never forgetting me.

And to my readers: YOU are the rock stars. I dream of a big sleep-over where we all show up with pizza and cheesecake and books and hang out. You're the best people in the world and I'm so, so thankful for you.

ABOUT THE AUTHOR

USA Today Bestselling author Adriana Locke lives and breathes books. After years of slightly obsessive relationships with the flawed bad boys created by other authors, Adriana created her own.

She resides in the Midwest with her husband, sons, two dogs, two cats, and a bird. She spends a large amount of time playing with her kids, drinking coffee, and cooking. You can find her outside if the weather's nice and there's always a piece of candy in her pocket.

Besides cinnamon gummy bears, boxing, and random quotes, her next favorite thing is chatting with readers. She'd love to hear from you!

Join the Locke List here.

www.adrianalocke.com

CPSIA information can be obtained
at www.ICGtesting.com
Printed in the USA
LVHW041614190919
631611LV00012B/967